House of the Winged God

William Xavier Chandler

First Paperback Edition, February 2026

ISBN 979-8-9945846-0-6

Visit thewilliamxavier.com
Instagram: @williamxavierchandler
Facebook: William Xavier Chandler: Author & Musician

Cover Concept & Design: William Xavier Chandler
Artwork: Mirko, @hugobass83. Italy

FURIOUS STYLES

ENTERTAINMENT, LLC

Publishing Division

TABLE OF CONTENTS

TABLE OF CONTENTS cont.

Part Two: House of the Winged God

House of the Winged God

Prologue

"How isolating, this existence. To be gifted with the power to manipulate and transform the secrets of the universe, but rendered powerless to share that gift. To be discarded by society and confined to the shadows... It creates a... need to vindicate. A need to eradicate. An appetite to destroy."

--- Aylash Revall

Part I:

House of the Gray Bear

Chapter One: Touch Down

Thirty-three thousand feet. Thirty. Twenty-four. Fifteen. Ten. Five. Lights coming into view. Buildings. An early morning cityscape emerging from the light fog and drizzle. Lower. Lower still. Wheels gripping onto the tread of the runway. I grip her hand and hold tight, but careful not to harm it. She's my safe place. Imagine that. Me, a seemingly indestructible monster, and she's *my* safe place. A drive to DFW, a commercial flight to Philadelphia, and a semi-private plane to Paris, France. All done in darkness. This is the only flying I've ever done, and my second touchdown is just as unnerving as the first. Trust is a dish best served repetitively.

"So this is Charles de Gaulle's airport?" I ask. Annie jerks her head toward me with an amused, quizzical look on her face, and I know I've said something wrong.

"De what?" She replies.

"De Gaulle's. You know, the name of the airport."

"You're pronouncing it 'D. Gallas.' Like Dallas. It's de Gaulle, like 'you have some deh gall pronouncing it like D. Dallas'."

"Cut me some slack. You've been here before. I haven't. I'm still very uncultured, compared to *anyone*, but especially to a globetrotter such as yourself... Why would you come here anyway?"

"The truth? Shopping. Croissants. Moulin Rouge. My mom rarely took extravagant advantage of our prosperity, two exceptions notwithstanding: Hawaii and Paris. We would take annual trips to each respective place, and my father would stay on his phone or his laptop while my mom and I would explore the city and indulge. I don't apologize for it – or her."

We make our way down the steps of the Gulf Stream and into a car waiting to drive us to our hotel, and as we make that drive, I'm taken aback by the... graffiti. And the rundown, post-industrial, post-apocalyptic looking ghetto surrounding the airport. I thought this city was supposed to be beautiful. I didn't expect my first impression to be so... unimpressed. The closer we get to our hotel, however, the more stereotypical my perceptions align. Cafes. Artists setting up early in the morning to peddle their works. Crepes being sold like the tacos at a food truck back home. Tourists. Lovers. Congestion. Commerce, pretentiousness, and freedom.

Beauty. Ageless beauty.

We eventually arrive at the Hotel Esprit Saint Germain, and it is *very* nice. I'd agreed to let Annie be our travel planner, so I don't really know how much this place, or anything related to our trip, costs, but I bet it's a healthy amount. Our room has separate living and bedrooms, and is cozy and romantic. Before this trip turns business, we've made time to visit the Latin Quarter and the still-in-renovation Notre Dame cathedral, among other landmarks. She's going to try and arrange for us to accompany a private, after-dark tour of the Louvre, but it seems like this event is exclusive to the really, really wealthy. She keeps giggling about something called the Crazy Horse, so she's no doubt got something up her sleeve. I bet it's a Texas-inspired steakhouse or something similar, to keep me from being homesick. I don't know about *any* of these things. I just know the people are supposed to be rude, and the Eiffel Tower's here. If we can visit it at night, I'm sure Annie is going to make me go.

It won't be long, though, before I have to feed, and not just on the dribbling open wounds Annie's been nice enough to carve into herself. But *really* feed. I'll need to visit the House of the Gray Bear. Sooner rather than later.

Maybe there, someone can point me in the direction of Le Bouffon. The Jester.

Chapter Two: The Map

Of all the things I'd found in the House of the Black Moon's bowels, none was as interesting as the map. The map contained all the origins, locations, and final known captains of the associated vampire "Houses", past and present. Even though Sinjin Pierce had claimed that eight total had existed, in all, twelve had been established. After my destruction of the Black Moon, only two remained: The House of the Gray Bear, established 1012, in Paris, France and the House of the Winged God, established 1,300 B.C. in Nis, Serbia, formerly part of Yugoslavia. Each of those two formed in different cities before eventually settling in their current locations. The other of the twelve Houses, in no particular order of formation (or destruction), were:

- The Stone Sword in New York; est. 1801
  Final Captain: Humbolt Brecht
  Ceased operations 1982

- The Iron Fist in Chicago; est. 1874

Final Captain: Silviano Corelli
Ceased operations 1993

- The White Swan in Montreal, Canada; est. 1901
  Final Captain: Miguel Trudeau
  Ceased operations 2021

- The Blood Fountain in Rome, Italy; est. 172, B.C.
  Final Captain: Antonio Giordano Medici
  Ceased operations 2017

- The Invincible Jade, which started in Kyoto but moved to Osaka, Japan; est. 775
  Final Captain: Hiromu Takamura
  Ceased operations 1947

- The Seeing Eye in Rangpur, Bangladesh; est. 1694
  Final Captain: Sangku Chaudhurani Singh
  Ceased operations 1905

- The Emerald Claw in Marrakesh, Morocco; est. 1394
  Final Captain: Yusef Hasan-Ali
  Ceased operations 1967

- The Dead Soul in Munich, Germany; est. 1503
  Final Captain: Elke Becker
  Ceased operations 1972

- The Burnt Phoenix in La Paz, Bolivia; est. 1888
  Final Captain: Mariana Domingo Rodriguez
  Ceased operations 2011

I was surprised to find that two of the Houses' last captains were women, but I don't know why. Maybe it seemed to me that vampires have a rather masculine, monarchy type of vibe, illustrated everywhere I'd gone by the fact that the leadership was male. In every case, there were no female leaders. By one fate or another, all of these Houses closed their doors, and their unified vampire communities ceased to exist. The collective dispersed across the earth or crumbled and faded into the ether. Another surprise was the lack of rhyme or reason to each House's final years of existence. Every location had its own unique reasons for closing the doors. The Seeing Eye in Bangladesh closed after a mutinous uprising killed almost every vampire on both sides of the conflict, while the Invincible Jade was crushed by internal, lasting fallout caused by WWII.

Aylash Revall was known to have formed or at least visited every single one of the Houses. He was practically creating the vampire race worldwide. I find it odd that he visited neither Russia, China, nor Australia. For that matter, he didn't come near Antarctica or its opposing pole. There is no record, not one, of him ever stepping foot in those nations. I figured a man that was over 4,500 years old would have touched, kissed, or stepped on every inch of the earth.

Chapter 2.5: Light Sleeper

Blacked out curtains. A handwritten "Do Not Disturb" sign taped at eye level to the front door. The sound of the ocean playing on my phone to counterpunch the assorted sounds of the city outside. None of these tools can alleviate the inability to become comfortable in my soul.

A few nights ago, I fed on some who knew me... Maybe. A woman named Courtney, twenty years older than me, according to her driver's license. She was cleaning the offices near my current hiding place, and I interrupted her, draining her completely. Before she passed, she looked at me, and croaked out, "I know you. I know who you are... She made the right choice giving you up. At least I'll die knowing you proved her right." Those words, genuine or not, have chilled and broken me ever since.

I'm trying to navigate this nocturnal, pretend human/real vampire existence with a straight face, taking care not to divulge any fears or crises to Annie. However, I feel like I'm slowly and quietly coming apart from the inside. Whoever Courtney Bunch is, she didn't help my existential torment at all. Moreover, being some fancy, levelled-up version of a vampire doesn't automatically provide me with an instruction manual on how to "be" that. I don't know what I'm supposed to be doing.

If I don't know where I'm going, what will I do when I get there?

Chapter Three: Research

I sifted through and acquired many documents in House of the Black Moon, and virtually none were thoroughly catalogued in any alphabetical or chronological order; nor were originals photocopied save for Aylash's personal journals. His, Sartep's, and Tulonus' journals were translated and typed up multiple times, but just thrown together in filing cabinets, posterity of the entries' dates unimportant. I have no idea why Alister Amaranth fed me some story about Aylash only living roughly 150 years after becoming the world's first vampire, but lie he did. It turns out that Revall ended up as a resident at the Horizon Vista Retirement Community, and things took a quick turn for the worse shortly thereafter. Residents and employees alike went missing; several were found dead. All this, Revall's doing. People had their loved ones removed from the facility and various authorities worked in unison to shut it down. Alister, working as a proxy, made sure to keep the property from being torn down or auctioned off, and it became a shelter for vampires in the area, as well as a secondary source of income for Alister and his House of the Black Moon. Enter me and the demolition of the House, the demise of Unholy Saint, and the beginning of the rest of my tormented existence. The discovery of a whole universe of vampires piqued my interest, and even though my initial attempt to regain my humanity had failed, Aylash Revall's many experiments and breakthroughs reinvigorated me. I'd grown so much closer with Annie these past months, truly in love with her, and any opportunity to return to the Land of Day and Sun, as Aylash named it, would have to be exercised.

Unfortunately, Aylash's trail had gone quite cold. There's no record of him transferring from the Horizon Vista, or exiting the country. He simply vanished. One thing that did stick out, and eventually led Annie and I to Paris, is an official grievance recorded by the House of the Gray Bear, apparently served to the whole of the vampire community some two years before Revall stepped back on American soil. Its main issue was continued and escalated conflict with both the House of the Blood Fountain in Rome, and the House of the Winged God in Serbia. The two vampires that signed this grievance, in blood, were a Reginald Duplante and a peculiarly named fellow – Le Bouffon. Annie said that in English, that meant The Jester. Both vampires were referenced heavily in all of the Gray Bear's files, but there is no mention of the Gray Bear after the date of the grievance, October 2016. Upon receiving and trusting confirmation from Sinjin that it still exists, I chose Paris as the first stop on my world vampire tour.

Chapter Four: As Relationships Go...

Travelling to Paris, France. Travelling anywhere. How the hell I was going to do that when I was basically restricted to moving around only half of the day?

Luckily, I have this smart, helpful, obviously deranged "girlfriend" to help me figure this all out. It still sounds weird, calling her my girlfriend. I'm more like her imaginary friend that she brings out from under her bed when everyone's asleep. We haven't even made love, yet. I call her deranged, because, you know... she's dating a fucking *vampire*. Once returning to Abilene, I got to stay in an empty four-office business suite Annie's father leased for his continually expanding company and then did nothing with. At least hasn't done anything with yet. I just couldn't return to Mona's house, even though it was now technically my house. There would be people asking where I was or how I'm doing. They would notice my skin, notice that I'm absent during the day, or not in town at all. They would ask if I had a job, and where. So, I sold it via a third party to a family in need, for less than half of what it *could* sell for, even in its meager condition. Here we are; abandoned building it is. I've by now grown accustomed to such an environment. Annie got a complex set of locks put on the door, and I'd been squatting in it for three months as we read page after page of the Black Moon's mysteries, and planned and plotted this two-stop trip to the other side of the world.

"How is this going to work?" I pondered, not having a clue.

"Well, how did Aylash Revall manage to make it work?" Annie replied. "He travelled all around the world, most of that time before there were airplanes and huge technologically advanced ocean vessels." *Good Point.*

"Good point. Speaking of airplanes, that might be a problem."

"Why? What do you mean?"

"I mean I might be afraid of getting in one."

"Why would you be afraid? You've never flown before."

"*That's* why."

I could tell she wanted to laugh out loud, but she bit her lip and held it in.

"Davis, flying is really no big deal. Thousands of flights take off every day, and thousands of flights land every day. The number of plane crashes, or even plane malfunctions, is much, much lower than car wrecks."

"That's just because there are only thousands of planes compared to millions of cars. Look, I know I'm going to have to do it, and I will. It's just something that's always kind of scared me. That's all."

"OK. No problem. I'll help you through it."

Annie put her hand on mine gently, and then we leaned into each other for a sweet, passionate kiss.

"Anything going on down there?" she inquired.

"You know I have to feed for that to happen."

"OK. I was just hoping that there would be some breakthrough."

"It is what it is. I'm a vampire, and vampires' parts don't work that way. I wish they did."

"Me, too."

As relationships go, I could say Annie's and mine was easily one of the weirdest, restricted, and destined to fail ones I could ever think of. And yet, it was working. *We* were working. Annie volunteered at a battered women's shelter in the evenings, so she could sleep in the day as much as possible. That way, our schedules would align easier. She would then come over to the office building, and she would eat her dinner/lunch before opening her skin to allow me to drink of her. I promised to try my hardest not to leave the premises and end anyone's life, but on one occasion, the urge was too great, and I busted out of the building at sundown and fed on an overnight cleaning lady. On another occasion, Annie and her parents left town for a wedding, and I was left to my own devices for three straight days. I drank of four people that weekend. When she returned to Abilene, she didn't ask, and I didn't offer. We just ignored that detail and got into the routine of planning our trip, as if it was a normal summer vacation for two love birds seeing the world. As previously mentioned, our relationship was... different.

The weeks stretched into months, and the trip had materialized quite nicely. It was basically all coordinated. Flights purchased. Hotel rooms reserved. Rental cars. Travel routes, etc. The only thing we *didn't* really have was an interpreter, in either country, that we could keep in the dark and still trust. We wouldn't have a way to pinpoint the House of the Gray Bear until we landed and started snooping around Paris' nightlife. I figured my sense of smell, or my own scent, would eventually lead me to the right person.

I was correct.

Chapter Five: City of Lights

This city is so beautiful. So intriguing. When you've never left America, you don't really have anything to compare it to. It also appears relatively safe, a few terrorist massacres aside. The architecture here is so painstakingly crafted, meticulous, and timeless. Right before I drift off to sleep in the morning, Annie and I sit outside a café and she has a coffee and some pastry, while I just sip on my water, supplied from a carafe. Then I hole myself up in the hotel room while she goes out like Inspector Gadget's niece, looking for clues - and baguettes.

We walked around the Latin Quarter our second night in town, and nothing special, just some cool statues and landmarks. But we stopped at a really cool, really dark, hole in the wall restaurant that Annie says is actually the best food she's ever had in Paris, so it must be really good. I wish I could actually stomach to taste it. We took a walking tour through the heart of the city, and learned about so much stuff. Stuff I'd let slip in and out of my ears in school. And that was just in a two-mile radius. We hadn't even ventured out with a car, or used the mass transit system yet.

The third night was a test. Of my restraint, our relationship, our feet. We did go to the Eiffel Tower, taking the elevator all the way up to the observation deck. We walked all the way around it, taking in the beauty and romance of it all, and I took a picture of Annie with the city behind her. I refused to be included in any pictures, for obvious reasons. The Luminastra Namtudari may have improved my physique considerably, but it did nothing to improve my perception of how I view myself. Annie did manage to sneak a selfie of us as we kissed. Turns out she's quite the sneaky bastard. I don't know how she did it, but she was actually successful in getting us added to the group of participants enjoying a private late-night tour of the Louvre. Among a group of twenty, I immediately felt out of place and out of my element. If I was uncomfortable around Bob Moore, I was ten times more uncomfortable among these extremely wealthy, extremely snooty socialites, while Annie seemed right at home rubbing elbows with them and commenting on the works. I vaguely recognized one musician and one actor, but I couldn't name them to save my life. Even with the museum to ourselves, and our tour guide providing a brisk pace, in four hours we only saw a fraction of the museum, only entering the Richelieu Wing. Annie cracked up when I tried to pronounce that word. I did notice, both there and at the Eiffel Tower, other patrons eyeing me with shocked or sympathetic eyes. Annie told me that a woman stopped her in the ladies' room and told her it was inspiring to see me keeping up my workouts and physique when I obviously have cancer eating me alive. Who would say that to a stranger? And how long have I not been the only one perceiving that I look different?

Taking on such a busy evening provided many tactical problems, mainly surrounding my need to drink fresh blood. After the Eiffel Tower, I was very antsy, and while we couldn't get back to the hotel in time to still make it to the Louvre, we were able to go into a restroom at a bar so I could get a quick fix via Annie, *once we paid for a drink*. We weren't granted access until then. Walking around that museum for so long, though, got me completely starving, and we couldn't have finished a minute later than we did. I got Annie to let me feed a little more before we got to the subway, but while inside the station, I made her go to the ladies' room and occupy herself while I found a victim. Her protests against such an action were noted but overruled. I couldn't go any longer without proper sustenance. Annie's main concern, aside from her obvious moral objection, was the possibility of getting caught. A string of international murders and missing persons' reports is not exactly the impression Annie wanted us to leave in France, and it could make things rather difficult for me in my search of "my kind."

However, I wouldn't be alive to have anyone to search *for* if I didn't have a necessary transfusion, so I entered the men's room in the subway, found a ragged, heavy-set gentleman sitting on a toilet, and got to it. His eyes when I burst in on him told a tale of surprise, then confusion, then fear, then acceptance. He seemed to be more *ashamed* of his ending than terribly shocked at how it unfolded. After I was done, I gazed upward and through the ceiling, looking out to some imaginary place of forgiveness and peace. I wondered if such a thing was possible for a creature such as myself. The man's name was Luca Dobrev. I'll always remember that he had completely taken off his jacket, shirt, and pants to use the toilet, leaving only a white "wife-beater" undershirt on. His chest was a sweaty, hairy mess, the reason for which I don't know. His sweat glistened on his long chest hair under the dull, yellow, fluorescent lights of the subway men's room.

We made it to the Louvre two minutes before our scheduled tour was to begin.

One final night of fun and tourism was on the schedule before we really got down to my purpose here, and we saved it for the Moulin Rouge and the Crazy Horse. Finally, I was going to get to pretend to enjoy a real Texas steak. Just like the night before, Annie's enthusiasm booked our itinerary pretty tightly, and we arrived at 8:00 to one place with an official start time of 9:00, and had to be at the second by 11:15 for a Midnight start time. That meant I was going to have to exit the Moulin Rouge, identify my prey, isolate them, feed and dispose of the victim in a minute or two around 10:45, not get noticed, not get filmed, and get our asses to the Crazy Horse, which would take at least nineteen minutes to get to from our starting point. A vacation? I think not.

The Moulin Rouge show was different than anything I'd ever seen before. Or maybe it wasn't; I'd never really *seen* anything before, save for two Unholy Saint concerts. I got lost a few times, not understanding French and therefore what was going on, but it was alright. Somehow, I managed to carry out all my tasks to the best of my ability (my apologies to the family of Marie Beaubois) and still got there no sooner than 11:35. I had Annie go on ahead of me to secure our table. I was confused as to why a steakhouse would be taking dinner reservations for midnight, but figured it was just something that the French do. *Wait, what?!*

It appears my prediction for this place was all wrong. Annie had made me promise not to Google it beforehand, and I complied. How naughty she is! Not ten minutes after we'd been seated in a comfy spot dead center, one row back, with a bottle of chilled champagne, did the stage fill up with beautiful women wearing almost nothing. I look over at Annie, who's grinning ear to ear at my shock. But this isn't a "strip club," per se. I don't know *what* to call it. It's like art, or dance, or an R Rated lip sync performance; but a "cute" Rated R. The women are stunning. Thin but not too thin, strong but not too strong. With each passing number, the individuals in a given routine ensemble appear almost identical. Same height and measurements, same wigs. A couple of girls get to perform solo numbers all by themselves. Annie's uncharacteristically drinking freely from the bottle, and I can smell her blood go from sober to tipsy to drunk in just under an hour. It's obvious she needed this night to get away from our purpose here. To just be in each other's presence as a couple. And admittedly, it's been very beneficial for me, filling every moment of waking time with a benign distraction from all things vampire.

For the last routine, there are over a dozen girls lined up in Rockettes-style syncopation. That's when I get a whiff. Fourth girl from the right. She's not human. She's a vampire. And at precisely the same time, she catches my scent, stares me dead in the eye, and winks.

This is my first interaction with Magdalena, a wolf in...

Chapter Six: Sheep's Clothing

It's after 2:00 in the morning, and Annie and I are hovering around the Crazy Horse trying not to resemble deranged stalkers. I want to talk to this mysterious young lady. Young might seem a relative term.

"Are you *sure* she was a vampire?" Annie asks puzzled.

"100% sure. And she knows I'm one, too. Just trust me."

Just then, I smelled her flesh, and turned to find her staring at the two of us from some 50 yards away at the end of the block.

"I thought you might be waiting for me," she oozed out of her lips with a sultry French accent. 'You're Americans?"

"Yes. Can we come closer?"

"Why?"

"I have so many questions I'd like to – I need to – ask you."

"I can sense that I should tell you both to fuck off, but I'm always in need of entertainment and a good story. But if we're going to have this conversation, I need to get off my feet. We need to go to Henri's."

"Is that your boyfriend's house?" She giggled and shook her head.

"No. That is a café on des Petits Champs. You can follow my scent there, no, Pepe le Pew?"

"We can Google it" Annie interjected with a slight hint of attitude.

"Oui. See you there in twenty."

I looked at Annie, quietly studying her facial expression. I said nothing.

"What?" she blurted out grumpily.

"Nothing. I said nothing." I had a tiny crack of a smile on my face.

"We'll finish 'nothing' later."

We walked into Henri's, which I was surprised was still open in the middle of the night, and didn't see our new friend anywhere, but I could smell her. Only the person whose scent I'd locked in on looked completely different. She went from a short blond wig and a beige trench coat to long, deep red and auburn wavy locks that hung down past her shoulders and a black, form-fitting mini dress. Her complexion was of course pale and white, and her eyes were such a dark brown they were almost black. My eyes caught a larger than normal number of moles laced atop her arms and shoulders. Like all the dancers at the Crazy Horse, she was stunningly beautiful.

"Are you surprised I don't look exactly like I did on the stage?"

"No. No, I... well, yes. I guess so." She shifted her attention to Annie.

"Let me guess; you're the more experienced of the two? More travelled?"

"Good guess. My name's Annie, and this, the *less* experienced of the two, is Davis. Davis McCarty."

"I'm sure we can change that." She looked at me with deep, deep eyes, their entendre not completely decipherable. "Why are you with a beast of the night? Can't you find a nice man of your own kind? I mean, aren't there millions of people in Texas?"

"How did you---" I started, when she held up her hand and stopped me in mid-sentence.

"Because it's overwhelmingly obvious where you

come from. It's basically tattooed on you."

There was an immediate and quite palpable tension between Annie and the intuitive redhead, who hadn't yet actually revealed her name.

After over three months together, I was finally starting to pick up on all the female secrets I'd never really known before. *Talking with nothing but your eyes. Being mad but denying you're mad. Silence speaking louder than rage. Judging and measuring yourself against a rival while adorning them with compliments.* It all seemed complicated and unnecessary to me. Right when I was going to try and relieve the tension and ask the vampire her name, a gentlemen approached our table.

"What can I get you? You must be very bold, or very foolish, for keeping Magdalena's company. I'm Henri."

"The Henri this place is named after?" Annie asked.

"The same" he replied. He looked like a nerdy but charming college professor. Thin, tall, receding hairline, designer spectacles. If we were in the States, he would live somewhere like Oregon or Maine. 'I'm guessing at least one of you is... unable to get a tan?" I understood his implication, stretched my torso, and raised my hand.

"Yes. That would be me."

"Well. Paris is a different kind of place, no? Maybe one day, we'll all be vampires."

"Perhaps, but I really hope not."

"Madame, would you like a wine, or a coffee?"

"Just a water, please. I need to sober up a little after the champagne."

"Ahhh. You saw Magdalena at the Crazy Horse! She's very talented, yes?" Annie answered Henri's question while looking directly at Magdalena.

"I don't know. I really couldn't tell her apart from anyone else up there."

Shit.

"Can I also get a water?" I hoped my request would end the friction and get us to the 50 questions part of the night. Magdalena nodded her head at Henri in a manner that said, 'Give us some alone time', and he pivoted on his heels and turned to tend to other customers.

"What can I do, or what can I... answer, for the two love birds?"

"Where is the House of the Gray Bear?"

"Mon Dieu! What would you want with that place, and how do you know about it?"

"I found out about it, and the history of the vampire... when I destroyed the House of the Black Moon."

"Destroyed? You? By yourself? Well, it *was* just a kiddie house for kiddie Americans. I guess it's possible."

I could feel Annie's body heat rise, and knew this was around the time she was---

“Kiddie Americans? That’s rich. What makes the Gray Bear so special?”

“It *has* managed to stay standing over a thousand years. How long did your Black Moon stick around?”

Silence.

“Yes. Precisely. The fact that one vampire managed to bring it down all by himself tells me all I need to know.”

“He’s not just any normal vampire.”

“Annie, please. I’ve got thi---”

“He’s got the Luminastra Namtudari.”

“Oh, mon putain de Dieu. Please tell me you don’t subscribe to the myths and legends of Aylash Revall and his fanatics.” I placed my hand on Annie’s and took over.

“So you know that name, and have heard the myths?”

“Oui. From time to time, some idiot vampire will mention the bastard Aylash and speak of his exploits.”

“Well, I don’t know a lot. I’ve been a vampire for exactly six months, two weeks, and five days. I do know what happened to me, though. To my body. I’ve undergone the Namtudari, and you not believing it doesn’t change a thing.”

Magdalena sat there, thinking unvoiced thoughts, judging the country boy from Texas with her gaze. She would alternate her stare, darting her dark brown eyes between me and Annie, finally settling on her next words.

“What exactly is it you hope to find at the Gray Bear? Do you even know what you’re looking for?”

“I guess, ultimately, I’m hoping to find Aylash Revall.”

“Well you will most definitely not find him in Paris. That’s for damn sure.”

“Would that have something to do with the grievance that the Gray Bear filed with the... Where does something filed go? Who does it go to?” This caused Magdalena to throw her head back, closed eyes to the ceiling, and laugh aloud.

“That is a very good question. The short answer is that they wrote the letter – grievance – and sent it to the three other remaining Houses. Unfortunately, the diplomacy Reginald exhibited was not reciprocated. It started a war between Italy and France, and then the Winged God ended it.”

“The House in Serbia? They ended the war?”

“Aylash Revall. He is the Winged God. He named the fucking House after himself. But yes, Serbia.”

“I thought he was referred to as the Lower God.”

“Lower God, Winged God, Hostile Savior, Demon Christ. And on and on. Do you want to hear this or not? By the time it was all said and done, the House of the Blood Fountain, in existence for over three thousand years, was no more. The Gray Bear lost more than half of its members, and the Winged God – Revall – had completely transformed from founder and champion of the vampire to cruel, isolated monster, capable of destroying us all with no sympathy or compassion. He underestimated the backlash of his actions, though, as well as the surprising amount of damage he undertook during the conflict. He became a target to the rest of us in Europe, so he left the House of the Winged God and disappeared. Some say he went to America."

"He did. To California. He stayed in an old folks home near the House of the Black Moon. Saying that sentence out loud makes me realize how ridiculous it sounds, but it's true. Things... didn't go well."

"Big surprise."

"Do you know why he wouldn't have just stayed at the Black Moon?"

"I have no idea. I can introduce you to Reginald Duplante. He is the captain of the Gray Bear, and he can fill in the blanks. I will need to talk to him first, to make sure he is OK with this."

"So you're close enough, then?"

"We used to be lovers. So the more accurate term would be *familiar*. We're not so close anymore. Where are you staying? I will get back to you once I've spoken with Reginald."

"I'll give you *my* phone number" Annie offered. "You can call *me*."

"OK, then. I will ring you, the vampire's gatekeeper."

Before Annie could react sarcastically or otherwise to that remark, Magdalena rose from the table and bid us adieu.

"I have to feed. Hopefully, there are some drunk teenagers out in the streets." And she was out the door.

I had to feed again as well, so I could get some good sleep before having a hopefully eventful night speaking with Reginald Duplante. I motioned over to Henri for the check, and took Annie by the arm.

"I need to go now, too."

"Can you do that while I stay here?"

"You don't want to go back to the hotel room?"

"Not right now. I need to decompress and just chill without all this vampire shit in my head." Just then, Henri made it to the table.

"Two waters and some bread? There's nothing to pay for, my new friend."

"OK. I need to step out for a bit. Can you make sure Annie is OK while I'm gone?"

She looked at me pissed off, and Henri looked at me amused. Annie began to argue as I stood to leave.

"I don't need a babysitter. I've been to Paris over a dozen---"

"Gotta go. I'll be back."

"He's going to feed?" Henri quizzed Annie.

"Yup".

"A word of advice. He should steer clear of Montmartre."

"What? Too late, Henri. He fed there earlier tonight. Why?"

"Oh. That is unfortunate. He'll face Le Bouffon soon."

"He's actually *hoping* to face Le Bouffon."

"Well... Then it was nice knowing you."

Chapter 6.5: Tingles. Bad Tingles

I fed on two teenage boys/young men, as both a matter of circumstance and as a challenge to my newfound body's strength. It was actually quite easy to drain one while I held the other down, hand over his mouth. I made it back to Annie to find her in the same seat, talking it up with Henri. As we left his cafe, he bid us a fond farewell and said, "If there's anything I can do for you, just let me know." I noticed him caress Annie's hand ever so subtly. He probably thought I wouldn't notice, or notice her bodily reaction to such a gentle movement. I also detected that his words of assistance were directed mainly at her, not me. *What the hell is going on? Is he hitting on my girlfriend in front of me? And what is this feeling I'm having, just thinking about it? Am I angry and... jealous?*

Conversely, I observed a virtual pissing match between Annie and Magdalena, and I don't know why. She didn't flirt or give me "come hither" eyes, or anything. I believe she mainly insulted me in an overt but playful way, one comment aside. I know without even having to ask, though, that Annie does NOT like her. What I didn't expect is that I... would. On the two occasions that Magdalena just stared into my eyes, I got tingles. Bad tingles.

Chapter Seven: The Jester

I'd seen his name in the accounts of the Gray Bear and saw his signature on the grievance to the Blood Fountain and Winged God, but I didn't know much else about Le Bouffon, this man with a nickname for a name. Annie told me about what Henri had said, and I honestly didn't pay it any mind. I was growing ever confident in my ability to face and defeat a challenge, even one that might be hundreds of years older than me. I was intrigued, though, to say the least. I had agreed to let Magdalena arrange a hopeful meeting between me and Reginald Duplante, but there was no mention of the Jester, so I thought I would set a trap for him in Montmartre. After pulling the locked door open rather effortlessly, I tiptoed my way into the famous Bateau-Lavoir with a mouthful of Annie's blood seeping out the sides of my lips and waited for my mysterious guest to join me there. This small building was after all a hallowed set of walls in Montmartre, which seemed to be the Jester's haunting grounds.

I sat cross-legged in the center of the room for a small eternity waiting for him, listening to a singular, repetitive drop of water as it fell from a distant faucet every 3.8 seconds. Just as I was about to give up for the night, a sense of dread clawed up my arms, out the back of my shirt, and onto my neck, and a foul smell of sulphur and soggy, mossy leaves floated on my nostrils. A glass broke behind me to my right, and then the sound of wood snapping erupted on my left, and before I could investigate either, two hands were gripping my cranium from behind, and two lips were eerily close to my left ear, exhaling a putrid, long-dead breath into its canal.

"Why are you here? What game is it you are playing?"

Before I could blurt out any reply...

'I do not play games. With vampires, or humans. I am Le Bouffon, and if you wanted to meet me, there are more mature, respectful ways."

He tossed me to the floor by my head, and as I lifted it and turned to face him, he was gone.

I stood there, dumbfounded, analyzing the room, his possible entry way, and subsequent exit route. *How was he able to infiltrate and overtake me so deftly?* He had to have been considerably faster than any vampire I'd previously encountered, able to move laterally as quick or quicker than I could run in a straight line, and I ran fast enough to wind soar. I called Annie to give her an update.

"Hi. Did you find him?"

"He found me, and he was *not* pleased."

"How so?"

"I'll fill you in when I get back. I have to---"

"Feed. Remember, Henri warned that you shouldn't do that in Montmartre."

"So he did. So what?"

"It's not *his* rule; it's Le Bouffon's."

"Well, then maybe we'll meet again tonight."

"Something tells me that might be a bad idea."

"I'll call you later, if I run into him."

Silence. She was debating on whether or not to give me advice. She knew I wouldn't take it, so the conflict was over how much wasted breath and time it was worth. She chose conservativism.

"Bye. I love you."

"Love you, too."

I headed to Montmartre's beloved Sacre-Coeur Basilica and scanned the heat signatures for anything promising. Sure enough, a young couple was holding hands as they roamed across the basilica's promenade on the bridge. They figured no one would be out this late, and maybe planned for some risqué romance. I slowly approached them, measuring my steps in a comfortable, confident rhythm. Their backs remained to me, completely unaware of my impending onslaught. Almost six months as a vampire, and my empathy had worn away to virtually zero. I'd come to grips with my situation and the unfortunate but necessary aftermath that it produced. Closer and closer I got to them. I was fortifying my strategy when the girl turned abruptly to face me.

"He fell for it," she yelled aloud in French at the night. 'Take him."

"I want to speak to him, first," a voice replied. A voice I'd just heard whispering in my ear earlier. The couple smiled at me arrogantly, like they were in on some prank being played on me, or that they were happy that some foreign invader would soon be disposed of. They then strolled lazily out of view, into the darkness.

"What do you want, intruder?" he demanded. "Why are you here, and what you do you know about me?"

"I know you're Le Bouffon."

"Then you know nothing I haven't already told you."

He stepped closer to me, slowly. He was not afraid of me; I think his pace was so that I wouldn't be afraid of him. At first, it looked like he was wearing some harlequin-style jester's hat on his head, it covering his eyes like a mask. As he got more in view, however, the skin on his face and the hat appeared to meld together. My perception was that it was unremovable. He had a bulbous nose with large nostrils, and big, full lips. He wore a dark purple, orange, and green satin shirt, each color fighting for supremacy. It was covered by a black cloak.

He seemed etched in time. I thought that rapid fire questions were best to get his attention and maybe keep him from wanting to rip me apart.

"Where is the House of the Gray Bear? Why did it file a grievance against the Blood Fountain and Winged God? Where is Aylash Revall? How soon can I talk to Regin---"

"Silence, hillbilly. You ask a lot of questions that you may not want the answers to."

"I flew across the Atlantic for the answers."

"How modern of you? Very serious, your situation must be. Do you know that before we went to war with the Blood Fountain, I'd never travelled farther than three hours away from my hometown?"

The Jester stopped and looked downward and away for several seconds, the silence within each second growing to a deafening pitch between my ears. I had no idea what caused his pause, or what his next move would be. I just knew I had to be patient.

My patience left me rather quickly.

"I've learned a lot these past few months, but I'm smart enough to know that I still have a lot left t---"

"You could live for centuries and not know all there is to learn from this city, from the Gray Bear, from the past. The problem is that even if I let you live, vampires have become too stupid, too childish, to make it past anything resembling a 'vampire adolescence'. Your landing here in Paris with no permission asked or granted is proof of that."

"Permission? Why would I need permission to travel to another country?"

"Because there are rules that vampires must follow. Rules that cannot be broken for fear of self-destruction."

"It looks like those rules have been broken right and left. There were twelve vampire Houses; now there are two."

"That's precisely my point. Around the 800's, vampires worldwide finally learned how to survive, to thrive, for more than the standard ten to fifty years before dying. We built more 'infrastructure', if you will, and communicated as a race, not just a scattered band of mutants. Something changed in the 20th century. Vampires shadowed and embodied the human ways of life, instead of cultivating what made us adaptable and unique. We, especially the American vampire, became selfish and delusional, as novels, film, and eventually television, something I never watch, turned us into a romantic, mythological, superhuman nightmare."

"Well, isn't at least some of that true?"

"10% of the truth does not make it the truth. The vampire community once stuck close to the shadows; played in the darkness. They started to come out, to socialize. They also got gluttonous in regard to feeding. They started hunting for sport or whimsy rather than for life. I never took a life that I didn't absolutely need to take, for my continued existence. Today's vampire is a child. A bastardized version of Revall's original vision. I will take solace in knowing that the end is all too soon for this kind of creature/person hybrid."

"Do you know where Aylash Revall is now?"

"Of course I do! He's barricaded himself in that grotesque fortress, the House of the Winged God." Just saying the words caused a physically adverse reaction in The Jester. His lips tied themselves together as if stitched by a doctor, and his fists clinched tight, until it appeared his fingers would gouge through their own palms. His head hung low with shame and regret.

"What exactly is your history with Revall?" I sheepishly squeaked out through one side of my mouth.

"I should kill you for asking such a question, as if we were long time friends. But I must be getting sentimental in my old age. Don't you need to be getting back to your fancy hotel and your girlfriend, so you can suck on her exposed arm, or breast?"

"I've got time."

"You sad little boy. Every vampire thinks they have time. That is Revall's greatest betrayal."

Le Bouffon looked me over, held out his hand, and as I came forward to take it, he thrust one arm below my left armpit, his fingertips planted firmly on my back, and then he ran toward the basilica holding me ever closer to him. Inexplicably, he "scaled" or climbed the walls of the basilica with only his legs and left arm, virtually flying to the top of its dome. This is where he would tell me a story I'd never – ever – forget.

Chapter Eight: An Origin Rooted in Pain

The Jester unhanded me, letting me gently catch my footing in the dome of the basilica's highest tower, as a smattering of birds were hastily awoken from their sleep. He inhaled a few deep breaths, indicating that he was unpleasantly surprised by the effort needed to carry me such a height, and paused to make himself comfortable before delving into the past.

"I do not know where I was born, but I grew up in a village in Limeray, which is just under three hours from Paris by automobile, but significantly faster if you use the train. I was born an orphan in 1704, raised in the church, and on my own by aged nine. I worked where and whenever I could, doing what needed to be done to allow my belly to sleep without starving. My attitude, though, was a problem for many in Limeray, and I soon turned to petty crime and public entertainment for my income. I was very flexible and uncharacteristically strong, so I would perform these crazy feats of strength or dexterity, and was soon equally applauded and ridiculed for my talents. Instead of work the land for my shelter and food, I would sneak around and take what I could. I was branded a delinquent and a villain, but the King's men in the countryside could never catch me. Eventually, the people started calling me Le Bouffon, even though I was not the Kingdom's or any court's official jester. It stuck, and I hated it at first, but in time I would turn the name into something to be feared. I started working as a kidnapper and assassin, a shadow that would enter a home and exit with a family member, or your jewels, or your family steel. I slept where I could, usually in a barn, or an inn by a brothel, but always on the lookout for the authorities. They were always hoping to catch me after a drunken night with a mistress. Only once was I captured, but I managed to escape, and kill my way out, scurrying to Amboise. That is where I met my curse. Where I met Aylash Revall."

"When was this?"

"I was twenty-two years old. It was March of 1727. I had snuck inside the chateau at Amboise, into the grave of Leonardo da Vinci. I was taking a piss on his tomb when a gust of wind blew in and almost knocked me off my feet. It was followed by hands on the back of my shoulders. Something lifted me up in the air and threw me into a wall. Before I landed to the floor, it was cradling me like a baby. A full-grown adult baby. I tried to move, but was secured tight to this creature. He spoke, and I realized it was a man. I *thought* it was a man. He said, 'Do you think it is acceptable to desecrate the resting place of one of the most brilliant and marvelous examples this human world has ever created?" I had no answer; all I could do was tremble and cough. He continued. 'He was not my friend, but we had a mutual admiration for each other. I have a mind to reach down your throat and pull your heart through your mouth, but I'm going to give you a second chance, and lifetimes to pay your respects.'

"He let my legs fall toward the floor, but held my upper body in his arms, and he bit down on my throat with a forceful jaw, piercing my skin and flesh effortlessly. Blood flooded out of me into his mouth, and just seconds later he dropped me like an unwanted toy. I was in shock, and I backed up against a wall, grabbing for my neck, trying to stop the bleeding when a pain seared through me like acid had been poured into my veins, rushing like a river gone mad. I writhed and convulsed, unable to control my movements or my pain, and I lunged toward this demon, reaching my hands out to him for resolution. Absolution. I clutched his garments, and he swatted my hand away just as the night's guard rushed in to investigate the loud noise disturbing the peaceful chateau. In a split second, Revall was contorting the man's neck, paralyzing him, hopeful that more guards would not be following close behind."

'You will need to drink this man's blood if you're not to starve to death. Luckily for you, I made him less resistant to your advance.'

"I couldn't fathom what he was saying, but yet I somehow knew to follow his direction. I crawled my way over to the guard, who was now alert and staring at me, his fractured bones and severed spinal cord refusing to let his useless body fight for life. I laid myself atop his chest, and positioned my torso and head so that I may lean down and take a mouthful of his exposed neck. The look of terror in his eyes radiated that fear into the open air, and he tried to gurgle out some words convincing enough to stop me from my purpose. All I heard was the loud white swirl of pain as it coursed through my veins and out my pores. I bit down on his throat, and Aylash Revall guided me through my first kill. I drained the poor guard dry, and afterward I was intoxicated by the blood keeping me alive. I didn't have too much time to feel the high of the effects, as Aylash Revall grabbed me by my collar and lifted me up on my feet. He turned me, so my back was to him, and then completed the punishment he'd started by making me a vampire. 'You consider yourself a jester?' he whispered in my ear. 'Well, forever, you will be one.'

"He then took some silver liquid from a sealed jar in his pocket, wrenched my jester's hat down over my eyes, and smeared the liquid over my face. It seared my skin, and melded the fibers of the mask to my face. Aylash then ripped holes into the hat so I could see through it. I screamed in agony as the liquid infiltrated and dried upon me. I tried to break free from his grip, but Revall just held me there like he was holding a two-year old who didn't want to get dressed. As the liquid bubbled on my cheeks and smoldered until its process was complete, Aylash brought me eye to eye with him. He told me that I could be a monster or that I could be a god, but that I would always be the jester, and then he vanished. Two guards appeared in Da Vinci's tomb, and grabbed me, trying to make sense of what had just happened. Seeing their fellow man on the floor dead angered them, and they began kicking me in the sides, until I rose, grabbing them by their heads. I did not yet possess the superhuman strength I would grow into, but I was manic enough to smash their heads together repeatedly until they were both dead. I then escaped into the night and hid in the forest until daylight came, using a knife to cut more accessible eye holes from my now permanent accessory turned appendage. That morning's sunlight brought the discovery of the unbearable torture that the sun would now inflict on me. You must remember, this was all before your Nosferatu and your Dracula. I had no idea what a vampire was, and had to learn by trial and error. It was over twenty years before I encountered another of our kind. I didn't see Aylash Revall again for over a hundred years, when he walked into the House of the Gray Bear one night like it was his personal French vacation home."

"Why is it named the House of the Gray Bear?" I interrupted.

"Soon you will find out, but not now."

"Do you still keep in contact with Reginald Duplante?"

"Soon you will find out... but not now."

What are you going to---"

"Soon... but not now."

Chapter Nine: A (Brief) Sit-Down at Henri's

So, to my surprise, the House of the Gray Bear is not actually in Paris. It's technically closer to Versailles, which I'd heard of, but don't have any recollection as to why I've heard of it. This small but vital detail of the Gray Bear's location was relayed to me the night I finally met Reginald Duplante. Two days after our first conversation with Magdalena, she'd called Annie and told her that Reginald agreed to meet with us at Henri's later that night, that he would meet us at 11:00, and we should not be late. She also said he would be guarded, short in his words, and easily agitated. He didn't like Americans, and he liked American vampires even less. What a great impression to have before even meeting the guy.

Annie and I arrived five minutes to 11:00 that night, and were seated right away when Henri saw us walk in the door.

"How did you get to this point?" I asked him. "Where you're keeping your café open all night, and becoming some vampire concierge?"

"A chance meeting one night in the park. I stumbled upon a vam... Wait. Didn't Annie tell you all of this already?"

"All of what? How would she know?"

"We spoke the other night, after you left to... you know. To feed." I stared a hollow, blank gaze through the back of Annie's head. She had her back to me, but I could feel her tighten her shoulders and bring her arms into her ribs, like she knew she was in trouble for something.

"Oh. No. She must have forgotten to mention it."

Henri led us to a table in the back of the café, half shrouded by a curtain for privacy. I felt like a VIP.

"Davis, Annie, meet Reginald Duplante, captain of the House of the Gray Bear."

I stuck my hand out to shake his, and was met with a slight lift of his head and a side eyed stare. Reginald didn't stand to shake my hand, or move at all. He projected a grizzled and ornery persona. He had stylish brown hair, peppered with gray streaks, and a quaffed beard to match. He wore corduroy pants, and his tan and caramel tweed jacket had oval patches on the elbows like from the 1980's. I've found that vampires tend to find a decade or a style, and it becomes theirs. They hold onto it forever.

"Hello, Mr. Davis. Ms. Annie."

"Hello, Reginald. Thank you for meeting with us."

"Don't thank me, yet. I understand you come all the way from Texas. Do you know J.R.?"

"What?" I was baffled. Thank God for Annie.

"I think he's talking about an old TV show."

"Ah. Ding. Ding. Ding! She gets it!"

Reginald's sarcasm and patronizing tone quickly dissuaded me from being reverential and overrun with pleasantries, so I thought I would get right to the point and barrage him with an overlapping volley of questions.

"Why did the Gray Bear file a grievance with the Blood Fountain? Why did you have to go to war? Why did the Winged God become involved and why and how did they end the war? How many vampires died? How long have you and the Jest---"

"Patience, little boy." Reginald gritted his teeth and pounded his fist on the table just hard enough to make a point, causing Annie to lean back in her seat, and dip her chin to her chest. I could hear her mouth emit a low-registered 'ooooh', like one would in elementary school right before a fight erupted on the playground.

"Patience is not something I have a wealth of. I'm trying to get to the heart of Aylash Revall's secrets, and eventually come face to face with him."

"Congratulations. That is truly the stupidest thing I've heard anyone say in quite some time. I am over 700 years old, and you really... how do they say?... take the cake. Good job, little boy."

"If you call me little boy one more time, I'm gonna take something el---"

Annie, and Henri, who couldn't help eavesdropping from just outside the curtain, both sought to lighten the atmosphere, but true to Magdalena's warnings, Reginald stood abruptly and declared that he would be leaving. Turning to address Henri, he spoke the following:

"You shouldn't allow just any vampire in here like a starving, stray puppy. It will eventually catch up to you. They bite."

And turning back to the table, he glared at me.

"And you. You have so much to learn about what we are and why we're still here. Hunting for Aylash will only lead to destruction. Fucking Texan."

With that, he left everyone at Henri's, and Magdalena shot a bewildered, judging glance at both Annie and me.

"I told you. I told you what he was like, and what he would do. You knew he wouldn't tolerate some---"

"Back your ass up a minu---" Annie started to say, when Magdalena grabbed her by the throat, and pushed her up against the wall, eyes ablaze and teeth showing.

"You have no business being in my city, in my café, in this conversation! You are an insect that I step on, on a daily basis. You are the weak. The pitiful."

"Well that was a fucking mistake," I interrupted. "You're going to unhand my girlfriend now, and refrain from insulting her any longer, or you'll end up in eternity as an afterthought."

Henri, knowing that he was also an "insect" in this scenario, kept his distance while attempting to keep the peace.

"Please; Magdalena, Davis. We can be civilized about this, yes?"

"I don't know, Henri. Maybe we can't. Maybe we're just savages who know only death."

I could tell that Magdalena's grip on Annie was only at human level strength; otherwise she would have corkscrewed her head right off her neck. She'd also eased her down from suspended in air to on her feet. But it was still strong enough that Annie's face was quickly changing from skin toned to purplish red, which boiled my insides like nothing had in a long time.

"I'm giving you only a second or two before I unleash some fancy, dominant electric shit from my hands and turn you into a popsicle of ash and regret."

"If you can't keep your girlfriend from making a fool of herself, or protect her from a vampire's advances, what makes you think *you* can even survive me?"

Just then, that same smell of Sulphur and soggy, mossy leaves I'd inhaled a couple of days prior permeated the room, and Le Bouffon's hands were ripping Magdalena off of Annie, and stiff-arming me back another five feet.

"Because he has the Namtudari, or can't you smell its pulsing, aggravated need to unfurl and wreak havoc from his veins? Can you not see the Christopher Lee fangs jutting from his gums like he was a little boy at Halloween?"

Magdalena stood, unimpressed, left hand on her hip.

"It's very unexpected to see you so close to humanity. You must be careful, my phantom. Everyone has a camera these days. It would be a shame to cheapen the legend of Le Bouffon... The Namtudari is a myth."

"You stupid child. You chose not to fight the Blood Fountain. You chose to spend your time galivanting and burlesquing among the humans. You didn't see Aylash utilize it to end the war abruptly. Reginald has told you, I'm sure. The Luminastra set your countrymen afire, froze them, *and* disintegrated them in mere seconds. It's something I still cannot shake from my mind's eye, and I've been around to see the unbelievable."

"It doesn't change the fact that he's dooming himself and everyone around him by letting his pet get too close, and too authoritative."

The Jester turned to me. "She's right, you know? This thing you have with your human girlfriend. It is destined to fail. She may very well be the cause of your demise."

"That's between me and her. It ain't none a 'yer business."

"Then go back home. Stay out of *my* business. Leave France. Leave the House of the Winged God behind. Leave Aylash... Behind."

"I can't."

"Of course you can't. You're a child in this upside-down world. And children do not do what they're told. So, if that's the case, you'll need to go to---"

"Don't say it" Magdalena intruded.

"---the House of the Gray Bear".

"Let's go, now" I demanded.

"No, you'll have to wait until tomorrow night. It's too far away."

"What do you mean? You have a good transit system here, and we can run long distances very fast."

"It's not here. The Gray Bear is in Versailles. See you there."

"When?"

"Tomorrow."

I looked at Annie, and she looked at me, our eyes each saying to the other 'Looks like we're going to Versailles', and when I turned to confirm with Le Bouffon, he was no longer there.

Magdalena shook her head. "Fucking Texan," was all she said.

Chapter Ten: The Gatekeeper of Versailles

Annie procured a rental car, and we set out for Versailles at sundown. It was just a forty-minute drive from Paris, but then we would have to "discover" the House of the Gray Bear, and who knew how long that would take. It gave us some time to talk.

"Why didn't you tell me about your conversation with Henri?" I asked, frankly.

"Oh," Annie replied, deflated. "I was wondering when you were going to bring that up."

"So?"

"There was nothing to bring up. He just told me about how he ended up opening a café, and how he ended up... palling around with vampires. No big deal."

"Obviously. It's something I hear about every day. On the news. On Facebook. It's basically such a boring story now. Frenchman aligning themselves with vampires. So passe."

"Babe. You used 'passe'." *Is she patronizing me?* 'Oh wow. You're really jealous. I've never seen this."

"I'm not jealous... I'm just... I'm protective. I don't know what his intentions are. And neither do you."

"Awww." She was grinning a mile wide. "Who cares what his intentions are? I'm *your* girlfriend. And you're my man. Got it?"

"Of course I got it." *I think*.

Annie's head shifted downward and towards the window. She was biting her bottom lip. And 3-2-1...

"So what's going on between you and Magda-whora? Oops; I mean Magdalena."

"What do you mean? Nothing's going on."

"Oh really?"

"Now who's jealous?"

"I fucking am. Me. *I'm* jealous. I mean, *protective*. I saw the whatever it is between you. The 'spark'."

“Get the fuck outta here with that. Spark? Spark, my ass. She thinks I’m a fucking idiot.”

“She was attracted to you.”

“That’s straight bullshit.”

“She said ‘I’m sure we can *change* that’, in that sultry, seductive ass voice. Staring you right in the eye. You don’t have a lot of experience with catty, no-good bitches, but I sure as hell do.”

“She was just messing around.”

“Her nipples got hard! Did you think I wouldn’t notice that? I thought vampires had to feed to get aroused.”

“Nipples? I didn’t notice anything like that.” I *had* noticed it. ‘Maybe she got cold. Vampires are cold by nature. You’re acting a little crazy now.”

She started to say something, but then stopped herself. Annie was mulling something in her brain, gnawing on that bottom lip, trying to formulate the correct string of words when I infiltrated her train of thought with a preemptive strike.

“Look. I love you. I love you more and more every day. If you say Henri’s harmless, then so be it. And I’m telling you that Magdalena’s no threat. Either physically or romantically. It’s you and me, Annie. You and me.”

She breathed in deep, and exhaled frustratingly.

“OK. If you say we’re good, we’re good. I love you, too. Now let’s find this fucking Gray Bear. I’m nervous.

And I'm getting hungry."

"Well... There, you'd probably end up being the meal instead of the clientele."

"Clientele? You're getting so vocabulary all of a sudden. Asshole."

Once inside the city limits, we drove around, and I let my nose guide me. Annie needed to eat, so her nasal passages, and Google, were scoping out restaurants, when I caught something.

"I found the scent."

"What?! Where?"

"That place in the center of the street. Inside there. There are two, no, three vampires."

"That's Dorian's Pub. Are you sure?"

"100%."

"OK, then. You go in there. I'm going to go to the pizza place two doors down."

"Wait a---"

"BEFORE you get all protective, I'm just going to be two doors away from you, and when I'm done with my pizza, I'll come over and find you. If your vampire friends try to take you out of there, or something goes funny, you call me. I'll do the same. OK?... OK?"

"Fine. Order, eat, and come over as soon as you can."

"Will do."

I parked, and then Annie and I went our separate ways, but I waited until she was inside the pizzeria before entering Dorian's Pub. Once inside, I scanned the establishment for my contacts, and found them rather easily. They didn't exactly look inconspicuous, their getup resembling punks out of '70's England, so I might have even been able to identify them without the wisp of death floating on their flesh.

"You look like a fish out of water" one of them spoke, in English but with a heavy French accent.

"Is it that easy to tell?"

They looked at each other, and then broke into a brief collective laugh.

"Yes, it is. Where are you from, my friend?"

"Texas. Abilene, Texas."

"What is Abilene?"

"It's not important. Just my home, is all."

"What are you doing in Versailles? A vacation with the wife and kids?"

Again they broke into laughter. These were very clearly not the serious, integrity-filled defenders of the vampire race that Duplante and Le Bouffon seemed to be. These ones were younger. More carefree. Therefore, more dangerous.

“I’m here looking for the House of the Gray Bear. I’m looking for Reginald Duplante.”

Their laughter and smug atmosphere came to a rapid halt, and they looked at each other again, this time with a grim seriousness to their expressions. There still only appeared to be one member of the group designated as the spokesman.

“Perhaps... Perhaps that’s not the best decision to make. Maybe, instead, you should think about going to Paris. Visit the Eifel---”

“I just came from Paris. I already saw the Eifel Tower, and Le Bouffon told me to come to Versailles if I wanted to find the Gray Bear. I *want* to find the Gray Bear, and I want you to take me there. Now.” The spokesman put his hand over his mouth and started tapping his hand on the table, while the other two kept darting their eyes between themselves, him, and me. ‘Do you guys always have to have some silent committee meeting before one of you talks, or can you speak your mind without some secret permission?”

“Easy. Easy. You don’t have to get... agitated. We will take you to the Gray Bear. We just have to wait on a couple of our friends. They will be here soon, no?”

“OK, then. I’ll just ease into this chair with you guys and wait.”

I texted Annie to get an ETA on her arrival, when she walked through the door of Dorian’s Pub with two other people. Two other vampires. One of them was a woman, dark haired, wrinkled, and irritable looking, and the other a man, well-dressed and stuffy looking. He looked more like a librarian than a vampire. He was clearly the intellectual alpha among this group.

"Look what we found wandering the streets; a young American woman who wreaked of vampire. Does this pet belong to you, sir?" This librarian was English. Or British. I don't know what the difference is, if there is one. Annie wasn't overtly frightened, but she immediately grabbed a chair and sat beside me, grasping onto my arm.

"She's not my pet; she's my girlfriend. I'd make sure I know the difference."

"My apologies, good sir. I didn't mean to offend either of you. I should know to speak with more... I'll address her more properly in the future."

"Please do. Thank you. Now that you're here, can we get onto the House of the Gray Bear?"

"In good time, sir. First, I have a few... *screening* questions for you. A harmless but necessary procedure, I'm afraid."

"Okaaaayyy." I could feel my arms ache with impatience, and my temples seize with severe annoyance. 'Proceed."

"What is your name, and why are you here?"

"My name is Davis McCarty, and I'm here to find out all I can about the Gray Bear and its conflict with the Blood Fountain, and to locate Aylash Revall."

"What do you want with Aylash Revall?"

His teeth ground against each other, his veins engorged and penetrated the barrier of his skin, and his age spots and freckles fought a war with the goosebumps now emblazoned across his body. The mere mention of Revall's name touched a nerve. A bitter nerve.

"Hold up a second. What is *your* name?"

"Fuggerton."

"Fugger-what?"

"Fuggerton. Edsel Antony Fuggerton."

"Hmmm." I didn't know why, but his name wanted to make me crack up laughing. Loudly. Annie could sense this, and she gave me a nudge with her elbow. Luckily, I was able to ascend to a place of inner peace and discipline. I did have to get at least one comment off my chest, however. "Is your nickname 'Mother'?"

"Mother? Ah yes, how very clever of you. As in Mother Fugger – ton. I've never heard that joke... a thousand times."

"Sorry. I can tell it's a touchy subject. Resume your inquisition, Edsel."

"What do you want with Aylash Revall?"

"Answers."

"To what?"

“A million things, Fuggerton.”

“Name one.”

“Like why the hell do I have the Luminastra Namtudari, did he create it, if he did, how come that process isn’t covered in his journals, and how do I control it?”

“Hmm. That’s more like four things. Very well done, Davis. Before I get to the very intriguing subject of the Namtudari, how did you find out about the Gray Bear?”

“From the journals I found in the underbelly of the House of the Black Moon.”

“My goodness. Ladies and gentlemen, we have in our presence the man who destroyed the House of the Black Moon.”

The four other vampires shot each other angry, almost menacing stares, and then they all focused those stares on me.

“At one point in time, such a revelation would lead to us all devouring you, pulling your limbs from your body, and dumping whatever remained of you in a river, to flow into the sea and be consumed by its scavengers. Only now, after everything’s gone to shit, the former rules no longer seem to apply. Younger vampires emerge, as they always do, and with them, new societal norms.”

“Are you saying you all used to be more unified?”

“Indeed. All of Europe’s vampires coexisted

peacefully, and we were even rather cordial with our brothers and sisters in Asia and South America. Unfortunately, things change."

"Things don't change, Fuggerton."

"I'm sorry?"

"People don't change, and things don't change. People change *things*, and things change *people*. So what 'thing' changed the vampires?"

"Just the opposite, my young friend. A 'people' was the catalyst in this situation. More like four people. Antonio Giordano Medici, who rose through the ranks of the Blood Fountain's leadership, corrupted and crippled its relationship with our local vampire communities and the other Houses, and sought undue favor with Aylash Revall. His becoming the captain of the Blood Fountain is the single most destructive moment in vampire history. Aylash, who by now you know, was the first ever vampire on earth, and for a time was our example to learn and live by. Something changed in him as the last 500 years or so droned on and created new nations and new cultures. He became disillusioned and began to lash out at both human and vampire alike. I believe he was tired of living in the shadows, and wished to become "famous" for lack of a better word."

"Acknowledged?" I offered.

"Yes. Perhaps, that's a better description. Anyhow, those two, Lenora Jeffries, an ambitious, bitter woman in London who petitioned staunchly for a House to exist in

England, and an American, Warren Winston. These four vampires, individually, and sometimes directly aligned, helped take twelve vampire Houses, twelve strongholds, and reduce them to almost nothing. And with a little help from you, now only two exist."

"I know of Warren Winston. I learned his story as I experienced mine. Antonio Medici is in files related to the House of the Blood Fountain, but I have no idea who Lenora Jeffries is."

"That's probably for the best. She still exists, unfortunately. So I pray that you never cross paths. She's a cancer, and extinguishes every relationship she tries to cultivate. You'll have no such problem with Medici. The Jester ended his reign as captain of the Blood Fountain, along with his existence on this earth."

"Thank you for the history lesson, Edsel. Can we start heading over to the Gray Bear now?"

"Such an eager student. You've certainly waited long enough. But I do have to ask, do you have the Luminastra Namtudari?"

"Indeed I do."

"Please explain. What's it like?"

"It's like the feeling you get when someone you're secretly in love with enters the room. Your heart races and pumps a gallon of blood per second. Your palms itch and sweat, and you can't focus on any one image longer than a fraction of a second." Annie grabbed onto my hand after hearing these words. Her touch was gentle and warm. "But instead of thinking about that person and feeling loving gooeyness, a freezing yet burning, mystical electricity forms from within your body and exits through your hands, impressively annihilating anything it touches."

"Outstanding. And why did this elusive gift get bestowed upon you?"

"That's one answer I'm hoping Aylash Revall can answer?"

"Well, I hope that you'll get your chance. I haven't seen him since the day he used that very gift to slaughter many of my friends. Friends that enjoyed their freedom and their anonymity in the very House we're leaving for now. The five of us will be taking two cars. You can follow, but you'll have to keep up."

"Can't you just give us the address, so we can put it in the---"

"Like I said, you'll have to keep up. Let us depart."

As we rose and started to exit Dorian's Pub, I couldn't help but sense the wrinkled woman with Fuggerton, and her cold stare as it remained fixed on me. I chose to engage.

"Penny for your thoughts?"

"Gold would not be enough, for my... thoughts."

"Fair enough."

Chapter Eleven: The Gray Bear

As we took the short but winding drive through the countryside to the House of the Gray Bear, Annie held my hand tight, but looked out the window.

"I can't see a thing, but you can tell that place must be beautiful in the daylight."

"Feel free to go out tomorrow. We can stay here tonight."

"I don't trust staying here."

"We don't have anything to cover the windows if we drive back to Paris. I think we may have no choice."

"We'll see. Necessity creates choices out of thin air."

A large row of trees along the road did well to cover the large estate tucked back into the nature of Versailles, and soon we were coming to a large, graveled driveway, where a solemn faced but handsome valet was waiting to take our rental and park it for us. He welcomed us in French.

"Sorry, senor; I don't know what the hell you're saying."

You'd be able to see his eyes rolling and the look of dismissive disgust on his face from a NASA space station, but he composed himself and changed his demeanor. It was obvious that he'd been disciplined enough to take his duties seriously.

"My mistake," he said in English. 'It was wrong of me to assume that you were French. Please hand me your keys. Your car will be in good hands. Please retrieve it by 30 minutes before sunrise, or there will be no valet available to return the keys to you."

Another attendant waived us forward and opened the large doors to the House of the Gray Bear so we could make our entrance. He did a small doubletake when catching Annie's scent and discovering that she was a 'normal' human. Similar to the Black Moon, a large dance floor was the centerpiece of the establishment, loud music pulsing and pushing gyrating partygoers who mashed and moshed and stomped on its multi-colored marble slab of a foundation. There were covered hallways adorning each side of this large room, and they all led to other smaller rooms hidden away behind ornate wrought iron and glass doors. At first glance upward, there appeared to be at least five levels to the Gray Bear, but it was difficult to assess exactly how big the place was. It was much more expansive than the Black Moon, but then again, it *had* existed for over a thousand years.

At precisely the same time, I could see Edsel standing at an opening behind the dancefloor with Magdalena of all people, while one of the punk looking vampires from the pub was walking towards us. It dawned on me that I didn't get one name from the group of three.

"Hello, Davis. Come with me. Reginald and some others are going to meet with you in the great hall in about twenty minutes. I am Jean Luc, by the way."

"The great hall? Well, what the hell is this room, then?" He didn't answer; he just chuckled a little to himself.

"Young mister Davis" Edsel bellowed as loud as he could atop the music. "How wonderful of you to join us."

"Sure. Whatever."

"Young lady, can we get you anything to drink. I assume you're still full, from dinner. Davis, on the other hand, must be feeling the pain of addiction flow through his body right about now."

True enough, I'd gone too long without feeding. I needed something quick, but didn't know from who. I only knew that I *didn't* want it to come from Annie. That seemed too intimate now for me to share that exchange in front of a bunch of strangers that I didn't trust or even like yet.

"Do you have a room where humans will let us feed on them?"

"Yes, as a matter of fact we do. It may not be what you're used to, though. Please, follow Jean Luc to the feeding room. We can become more acquainted with your girlfriend."

"Whoa! Whoa!" she erupted. "I'm not going anywhere in this place without Davis, and vice versa. He usually feeds on *me*."

Magdalena, who'd been silently studying us with ever blackening eyes, interjected.

"That's not how things are done here at the Gray Bear, I'm afraid. You will be well taken care of out here, while he's well taken care of in there. I will guarantee it."

Magdalena looked at me, and her expression immediately morphed from playful to serious. She gave a slight head nod, a gentle sincerity in her eyes telling me that Annie would be safe.

"Annie. It's alright. You can trust her. You'll be OK."

"Trust her?! She choked the shit out of me, and would have choked the life out of me had you not been there."

Magdalena giggled a little but then stopped herself, cupping her hand over her mouth.

"It's true. That was wrong of me. I won't do that again. And if you look around, you will find that there are a fair amount of humans just like you in the house tonight, every one of them safe among the beasts. You're more than welcome to strike up a conversation with any of them. No harm will come to you... Annie."

Annie wasn't convinced, but she was also well aware that I wouldn't let anything happen to her, and wouldn't dare leave her alone in a den of vampires if I thought it was dangerous for her. In my peripherals, I could sense Fuggerton growing a little impatient, looking at his watch.

"Please, we must decide quickly. Time is of the essence."

"Alright then," Annie conceded. "Show me a good time. I'll have a Cape Cod." Fuggerton relaxed his shoulders gratefully.

"Perfect. Maggie, please lead Annie to the bar and instruct Roland to provide anything she wants free of charge while keeping a trained eye on her. Jean Luc, please lead Davis to the feeding room. Davis, please try and be as efficient as you can. If we delay once Reginald is ready, he will be a sore, petulant child the rest of the night."

Jean Luc led me through one of the covered, tunnel-like hallways past several rooms, including one that looked like a music venue, and then down a staircase to a catacombs-style underground lair. It was very reminiscent of the underbelly of the Black Moon, although much more well-kept. At the end of the line stood a curved wooden door with a large round ring on it, and a slot through which one could peer inside. It was as if I was thrown back in time to a castle in the Middle Ages. The assorted smells of vampire, human, wine, and blood wafted out of that slot, and my throat grew thirsty and anxious. Jean Luc's smile widened as he watched my hunger overtake me.

"In there, Mr. Davis. Your meal awaits."

He knocked the huge iron ring against the wooden door, and someone on the inside opened it. Blasted by a warm humidity and the sounds of clinking glass, chewing and suckling, and whispered conversation, I walked inside to find a much larger room than I expected. Also unexpected were vampires feeding on humans, but not like in one of Sinjin Pierce's establishments, nor like the dungeon that Alister Amaranth kept kidnapped victims locked inside. This was murder, to be sure, but a consensual 'pleasant' kind, if that was possible. I tugged on the doorman's arm, and asked a question that made him look me up and down, before smiling and shaking his head.

"Can I just drink of an open wound without killing anybody?"

"No."

"OK. So then... how does this work?"

He grew frustrated very quickly.

"Have you fed on someone before?"

"Yes, of course."

"Then you know how it works. You grab someone,

you expose their throat, you bite through the skin, you suck the blood." His expression was one of exasperation, but his accent intrigued me. There were plenty of non-French vampires in the House of the Gray Bear.

"Where are you from?" This question threw him off, and I believe he was genuinely pleased someone asked.

"Poland. Drink."

"Just anybody?"

"Anybody."

The menu's ratio was about 60-40 female to male, and they all just lazed about calmly, drinking wine. They seemed intoxicated or under some other influence. Otherwise, they would most likely be screaming and crying, pleading for rescue or escape. I scanned the room, hoping to find the most willing to die, and settled upon a young man who just looked at me with an ambiguous smirk. I looked at the doorman, who nodded at me approvingly, and I looked back at the young man, who just motioned me over with his left hand. My instincts wanted to select a young lady, but I chose a man. I felt that feeding on a woman in this environment was like 'cheating' on Annie. I didn't know exactly why, but felt that way, nonetheless. The young man's eyes told me a story of melancholy and surrender. He knew his fate, and he was ready for it to consume him. He confirmed as much with a few words as I sat down on my side, on a hard, damp stone floor, and grasped his lush brown hair in my hands.

"It's time, friend. Do it."

I held his body in place against the wall with my own, clinched my teeth down on his throat, and drank like I'd never drank before. He let out a frightened sound at first, jolting out his stiffened arms and legs from his torso. His sound then transformed into a moan, like his end was becoming pleasurable. His right hand grasped onto my bicep and held it comfortingly. His aroma was a mixture of sweet perspiration, 90's cologne, and unclean filth, telling me that he'd been down in this room for several consecutive days without a shower. Edsel's warning about time echoing in my brain, I finished the process in about half the time I normally would, and stared at the man's face when he went still. His eyes looked into mine with an empty satisfaction, his ordeal over.

I rose to my feet and wiped off any dirt or debris from my clothes, looking back awkwardly at the doorman.

"I guess that's it."

"Yes."

"You didn't know his name, by chance, did you? The young man?"

"Would it matter?" He spoke to someone through the slot in the door. "Take this last one to The Abomination. Take our guest to the great hall."

As I got to the door, the doorman stopped me, placing his hand on the center of my chest. I didn't know if things were going to turn negative for a second, when he spoke as softly as a grumpy, Polish vampire could.

“These people. They have nothing left to live for. Their lives outside this room... They... Not good. This is respectable. No more pain. The drink is “touched.” It makes the process easier.”

“Sure. If you say so. Have a good night.” As the door closed, I turned and asked, “What is The Abomination?”

“You’ll see” was the muffled reply from the other side of the closed wooden door that resembled some Robin Hood inspired horror story.

Chapter Twelve: Conclave

Jean Luc, now rejoined by his fellow punks, including the 'spokesman' from Dorian's, who I learned was named Marcus, led me back up the staircase, and down one hallway to another on the opposite side of the estate, where we took a left turn into the aforementioned great hall. I tried to find Annie as we walked back among the general population, but I couldn't locate her image. I did manage to catch her scent, and it was still alive and free of blood, so I figured she was still safe and partying it up. Jean Luc announced my presence to the room, and ushered me in, closing the tall double doors behind me. I was face to face with what I assumed, after the war with the Blood Fountain and Winged God, remained of the leadership of the House of the Gray Bear. This was a large but cozy stone and wood grained meeting room, equipped with an oversized fireplace and the busts of slain animals on the walls. The ceiling was at least twenty feet high, and the hall was overall very welcoming. The eighteen vampires all staring sharpened, figurative daggers through my heart, on the other hand...

"Mr. Davis McCarty" Reginald Duplante welcomed me. "Please grace us with your presence and amaze us with your tale of poor, lost child to omnipotent, ambitious detective. We are the House of the Gray Bear, and in time you'll be introduced to us all individually."

I scanned the faces looking at me in various forms of peculiar, measured interest, distrust, or ambivalence, and noticed that Magdalena was now in the room, leaning against a distant door, even though she didn't appear to be in any leadership role. Also in the room, Le Bouffon hung defiantly atop one of the beautifully complicated chandeliers as far removed as possible from the large rectangular table the rest of the assembled group sat around.

"Thank you... Thank you for the opportunity to come here, and... talk to y'all... about... about, you know. The House of the Winged God, and Aylash... Aylash Revall."

"Why are you so nervous, Davis?" Reginald was confused. "There is no reason for hesitancy. I mean, you can destroy us all, yes? We are no match for the Texas Luminastra."

Almost everyone gathered busted out in laughter, which caused my newly ingested blood to boil. I'm *not* one for being the butt of jokes.

"Is something funny, Reginald? Maybe I'm not up to date on the French sense of humor. I don't know why I'm nervous; I guess I'm not comfortable with public speaking... And yes, I *can* destroy you all, comically easily, with one blast from my fucking hands."

Their laughter stopped instantly.

"Who is this child?" one of the men asked incredulously. With that, several other voices rose, until a cacophony of undecipherable protests occupied the room. Reginald, remembering our meeting at Henri's, grew a big smile across his face.

"Be careful" Reginald silenced everyone. "Davis doesn't like such descriptions. He is a man, after all."

"Then treat me like one."

"In our defense, all of us here are much older than you, and some of us are much older even than the country you call home. Relatively, you are a child compared to the vampires of the Gray Bear. In all seriousness, tell us your story, briefly, and if there are any requests contained therein, we will discuss them and come to a decision."

At Reginald's direction, I did just that. Trying to be as succinct as possible, I relived the day of my transformation, the immediate aftermath, the road trip across America searching for Unholy Saint, my inability to shake the love from or for Annie, the culmination of my search at the House of the Black Moon, and the subsequent data I took with me.

"All of that story has led me here, to this place, in front of all of you."

“Don’t you mean, ‘y’all’?” a thin, pale, sharp featured man jested for the group, resulting in yet another round of boisterous laughter at my expense. My teeth clinched hard, and my hands became fists. I’m finding that I don’t like to be made fun of. It happened enough when I was growing up, and I felt powerless to stop it. Now, though, I knew that stop it is exactly what I could do. So as the thin comedian threw his head back, mid-laugh, I flew at him in a controlled rage, taking his bony jaw in my hand as three of his compatriots seized me and held me against the table. I believe we were all equally surprised by how quickly we’d sprang into action.

“Mr. Davis, I should be in awe of how quickly you were able to get to Paul, but you should also understand how easy it would be, Namtudari or not, to destroy you. Any escalation in the Gray Bear will lead to a truly destiny-changing interaction with The Abomination. Trust me when I say that neither you, nor your girlfriend, would appreciate that interaction.”

“Let me go, and I’ll be cool. Don’t insult my home or my accent, and we’ll be jus---”

“We can insult anything and ANYONE WE PLEASE! This is *MY* HOUSE!”

Just then, a small smattering of hand clapping came from atop the chandelier at the opposite end of the room. The Jester was sarcastically applauding Reginald’s outburst. He now chose to involve himself, leaping from the suspended work of domestic art, landing quite gracefully.

"Why is it that you can muster a necessary anger at precisely all the times it is not needed? Why does that anger shrivel and disappear into your testicles when it would actually be beneficial?"

"I don't know what you mean, but I could ask you basically the same question. Why are you a member of this room or this community when it suits or amuses you, but not when you deem it an inconvenience?"

As The Jester walked slowly toward the assembled body, he and Reginald stared each other down silently, never leaving each other's eyes. A growing tension mounted on everyone's shoulders, and in their throats.

"I've given a great deal to this room and to this '*community*', so I don't appreciate my intentions or my loyalty being questioned."

"You've become a fairytale, and you preferred it that way even before you were a vampire. You've become a shadow. The shadow of Montmartre. It's amazing that you even left Paris to be here."

"I understand the importance of such a meeting. The gravity of what it could entail."

"And what is that, eh?"

"The chance to finish the job."

"You mean kill Revall?"

"Why not?"

Things got very serious within the walls of the great hall, and everyone started to whisper and mumble to each other. It didn't take me long to figure out that me and my fancy tricks were the lynchpin to The Jester's interest. Reginald sought to calm things down, but Le Bouffon had other ideas, addressing the whole of the conclave.

"Shouldn't you all want to jump at the chance to get the ultimate vengeance, the ultimate justice, for the *injustice* that was committed against the Gray Bear and all of France's vampires?"

"The war was fought, and it was finished," Duplante countered. "We won by not being completely obliterated by Revall, and he won by claiming victory and slinking back home to his fortress, before disappearing altogether. I don't need to fight the same war again, and I don't need to revisit the image of him setting more than half of my countrymen, my brethren, afire with the Luminastra. We are lucky to be alive."

"We are NOT ALIVE! Each and every one of us died the day we became vampires. I died in Amboise almost three hundred years ago, and I died again at the hands of the Lower God. I want my revenge!"

"And who says that Davis McCarty is here for a battle? And who says Davis McCarty would be on our side?"

Reginald's question stopped the conversation dead cold, and the whole of the room cast their eyes upon me curiously. A mere three seconds went by like it was a century. I broke the tension by creating more.

"Indeed. Who says I'd join you prim and proper fuckers, or that freak show with the clown hat?"

Le Bouffon stared at me, first with a look that told me I'd broken his heart, and then with a widening smile as he started to laugh quietly. His laugh then morphed into a cackling howl, as if he was watching a George Carlin special.

"Oh, Davis! You miserable Texas bastard!" Le Bouffon yelled, as he approached me. He grabbed each side of my face with his hands and kissed me on my right cheek. Seeing this let everyone breathe a sigh of relief, and then they all sort of started laughing, but a much more nervous laugh. Reginald stood up from his chair and stared solemnly, not uttering a word or making a sound, his hands on his hips. 'Don't you see?" The Jester continued. 'I think everyone here has become too desensitized to our lot in life. We don't have the connection to the human world that Davis does, except for maybe one of us." Le Bouffon glanced arrogantly in Magdalena's direction when sharing that last statement. 'Like an imbecile, he wants to try and become human again, for his Annie. He hasn't experienced the joys of immortality, or the advantages his condition gives him over the human world. He wants to go back to eating potato chips and drinking soda, yes? He wants a 'normal life'. That's why he wants to visit Aylash Revall. And, if he thinks he can attain this wish by killing Revall, that's what he plans to do."

Reginald Duplante put his head down, hand over his mouth, and stroked his beard several times before replying. "Does Le Bouffon's hypothesis ring true, Davis?"

“I’d be lying if I said it didn’t. But at the same time, I’m not looking to be a soldier, or a pawn, in someone else’s war, especially if it’s one you can’t win.”

The Jester’s eyes grew afire with delight and ambition. “Oh, but with you alongside us, Davis, we *can* win.”

“I came to find out where the House of the Winged God was, and to hear more about your war with the Blood Fountain, but I don’t plan on leaving here tonight with a decision, one way or the other, about fighting him, or much less waging an all-out war on him. I don’t even know what I’m in for, or what I, or we, would be up against.”

“If you and Annie stay at least one more night here, I can make your decision clearer for you” Reginald stated flatly. “You would have an idea of *exactly* what you are up against. And if you must know, I can also share the details about our conflict and eventual war with Italy and the Winged God. First, you must meet everyone, and take a grander tour of the Gray Bear. It would not be thorough enough without setting eyes on The Abomination.”

“What the hell is The Abomination, already?! And can Annie finally join me?”

“Oh, how sweet of you. Yes, we will get your Annie, and you can experience the Gray Bear together. It will be very... eye opening.”

Chapter 12.5: The War Council

After individually speaking with the eighteen vampires I stood and spilled my guts in front of, six stood out as highly interesting, highly suspicious, or potentially helpful. I'd eventually christen them, jokingly, The War Council. In addition to Edsel, Magdalena, The Jester, and Reginald, I made a note of:

1. Paul Lajoie – The rail thin comedian of the group who I had to restrain myself from decapitating. He kept a hard, scornful stare on me after our incident, and stomached no more than just a few seconds with me afterward.

2. Margerie Duplante – No relation to Reginald, she radiated a sort of fairy godmother vibe. Very joyous and thoughtful during our one-on-one, she expressed remorse for the circumstance by which I was turned, as well as for the loss of my

grandmother. I had never mentioned Mona, but Margerie still knew somehow.

3. Magnus Olruud – A large, burly whitehaired/white bearded man, he stood about 6'4" and uttered just one sentence to me; "If you kill him, I will help."

4. Sylvain Montreux – A good looking, very charismatic man, I would be surprised if he didn't succeed Reginald as captain of the Gray Bear... if it even continued to exist much longer. He said he would most likely not accompany any of us to Serbia, unless he was guaranteed no bloodshed would occur.

5. Thomas Richard – A twin who's brother was slain by Revall's Serbian army, and who himself was tortured by Aylash, Thomas is a bitter, angry man to say the least. There is a half-crazed spark behind his eyes that can either be a strength or a weakness for me. As much as he has a personal vendetta against the Winged God, he did not confirm whether or not he would assist in travelling to Aylash's House.

6. Tamlyn Bernard – An unfortunate vampire, she was only fifteen when she was turned, the circumstance by which was almost identical to mine. That caused an automatic kinship in my heart for her. But there's an odd, coldness I sense from her. Her quiet, distant demeanor is unsettling.

Chapter Thirteen: The Abomination

My head was still spinning from meeting everyone individually after having an already tense appointment with the lot of them. It's funny how even undead people have a phobia of public speaking. My throat was dry, my brain numb, and I felt physically drained. My speech teacher freshman year of high school would *not* have been surprised.

I had left the great hall in search of Annie on or near the big dance floor, so that she may join me on this grand tour of the Gray Bear, and what to my surprise would I find but her and Henri from Paris in deep conversation. Again, I saw him touch her hand in too dainty and long of a caress than I found to be acceptable. If I was a cartoon bull, a jalapeno red steam would erupt from my nostrils, and my bloodshot yellow eyes would shoot out of their sockets a good ten feet. I started to stomp my way over to the table they were leaning on when Magdalena grabbed my arm from behind.

"They're not doing anything, Davis. Be careful. You don't want to cause a scene here. And Henri is a friend to the vampire. Killing him would be a great loss and a fatal mistake."

"I know what I see, and *he's* the one who made the mistake."

"Please. Use your head." She took a glance toward Annie and Henri, and then stood between us, embracing me in a hug. A long, forceful hug. I awkwardly stood there, unsure if I should envelope and hug her back. She then took my hands and planted them on her ass at exactly the moment Annie looked over and saw us. In hindsight, she'd planned the entire display perfectly. I could see Annie almost spit her drink out and bolt from the table in my direction. I pushed Magdalena off of me and stared at her confused and a little pissed.

"What the hell was that?" I asked.

"Yes, what the HELL *WAS* THAT?!" Annie asked us both, but with her eyes firmly locked on me like they were attached by a rope of superglue.

"Spicing things up, maybe," Magdalena replied gingerly.

Just as Annie was going to give her a mouthful of opinionated Texas territoriality, Edsel interrupted. He could sense the tension. There was enough of it he had to virtually rip through its sticky, tough, ectoplasm hide.

"I hope everything is going well here, but we do have to get on with it. Annie, are you joining us?"

"I don't know. Davis, am I joining you, or have I been replaced?"

I just threw my head upward, made out the complex patterns in the ceiling's design, and took a few deep breaths to reset myself. Extending my hand out to take hers, I tried to quell the situation.

"We'll talk about this later."

"Fucking A, we will."

Edsel didn't need to ask, he knew the cause of our tension.

"Maggie---"

"I hate it when you call me that. My na---"

"Right. Maggie, can you please stay back and entertain Henri? I'll take it from here."

The three of us then went behind the bar, through a door and down another, less elaborate hallway, where we met Reginald, Sylvian, and Margorie. Together, they walked us through the House of the Gray Bear. It took almost two hours before we'd completed the tour. Reginald spoke of its formation, its once close ties with Aylash Revall, certain rooms and the several, very important historical figures who'd stepped foot through its doors. The entire time, any time I reached for Annie's hand or to touch her shoulder, back, or cheek, she brushed me away, and walked or looked in the opposite direction. I tried to not let our pending confrontation distract from the moment, and let her sulk.

I was very pleasantly surprised by the music venue inside the Gray Bear. No one was playing tonight, but Reginald ran down a list of artists who'd played it previously, making sure to mention fellow Texans, At the Drive In, their successor, The Mars Volta, and something called D.R.I. Other notable acts included Jane's Addiction, Nine Inch Nails, St. Vincent, and Superjoint Ritual. Close to the end of our walking history lesson, we came to the entrance of what I suspected was some hidden, VIP-type room, where I expected to find more vampires feeding on humans, but in a more stylish interior. Instead the door opened up to a balcony which hovered over a dark, cold, vile smelling cavern of a room almost as large as the Gray Bear's dance floor. It resembled a sort of animal den, but a man-made one. The smell of dead, exposed, decomposing flesh filled the room and our nostrils with its atrocious welcome. Across the expanse, at the bottom of the room, sat a gate on display by torches. A very heavy-duty gate, built into the natural stone that the House was built out of, it would have prevented the Kraken from Clash of the Titans from escaping. From behind the darkness of that gate, we heard an animalistic groan/roar combination, and Annie and I looked at each other, curiously.

"Would you like to go down for a closer look?" Reginald questioned, with a childlike gleam in his eye. It was the first time he didn't seem hundreds of years old. "Would you like to finally meet The Abomination?"

"Yes, please." My curiosity won the battle with my common sense, and as Annie nodded at me sheepishly, I saw in her eyes that her internal struggle was fought and won by the same player.

"Let us go, then." Reginald opened a trap door in the floor of the balcony, and pulled a lever, which triggered some staircase to protrude magically from within the walls, and we descended that staircase down to the bottom level of the cavernous quiet room.

As our feet touched the floor of the room, a much louder growl reverberated through the entire room, and I could swear I felt vibrations from the sound. Annie didn't ignore me anymore, instantly wrapping her arms around my right and snuggling her head on my shoulder.

"Did you not read of this in your documents you stole – I mean procured – from the Black Moon?" Reginald was puzzled.

"I never came across anything called 'The Abomination', if that's what you mean. He was otherwise fairly descriptive and proud of his experiments."

"Maybe this will reveal how 'proud' he was... Open the gate."

Sylvain and another vampire stood on a platform above and behind the gate, and turned two wheels on either side of it, which acted as a primitive lever and pully system, far less impressive than the staircase in the wall. The gate rose about half a foot every two seconds, and once it hit its limit, a pair of luminescent, scorching eyes emerged from the darkness, and the largest animal I've ever seen in person lumbered out of his cave-like domain. It was a bear, *sort of*, but not *exactly*. He set those glowing, vicious eyes on Annie and me, and he took off in a run right for us. Luckily, his hind legs were secured by ridiculously large shackles, and his sprint was halted abruptly when the chain they were attached to ran out of length. The creature's face hit the floor, and it lay there flat on his belly, whimpering a pathetic sound, which caused Annie to feel an instant sympathy for it.

"What the fuck is *that*?" she asked. Reginald put his hands on the bear thing's head and rubbed it like he was petting a golden lab in the backyard. It had fanglike teeth jutting out from both its upper *and* lower jaws.

"This... is the... Abomination! The Siberian/Polar Bear hybrid that Aylash Revall turned into a vampire. This is the creature that the House of the Gray Bear is named after."

We stood and just stared. Silent. In awe, but full of sadness and empathy.

"Why?" Annie asked weakly, like she was watching those late-night animal cruelty commercials with the sad Sarah Whatshername song.

"Several reasons. One, because he wanted to. Two, because he could. Three, because he was never satisfied with the way nature left things. He believed that evolution was moving much too slowly. It's the entire reason he ended up like he did. He performed many experiments on animals, including trying to merge two or more species into one. They include aardvarks, hippos, rhinos, horses, pigs, otters, etc. Most never succeeded. Any that did must be held proudly at the Winged God. But Ballou, here, he is a special case. And his name is merely coincidence, not some tribute to that mouse's cartoon buffoon. His name was Ballou some 1,100 years ago, when Aylash spliced his DNA with a Polar bear's, and possibly something else. After Ballou was full grown, Aylash transformed him into a vampire, the only animal vampire as far as I know. Ballou was unable to be tamed after that. He grew enraged and ravenous. But he can still eat normally, so in addition to his need for blood, his hunger for meat and other forms of sustenance grew just as great. He grew too chaotic for Aylash to control, so he left him here, proclaiming Ballou a gift for the first captain of the Gr... of France. The "gift" killed many a vampire, and many more humans, so as this House was being constructed, so was a container strong enough to hold our namesake mascot. His existence, as well as his circumstance, was soon found to be too abnormal to be pleasant, replicated, or sustainable. That is why he is known as The Abomination."

"Why not—" I started.

"Just kill him?" Annie finished.

"It's not his fault, what he is. It was not the former members' place to kill him, just as it is not mine, now."

"It's not kindness or mercy to let an 'abomination'

continue on living."

"Yet he does. He ages, he yellows, he's slowed down considerably, but yet he continues. He just needs help."

"He lives in a fucking cave behind a gate he can't open!" Annie exclaimed.

"We have to protect ourselves as much as we do him!"

"You're confining him, not protecting him."

"You will see it your way. That does not make it so."

At that moment, Ballou, The Abomination raised from his belly and stood on his hind legs. He was bigger than any bear known to man. I estimated his height to be easily fifteen feet, and more yellowish brown-white than gray. He had long-formed scars from clashes with vampire and human alike, and matted fur from centuries in captivity. We were a safe distance from him, but that didn't stop him from swiping at us aggressively multiple times or trying to break free of his shackles. My fear is that I would be in his presence when he was finally successful. Would the Luminastra Namtudari save me in time if The Abomination galloped at me at full speed?

Reginald decided it was time to continue on and leave the bear's den. He motioned over to Sylvain, and a corpse pierced by a long metal hook was lowered down to the floor and placed right at the entrance to the cave. Ballou turned his attention from us to the corpse and scurried over quickly to grab it. Sylvain pushed a button and the hook with the body still on it swished inside the cave by some invisible line, causing the bear to follow in after it. He and the other man then lowered the gate as quickly as they could, before Ballou could escape.

"Now you know a little more of the depth of Aylash's twisted, mad philosophy and its effect on the rest of the world. Do you still want to talk to this man?"

"Yes. Now more than ever, actually."

"Well. It's a discussion we can resume tomorrow. For now, it's time I fed and laid my head down until sundown. We don't want to make rash decisions on an empty stomach or with not enough sleep. I'll guide you back to the dance floor, and then you can go with Edsel to pick which guest rooms you like. We normally don't allow humans to stay over-day in the building, but we will make an exception for you."

"How accommodating of you. Thanks for the hospitality."

"Of course. It's the least I can do for the one who's been prophesized to lead us after the first has died."

"Wait. What?"

Chapter 13.5: Simmering

Fuggerton walked us up a spiral staircase to the second level of the Gray Bear, and led us down a corridor full of resort-style private rooms which overlooked the rear of the estate. Out their windows you could view lush gardens and a beautifully sculpted maze with comfy benches in its circular center. You know, for sunbathing... in the... moonlight. The room Annie and I chose was filled with plush pillows for sitting on the floor and vegging out like we were practicing Indian transcendentalism; at least, that's what Annie said. Long, multicolored cloth strips were tied to the wooden frame of a king size bed, and the lighting was dimmed for prime romance. It was the perfect atmosphere for a... fight?

No, actually. Our night ended with silence. Awkward uncomfortable silence. I wanted to say so much. To bring up her alone time with Henri. To explain what she thought she saw between me and Magdalena. Instead, we turned off the lights and crawled into bed defeated and resentful.

We lay with our backs two inches away from each other, but I felt a proverbial stone and brick wall growing between us. The heaviness was almost unbearable.

Chapter Fourteen: Triangles?

Annie woke some four hours after we went to sleep, and left the room while I continued my anguished attempt to outlast the sun. She later gave me her account of that time alone. She spoke of how quiet and still the Gray Bear was in the daylight, but also how beautiful. A few humans were on site, either cleaning, landscaping, or restocking inventory. Nothing much else. She walked out onto the backyard garden and meandered through its maze, nestled down on a loveseat, and enjoyed listening to the birds hold their conversations. A surprising tap on her shoulder from out of nowhere frightened her, and Henri of all people was standing there, with a smile.

“I didn’t mean to scare you. I was just taking a stroll through the grounds before I head back to Paris, and saw you sitting there alone.”

“You stayed here last night? I thought humans were prohibited from overnight stays.”

“Normally, yes, but I have special privileges. I’m a permanent guest of Magdalena’s, and it’s my café that supplies the food for the human clientele here at the Gray Bear.”

“Magdalena... I don’t think I like her.”

“Ah, yes. She has that effect on certain people. To be perfectly transparent, she told me about her little stunt last night, and you have every right to be angry. Hopefully, Davis was able to convince you that he was not complicit in her behavior, nor was he responsible for anything you should be mad at him about.”

“Actually, we didn’t talk about it. We didn’t talk, period. About anything.”

“Oh? Is everything alright between the two of you?” Henri gently touched Annie’s hand, and began to rub it. She finally got a sense of what might have upset me.

“Can you please not touch me like that?”

“I’m very sorry. I didn’t mean to give you the wrong impression. I’m only trying to be supportive.” He removed his hand from hers, but placed it on her shoulder, causing her to shrug it off.

“Why? You don’t know me. What do you care?”

“You seem like a good person. Intelligent. Loving. Beautiful. Faithful... I don’t know why you’re with a vampire, to tell you the truth.” This bluntness threw Annie off, and disturbed her.

"Well, not that it's *really* any of your business, I've had some form of affinity for Davis since I was 11 years old, and think that I may have actually been in love with him since I was seventeen."

"That is a long time. And how long has he been in love with you?"

"Don't know. Maybe just as long."

"And how long has he been a vampire?"

"Almost seven months. Seven, long, heartbreaking, life-changing months, Henri. And I've been here for him throughout that time, even when he didn't want me to be."

"He's smart. And he obviously cares enough for you to not wish this existence on you. I've seen a few vampires try to dabble with human love. It doesn't end well."

"So I've heard. And let me guess, you don't see us being the exception to the rule?"

"No. I do not. I see every reason in the world for you to stop accompanying him on this suicide mission, and live your life as it was supposed to have been lived. He became a vampire. You did not. Even if you were both human, he doesn't seem like he'd be your type."

"Are *you* the type of person I should be with?" Annie placed her hand on Henri's thigh, and he jerked back slightly, astonished, but kept her hand where it was. "Cultured. Well-read. Mysterious. Good with the ladies?"

"I would love nothing more than to prove to you that I am the type of man who would appreciate you, in the sun and the moonlight. I find you to be intoxicatingly attractive, and I've been pulled into your orbit like nothing I've experienced in a long, long time." The truth finally revealed.

Annie grabbed Henri by the belt of his pants, pulled him closer to her and then led him down closer to her face, yanking down on his tie. She made her eyes as harmless and endearing as a baby fawn, and then...

"Politely go fuck yourself, Henri."

"Understood, Annie. You've made yourself clear." Henri took a few steps back and adjusted his clothes. "I will not bring it up again, and will not bother you... Your bluntness almost passes for French. It's refreshing to see an American so polite *and* so direct."

"Glad I could help you out, there, Henri."

"Please do not make yourselves strangers. My café is always open to Davis and his kind."

Henri turned and walked away. Annie watched him as he did, and a flood of thoughts rushed through her mind like a river. *What if he's right? What if I shouldn't be here? Am I stupid? Am I wasting my young adulthood on a tragic story with a tragic ending? Should I be looking for a regular relationship with a regular, living, breathing human? Why am I not back at K.U. finishing my Masters? What the fuck am I doing?!* She propelled herself from her seat, and started walking forcefully out of the gardens and down a trail in the woods behind the Gray Bear. As she walked, her thoughts became more taunting, and she began to pick up her pace, until she was eventually in a full sprint.

Sweat beading up on her neck and chest, she pushed her lungs to their capacity, and ran until her exhaustion and a tree branch caused her to tumble to the floor. On her hands and knees, heaving and gasping, trying to inhale much needed oxygen, Annie began to cry. She lay down on the peaceful, cold earth, curled her knees up to her chest, and cried until her tears were no longer necessary. Visions of walking the stage to get her Masters, a big, illustrious wedding, a honeymoon on an island, childbirth, raising two beautiful children, and growing old with her husband as they watched the world go by from a quiet porch all swept through and out of her. These were the things she'd have to permanently give up if she remained at my side. She'd made a decision, and she would speak with me about it that night.

A half-hour before sunset, I was already awake, the night's miserable ending with Annie still fresh and stinging in my head. She was not in the room, but I could tell she had come in and taken a shower at some point. Her backpack was open, and clothes gone through. I rose, showered, and brushed my teeth, all trained behaviors I learned from her, and went down looking for my girlfriend. I hoped she was still my girlfriend.

There was a large breakfast area with ample seating in this monstrous chateau, and I found Annie there eating dinner. I gently eased up to the table as timid as a dog who'd been in trouble with his owner might. I set my face to puppy dog eyes mode, and nudged her with my hip. She just looked up at me blankly, and I could tell she had been crying.

"That bad, huh?" I asked, halfway hoping for some laughter to break the ice.

"Maybe. I don't know."

"What were you doing? How long have you been down here?"

"A while. The whole day, I guess. The staff was very surprised that a human was here so early. The chef had to scramble to whip me up some dinner... I spoke with Henri earlier." A rage boiled my stomach and started to rise up my insides, to my throat.

"That motherfuc---"

"Don't worry about him. You were right, though, about him. He did have romantic intentions for me. I let him know in as few words as possible that I didn't feel the same way." Her words relaxed me for a spilt second. Then...

"But he did make me think about some things." Rage-filled yet again.

"That motherfuc---"

"Calm down." Annie took my hand. "These were things I needed to think about, should have thought about, long before we even flew across the world vampire hunting. They were things you tried to get me to think about, and instead I just let my heart make all the decisions. My head finally realized it should put on the breaks."

"Whoa." I was starting to feel like she was breaking up with me, and a tight vice was churning around my heart, constricting with the force of an anaconda. "Are you doing what I think you're doing?"

"I'm not doing anything, but I have two paths I can walk down. First, before I do or say anything stupid, or that I consider final, you need to talk to her."

"Who?"

Annie pointed her finger past me, to my left. "Her" she said through narrowing, piercing eyes and gritted teeth. I turned around to find Magdalena sitting at the edge of the room's bar, legs crossed, smirking at us, in a black sequined dress.

"Oh. Her."

"Oui. Me," she called out in a half laugh.

"I don't have anything to say to her, Annie."

"I think you do. I can feel the physical reaction you have around her, so please don't insult my instincts with denial. And more importantly, you need to hear what she has to say to you. It's the only way for you to understand the magnitude of what you can have in your life vs. what you deserve."

I didn't completely understand what she meant, but I sort of interpreted it as 'I need to look at all sides of a situation before I can move forward in any one direction.'

"Alright, then. I'll play this game." I was just happy to have someone to play it *with*. Motioning to the courtyard, which was growing exponentially darker, I escorted Magdalena out its French Doors, which here I guess were just... doors. "I'll be back shortly, Annie."

"What happened between Annie and Henri?" Magdalena asked, but with a hint of mischievous attitude, like she already knew something I didn't. I was still new to manipulation under the disguise of love, but I wasn't falling for it.

"Nothing. Nothing happened."

"Are you so sure?"

"Nothing I've ever been surer about." We stared at each other silently for at least three seconds. "What is it you want from me? Are you pissed off that a vampire and a human are trying to make it work?"

"A little bit, yes. Because it's so naïve. I work among them, the humans. I see them living their stupid, busy lives, and I can't believe you would subject yourself to this hamster wheel they run on."

"I wouldn't even be here right now if it wasn't for Annie! She planned our trip, our itinerary. Everything!"

"So she's a good travel agent."

"I'd be careful. I love her, and have for a long time."

"Such emotion is something you will need to let go of, if you're to survive. Superhuman Namtudari or not. The people who cannot move on through life with you will anchor and drown you, if you cannot let them go."

"That's my cross to bear."

"You do not have to have a cross! You can exist without being resurrected... How long have you been a vampire?"

"Since earlier this year."

"Oh, you're still a bab---, still a beginner, to this. And how long have you been in a sexual relationship with Annie."

"We're not... We haven't been..."

"You have not had sex, yet!"

"No. Not yet. We're waiting for the right time. What does that have to do with anything?"

Magdalena put her hand over her mouth, and her eyes grew two sizes larger, like she'd just witnessed the Challenger explosion or the planes going into the Towers.

"My god. You are both still virgins?"

"Not both of us... Not her."

She licked her lips a little, and teased her hair with her fingers.

“Davis. I think I just felt something in my privates that I haven’t been able to feel for two hundred years without drinking blood. The thought of devirginizing a vampire makes me extremely horny.”

I was instantly embarrassed and uncomfortable, but secretly turned on. “Well, you can stop, because nothing’s going to happen between you and me.”

“Why not? Why can’t you indulge in the finer things in life? The things that make it worth living? I could teach you pleasure you didn’t know existed... No one said we couldn’t include Annie in the festivities.”

I was really in over my head now. I felt like it was the first day of seventh grade P.E. and I had to be in my underwear in front of everyone while we changed out. I’d never even made love to Annie, and this crazy nympho was talking about a threesome. I had to abort. I was just glad she didn’t mention---

“And maybe even Henri, too.”

That was it. Interview over.

“No way in hell. No way am I bringing anyone else into my bed. Ever. I love Annie and only want to be with her. And I sure as hell would never share her with another man. Especially not him.”

“Oooh. I’ve clearly touched a nerve.”

“You’re really good at that, apparently. Look, I don’t mean to offen---”

"There was something about you" she interrupted. "That night in the Crazy Horse. I could smell a vampire in the building as soon as you walked in, but I didn't know who until the end of the night. When we locked eyes while I was onstage, something surged through me, and I felt and instant attraction, even though one look at you and her on the street told me you were a bad omen. You have this aura, for lack of a better word, that surrounds you and draws vampires to you. Maybe even humans. I don't know if it's the Luminastra, or some Texas charm, but I wanted to be closer to it, even though you're a baby in this world, and you have this death wish to meet Aylash Revall. I still couldn't stop myself from getting closer. Do you know how long it's been since I've even been to the House of the Gray Bear? This is exactly my third time since their war with Antonio Medici and Revall. I had to see what was going to happen with you. I wanted to keep you here. My attraction to you is not just sexual. It's... sensual. Spiritual. I can't explain it, but I want to discover it. To unravel it. To---"

"I can't be your guinea pig." Now it was my turn to interrupt. 'Or your chosen one, or your guiding light. I can't even be just the kid you teach about sex. Whatever gravitational pull you're feeling to me, I'm feeling that same thing about the House of the Winged God. I *have* to meet with Revall, and I *have* to try and become human again."

"That is a stupid fantasy. Do you know how many vampires have walked the earth since Aylash Revall became the first? Do you know how many have managed to be cured of this affliction? None. Zero. Do you know how many have even wanted to turn back, once they realized how many gifts they were given by becoming vampires? Again, zero. You have been invited to the evolution of the human race, and you've apparently become its supreme specimen."

"You may tell yourself that, and maybe it's different here in France, but all I saw in America was sad, isolated, lonely vampires who were either running away from their existence or trying to paint a prettier picture of it. The reality is that it sucks. It sucks big time, and if I can have a regular life with Annie, who's been an amazing fucking person the whole time I've known her, and who was living a pretty glorious life before she fucked it up by falling in love with me, then I have to try... I have to."

Magdalena dropped her head and shook it slowly, bewildered by the fact that she was either failing to get through to me, or that I was turning her advances down to stay with Annie. Then I saw it. I saw the humanity in her eyes. I saw the despair of vampirism on her face.

"You're just as sad as the vampires back home" I opined.

"You don't know what you're talking about."

"Oh yes I do. I'm not some experienced world traveler, and I don't know dick about shit, but I know sadness. And that look is a lonely ball of sadness."

Magdalena swept her hair from her eyes and pointed her head up at the black sky. "Maybe I was looking for someone I could spend eternity with."

Here we go again. This reminds me of how Devin Sikorsky changed her tune on me.

"You just met me. You don't even know if you're going to be interested a week from now, much less an eternity from now. You vampires all seem to be attracted to power, or status. What this might mean for you. It's not about me at all, is it?"

"Of course it is. I'm attracted to you, and was, even when I thought you were giving me some bullshit story about the Namtudari."

"But now that you're convinced about that, I sure do look a lot hotter, right?"

"Please. I could give a shit."

"Well, actually it did make me a lot hotter. Bigger muscles and all. I didn't look like this before." Magdalena laughed, and a rising temperature eased up a bit.

"I think if Annie fell in love with you before you changed into a muscle-bound blood drinker, you were probably pretty handsome to begin with."

Those words shot through me like a 12-Gauge. Only, they worked in direct opposition to Magdalena's intent. They reinforced how much Annie loved me. How much she cared about me when nobody else did. When no one even looked at me, let alone made the effort to get to know me. They made me realize that Annie and I were meant to be together for the rest of our lives, no matter how long or short a timeline that might be. There would be no love triangles, or quadrangles, or any other polygons in my life. There would only be my love. My one love.

"Thank you! Thank you, so much! You don't know what you just did." The puzzled look on her face told me that she agreed with that last statement. I kissed her on the cheek and gave her a big hug. "I've gotta go. I've got to speak with Annie!" I tore off through the gardens, and back into the Gray Bear as fast as I could. Magdalena stood frozen in her spot, unaware of what the fuck had just happened.

Chapter Fifteen: The Vow

When I bolted through the French Doors of the Gray Bear's café, Annie was nowhere to be found. I looked left and right, but she was not near. For a moment, I thought that if I found her with Henri, I would tear his head off, his friends inside the place be damned, and fling it as far a distance as I possibly could. I went up to our room, and opened it to find her standing quietly in a ring of those big, comfy pillows, wearing a sleeveless, cream-colored, cotton gown. Candles were lit all around the room, surrounded by bouquets of flowers, and randomly strewn rose petals. Some soft mood music by something called Enya was playing, connected from her phone to some speakers in the ceiling, and the lights were dimmed especially low. A smile lined her face, but a tear streamed from each eye, down her cheeks. It was an image I'll always recall. I opened my mouth to speak, when a knock came at the door.

What the hell?

"Yes?" I snuck my head out and asked with the patience of a two-year-old. It was Fuggerton.

"Your Annie's delivery, sir. A bottle of our finest wine, 600 years young, in its original sheepskin cask, and the finest chocolates from both Belgium and Switzerland. Obviously, these appear to be for her. Oh, before I forget: the sharpest blade money can buy, perfectly crafted and specialized to open small, able-to-heal wounds. I believe this will aid in your feeding for the night. It is an *extreme* exception to the rules of the House."

She seemed to think of everything.

"I guess she thought of everything."

"Yes, sir. I suppose she did... This is a very important - no, monumental - step in your future together, sir. I am not a butler or a servant, but I wanted to be the one to deliver these arrangements. To let you know that... no matter what you may hear from other members of this community, I support you. I think that your intentions and your soul, still seem to be intact and good-natured. I wish for those days again. Treat her well, Davis, and she will do the same. She's throwing away her life by clinging to you. It's no small sacrifice."

"Thank you, Edsel. I think."

"No reason to doubt me, Davis. I speak only truth and praise. I'll even let you in on my nickname, if you like. I do not divulge it to just anyone."

"Sure. I would appreciate it. What's your nickname?"

"Mother."

This son of a bitch.

I closed the door and turned to find Annie still standing there, consumed by a small shiver and an invasion of goosebumps.

"Are you OK? Are you cold?"

"No, Davis. I'm scared, shitless."

"Of what?"

"Of what you're going to tell me. Of what happened between you and that redheaded demon."

I laughed out loud.

"Oh! Oh, baby! Ain't nothing happened with that redheaded demon!" I think tears might have now started to squeak out of my eyes ever so subtly, but they were tears of joy. "Nothing's ever going to take you away from me. Nobody's ever going to take you away from me."

"Aylash Revall might."

"What?"

"He's the lord, and king, and God of all the vampires, Davis. The very first, still roaming the earth after over 4,500 years. If you're in his presence, and he decides to, he'll erase you from existence faster than I can scream your name." I was speechless at this revelation. "So to that end, I want you to make love to me. I want to make love to you. Tonight. Now."

I stepped into her ring of pillows, holding the basket of wine and chocolates in one hand and the blade outstretched in the other.

"Annie, I promise from this day forth, no matter what destiny or fate is placed and sealed before us, I will love you with all my heart, and protect you with all my might."

I slowly laid the basket down, handed her the blade, and placed my hands on her waist, giving her the most tender kiss I could muster before giving her another, and another, and then...

Another knock on the door?!

This knock was followed by an intrusion from one Reginald Duplante. A very agitated looking Reginald Duplante.

"You. Davis. I need you in the Great Hall, now. You can bring your – her – if you like. She may not like what she sees or hears, mind you. You've been warned. Come NOW!"

My tormentor is not a vampire. It is timing.

Chapter Sixteen: Complications

Annie rapidly changed her attire, and we both bounded down the stairs to the great hall, curious and hesitant about what we might find when we got there. I tried to quickly wrap up some loose ends as we went.

"So, how and why did you coordinate such a romantic environment to deflower me if you didn't know for sure what happened between me and Magdalena?"

"One: I was hoping I was right. And two: no matter what happened between you and her, I think we were meant to be together. Cosmically drawn to one another. You were going to see how much *I* loved you. How much *you* meant to *me*. You were going to see it on my face. Feel it in my touch. Long story short, I guessed. I'm glad I guessed right."

"Good answer. Me, too." I stopped her on the stone

spiral staircase, pressed her up against its wall, and shared a long, wet, passionate kiss before we had to resume our dash down to the great hall.

Upon reaching the door to said hall, we both stopped, caught our breath, and looked each other over for approval before making our entrance. I opened the door for her, and we walked into a complete clusterfuck of chaos. Almost everyone was on their feet, yelling, pointing, and accusing each other of one vampire violation or another. Then, as if one mind was controlling all of them, they stopped and turned in unison, in my direction, before erupting again. They yelled at me, at Annie, at each other. Paul Lajoie was arguing so vehemently with three others that spit was exploding from his mouth and jutting in multiple directions. He included me in his drenching, doing me the favor of speaking English at least every third sentence. Magnus Olruud and Le Bouffon were more busy instigating than calming, and it appeared that they were in the minority in what Annie was able to decipher was a disagreement over helping me find Aylash. Half the group wanted no part of such a journey, a little less than that wanted to help as a matter of diplomacy, and Le Bouffon's contingent wanted to try and kill Aylash Revall as a matter of vengeance and their warped sense of justice. Just about everyone felt that all of this was my fault, just by me showing up on French soil.

Reginald Duplante had finally had enough, and as the ranking captain of the Gray Bear, he called an end to the conflict by firing a shotgun blast into the ceiling. Everyone fell silent and fell still.

“Don’t worry; I was going to renovate the ceiling anyway. Hopefully, the paint huffing punk rockers stuck in the 1970’s upstairs didn’t get one of their jackets ruined.”

His comment did conjure a few laughs, but the mood was somber, the nerves stretched raw, and any wrong comment would cause a tipping point. Reginald sought to prevent that, but a ceasefire would be short lived. Le Bouffon would see to that.

“Have we all become cowards, even when blessed with the gift of the Luminastra Namtudari. A weapon to counteract Aylash’s?”

“Do you honestly think that’s enough?” Duplante countered. “A relatively inexperienced boy vs. the oldest living vampire? Is it possible that we’ve all forgotten that the Namtudari is only the beginning of Revall’s arsenal of supernatural play toys?”

Annie whispered into my ear, “What’s he referring to? Did you read something in his journals?”

Aloud, I asked the group, “Is he talking about the Spectralis Invincibus?”

“Indeed, Davis. The Spectralis Reptilios Invincibus, also known as the Convergence. Maybe we’ve all underestimated the young man from Texas. He knows precisely what I speak of. Yes, Davis, the Invincibus is yet another of Revall’s experiments gone wrong. Or gone right, depending on who you ask.”

“What is it?” Annie asked, causing everyone to look at

her with disgust. Humans apparently have no right to speak in this room.

"What do you know of it?" Reginald inquired of me. 'What did your scriptures say?"

"From what I gathered, it's like some shedding of the skin, involving some sort of ancient, serpent-like snake, replacing an aging vampire's body with a new and improved one. But it sounded like Revall never confirmed it or attained it the way he wanted. At least that's how it sounds from the books."

"Well, he most definitely *did* attain it, Mr. Davis. He held an 'unveiling' for this new transformation, and a few of the highest-level vampires in the world were privileged to witness it firsthand. This was 1922. We'd only been out of World War I for a few years, and even the vampires were slightly afraid to tackle what would become the roaring twenties. Revall's isolation in the House of the Winged God allowed for him to resume his experiments on himself, on others, on animals similar to the one performed on our tormented, beloved Ballou. He'd been looking for new ways to cheat old age and death since his first success, and the Spectralis was the most advanced, most accomplished yet. The fifteen or so of us there watched him go from a wrinkled, old, faded, relic to a strong, chiseled, machine of death. His skin, his muscles, his posture all that of a young man identical to someone no more than 35 years old. What's more, his wings. They went from---"

"I'm sorry; what the holy fuck did you just say?" My

accent got terribly more west Texas than it had on the entire trip. "His wings?"

"Yes, Davis. His wings. Aylash had managed to develop wings through his magic. However, they weren't useful for anything other than a sideshow attraction at a carnival. They were wholly ineffective, and resembled a chicken's. Somehow, some way, through undergoing the Spectralis Reptilios Invincibus, those pathetic flaps attached to his shoulder blades were now as big, strong, and effective as the largest raptors in the sky. Aylash was able to fly, and the so-called 'winged god' could actually live up to his name."

"You're shittin' me."

"Oh, I sincerely wish I was, Mr. McCarty. Now, luckily, as a postscript to that development, and a brief detail of our last, unfortunate battle with him, those wings did manage to get severed during the fight. As far as I know, he was not able to regenerate them. *Un*-fortunately, the clipping of those wings is what propelled Revall to unleash the Luminastra Namtudari on us, eviscerating so many members of this illustrious House in an instant, ending the battle, and ending the war. He drove a permanent stake through the heart of the vampire community, no pun intended, and severed his relationship with virtually every other vampire alive, your music friends at the Black Moon notwithstanding."

"How did he manage to hook up with them, you reckon?"

"I have no way of knowing, and do not care, to be

perfectly honest. I can only assume that Warren Winston was somehow connected, even though he perished decades ago. The important thing is that he's returned to his home, and that you are dead set on visiting him. I cannot in good conscience allow you to do so without assistance from us. Some of us, understandably so, want nothing to do with such a mission. Others of us, also understandably, want to travel with you for no other reason than to kill Revall and end his monstrosity of an existence once and for all, using you and your powers as needed... I would be lying if I told you that I didn't think some of the vampires in this room were curious about your wishful dream that killing Revall might return you to the safety and ignorance of your former humanity. Maybe others in this room wish that same fate for themselves. There is no telling if a vampire who's lived hundreds of years would automatically dissolve into dust after such a return to form, but I believe that's probably an irrational reaction based more on fiction and superstition than physics. In any case, the Gray Bear is divided on this topic, and will need to vote. Since there are seventeen of us, there will most definitely be a majority rule, and that final tally will be just that – final."

"Wait. There were eighteen of you here yesterday, and there are eighteen of you here today. That means it cou---"

"Magdalena Minerva will not be voting. She is no longer a recognized, official member of the Gray Bear, nor was she ever in a position of leadership, no matter what her presence or influence might suggest." Reginald looked straight at Magdalena upon uttering that statement, and her gaze back was full of anger and venom, followed by the watering of eyes full of sadness and regret.

"OK, then. When is the vote?" I asked, oblivious to the sense of urgency in the now calmer room.

"Now, Davis. We vote now. Please take a seat if you wish."

I pulled a chair from the corner of the room and gave it to Annie. As she sat down, I stood behind her with my hands on her shoulders. I could feel the hunger of blood requirement filling my veins and salivary glands. *This vote had better go quick*, I thought to myself. *How can these vampires go so long without feeding?* also danced around in my brain for a bit before Reginald began the vote. He did so by walking to each member of the assembly and standing in front of them until each gave their answer.

"No" was the first reply.

"No" the second.

A "Yes" from the third and I breathed a small sigh of relief.

A "No" followed by two more "Yes" votes, and we were completely even before getting to Sylvain Montreux, who had given me a positive vibe the night before, but not a vote of approval for my journey. His vote, in my opinion, was a vital one.

"No" was Sylvain's vote. He looked at me and mimed the word, "Sorry" before biting his lip and turning his head to look away.

Magnus stood up and voted “Yes” with a loud, barrel-chested roar, and looked down at Sylvain with anger upon doing so. After eight votes, we were still tied, which gave me the hopeful impression that sympathy for my cause, or their revenge, had grown significantly since the night before. Then, three consecutive votes of “No” ended that perception quickly. All eyes were now upon Le Bouffon, The Jester, as it was his turn to vote. He did not open his voice quickly, instead choosing to leave us all in suspense. As the patience wore thin, and everyone started to feel uneasy, he finally spoke.

“Yes, of course. What did you think I was going to say? The only reason I would bring myself back to this godforsaken prison with the gruesome lot of you is to make sure that we are all on the same page, and that we go intent on ending Aylash Revall once and for all.”

His words drew the ire of some and the excitement of others, and the room erupted like they’ve been so prone to do. As the outsiders looking in, Annie and I sat and watched them tear into each other, and my mind wandered shortly, to some movie I’d seen where I think an Italian family sat around a dinner table and yelled like this at each other constantly. I wouldn’t be able to remember the name of the film, even to save Annie’s life. Reginald regained order, silencing the group, and reinforced his objective of getting through the last five votes.

“Please. Please leave your emotions and ulterior

motives at the door until we have finalized the initial vote. Then we will---"

"*Initial vote*?" I interrupted.

"Yes, Davis. This vote will determine if some or all of us go with you to Serbia. Then we will drill down and determine if we're going to attempt to *speak* to Aylash Revall, or if we're going to attempt to *kill* him."

"Oh. Shit... Well, then continue, I guess."

"Oh, thank you. Thank you for allowing me to resume speaking in the House I'm the captain of. So very gracious of you."

His sarcasm crawled up the small of my back, slithered across my spine, and settled angrily like a wasp's sting where my neck meets the base of my skull, and my instinct was to bolt right for him. Annie sensed this, and calmly placed her hand on top of mine. She didn't have to speak. That small gesture was all I needed to know that she was indeed in tune with me, and was most likely my soul mate. I let things go, and he resumed the *initial* voting process.

"Margerie, what is your vote?" Reginald leaned down and stared at Margerie lovingly, as if he was a gameshow host letting an elderly woman know he was granting her his full attention. Margerie, in turn gazed upon the expressions of the group awaiting her answer, and then took a long, hard look at Annie and I. Addressing me directly, her answer was:

“Davis, I’m sorry, but I do not want any more bloodshed. I want no harm to come to you or your lovely woman, and I want no further heartbreak for my Gray Bear. I love this House and my people all too much to replay that horror again. My answer is no.”

A collective deflation fell along the floor of the room, and even those in favor of staying the hell away from Serbia and Aylash Revall seemed to sympathize with me.

The next vote was “Yes”.

The one after, “No”.

Two votes left, and they both needed to be yes if I was going to have any help from the House of the Gray Bear, whatever my ultimate mission was, or whatever its resulting action from Revall. The last two votes belonged to Thomas Richard and Reginald himself. I didn’t have a great feeling, but at least I felt my chances were 50/50. Thomas, much like Margerie, looked upon the faces of everyone gathered, and then, much like Le Bouffon, intentionally kept us waiting in anticipation. I could feel that his answer would come with a bit of a monologue, clarifying and justifying his answer, and was not disappointed. He started methodically and solemnly.

“The Gray Bear’s unfortunate decision to escalate a perceived injustice at the intertwined hands of the Blood Fountain and Winged God left a dazzling, soul crushing anguish upon the members of this room and the members of our overall population here in Paris, and all of France for that matter. Every vampire from hundreds of miles away, from other countries even, who sought comfort and shelter here in Versailles, was left shattered. That this House is still standing is itself a small victory, but a hollow one. Instead, I believe it's more comparable to a stain, a scar; this cruel reminder that we are now alive but weaker than before. We've become a joke for Aylash Revall to laugh at from the comfort of his isolated castle in the mountain. We all suffered, but I maybe suffered a little more than you. I was tortured by that sick, deranged bastard, and am only here because Le Bouffon was successful in finding and freeing me. My twin brother was not so lucky, and I can still feel him here in this room, and know what he is thinking from some unseeable, unknown afterlife. I can see his ghost in my dreams and know that I failed to save him, to protect him... so what can I do? What can I do, Reginald? Just one thing. Avenge him. I can avenge him. I can absolve myself of internal, and eternal, guilt, and guide his soul to its resting place, wherever that may be. I vote yes, and now I believe that even if no one else in this room lifted a finger to help Davis McCarty, or if even he himself turned around and flew back home to his stupid America, I would travel to the Winged God alone and die or kill for my brother and the Gray Bear. This episode has reinvigorated me, and I am tired of sitting here bitter and broken. I am going to Serbia. I don't care if I cannot make it back."

This all left everything squarely on Reginald Duplante's shoulders. His was the last and deciding vote. The weight of such a swing hadn't hit him fully until now. It was oddly amusing to see the grimace of discomfort etched on his face. No holier than thou, or 'smartest man in the room' smirk; his face was one of burden and disbelief.

"What do you say, Reginald? It sure sounded like you wanted to help."

"I did not *want* to help you, Davis. I felt *obligated* to help you. That is a distinction that needs to be understood. As much as it divides us, as much as it could help rebuild us, the obligation feels very much like a double-edged sword. It could also mean destroying this House, and walking right into its destruction intentionally, when we in this room have all fought so hard to pick up the shattered pieces of what it once was and move on. And yet, that word obligation keeps popping back up on my lips." Reginald paused, and looked up to some imaginary picture in his head. It was as if he was arguing with some phantom of the Gray Bear's past. Then, upon making an internal decision, he looked over the room and decreed his verdict.

'As the captain of the Gray Bear, and the steward of its members, I vote... I vote Yes. We will assist Davis McCarty in some form or fashion on his trip to Serbia and the House of the Winged God." He tried to finish his train of thought as the volume once again rose loud enough to rival a small concert in a club. He had to increase his volume significantly to be heard. "We will recess in order to feed and recharge, and then we need to return to the great hall in one hour."

Paul Lajoie bolted up from his seat like a jack in the box, and started for the door. "I, for one, will *not* be back in one hour. I may *never* return." He did a military heel-step about-face and walked out, causing Le Bouffon to burst into laughter at the almost childish spectacle. His performance was not without positive reinforcement, however, as all those who voted no, save for Margerie, followed directly behind him.

"Well, Mr. Davis," Reginald began as the rest of the group slowly dispersed, looking for fresh blood. "It looks like you will get your wish, and get to drop in on Mr. Revall with more than just a human love interest as reinforcements. As we prepare for our next discussion regarding this trip, may I say something that you hold onto, and hold tight?"

"Of course, Reginald. What?"

"Sometimes it's the wishes that come true that turn into nightmares. Aylash Revall is one of those nightmares. An entirely unprecedented, frightening one you can never wake up from."

Chapter Seventeen: Uninvited Guest

One day in high school, I overheard a classmate describe the line for the men's room at a heavy metal festival he'd traveled to in Dallas. This is what I envisioned as the line to feed in the bowels of the Gray Bear stretched and multiplied. Not only had the assembled high order of the House been entrenched in a highly charged and volatile discussion, but most of the vampires outside the great hall stopped any activity and attempted to catch some words on the wind with their enhanced auditory abilities. Therefore, the lack of usual and consistent feeding resulted in a log jam of sorts once everyone gave in to their repressed hunger pains. The feeding room only has so much room, and so many willing or available menu items.

A side effect of this delay was that Ballou, The Abomination, went longer than usual without his carcasses to devour and gnaw on. Ever the punctual consumer, his ravenous nature gave him a double dose of adrenaline, and his already impressive strength increased even more. He rammed the large, heavily fortified wood and iron gate with one shoulder. He then reared back and did so again with his other, before hitting it full force a third time with both shoulders, his head, and every ounce of weight on his gargantuan frame. The impact caused others in the building to feel the reverberations. The third time was indeed the charm, and he caused the center most pillar of the gate to crack and splinter. Upon realizing his success, The Abomination back pedaled to the very end of the cave, and then galloped with all his speed and force to that very spot, shattering the post, and breaking through most of the two on each side of it. Ballou, enraged and starving, lashed out with his outstretched paws and tried to claw his way to freedom. Reginald was summoned quickly, me tagging along behind in anticipation while letting Annie go back to the room to rest. He made his way down to Ballou, clutching an annoying, inebriated human male who reeked of too much cologne and too much vodka, in one hand. He'd snagged him off the dance floor, and brought him down to the cave as a peace offering, an appetizer before Ballou's main course.

"You should consider yourself lucky," Reginald reasoned right before he tossed the partygoer to the cave's now vulnerable barrier. 'You're one of only five day walkers to ever be granted entrance into this room." Ballou then demonstrated why the name The Abomination was an apt one. No being, no creature, human or otherwise, should ever be able to be eaten, or even handled, by any creature that viciously. That easily. I would like to think that he felt no pain, or only felt it for a split second, but that would be a lie. Ballou gripped his dinner, injecting his fangs, and then tossed it from side to side, allowing it to crash and crumble against the unforgiving stone floor. A vampire Siberian/Polar bear hybrid is without a doubt the most alpha dominant animal to ever walk the earth. An orca whale would turn tail and swim the fuck away from Ballou, The Abomination. Fast.

He was far from satiated, and his growl and insane eyes paralyzed the handful of vampires in the room with complete dread. Reginald, however, just started singing some whimsical sounding song nonchalantly, his volume alternating between louder and quieter, harsher and softer. Ballou seemed to follow Duplante's lead, falling almost mesmerized to the sweet notes of the song. He laid down flat, his head poking through the damaged opening he'd made, and just rested calmly as Reginald rubbed and scratched his head, planting soft kisses right between his eyes. I was struck speechless, and humbly witnessed the two in extreme reverence. I knew, though, that he would only be this docile for a short amount of time, as his victim was merely a snack in the grand scheme of things. I was curious, though.

“How did you form this bond with him? He seems like he'd be the opposite of a ‘touchy-feely’ teddy bear type.”

“It took a lot of time and trust building. We were introduced just under 700 years ago, and I was presented by the former captain to Ballou as someone he could consider a friend. That's not to say that things went smoothly at first. It took over a hundred years and a lot of cajoling and treats to get to anywhere near this display of our current relationship. And that balance is still very fragile."

"By treats, you mean humans, right?"

"Indeed... Ballou is a representative of this House. He is a symbol of the pride we take in adapting and overcoming a situation. The members of the Gray Bear, the members of the French vampire community, we are not ruled by our circumstance. Nor have we ever been. We were not the first vampire House, but many a time throughout history, we've been the best. You might have perceived an amount of shame in The Abomination. In his existence here. The shame does not lie with him, at his feet. It lies with the tormented soul who created him. A man so vile he eventually ceased to be a man... Make no mistake, Mr. McCarty; Aylash Revall is a demon. An abomination far more condemned and malevolent than my humongous, furry friend here."

"Then why tempt fate a second time by traveling to his home?" an unfamiliar English woman's voice called from atop the balcony overlooking the Ballou's home/prison. Reginald didn't look up at her. Instead, he put his head down and sighed, before directing his closed eyes up to the ceiling.

"I know I should be surprised, but I'm not. I'm actually wondering what took you so long."

I didn't know what the hell was going on, or who this lady was, but I could gather really quickly that Reginald was unhappy, and that this woman's presence was a problem.

"Who is she?"

"This, Mr. Davis, is Lenora Jeffries."

Shit.

I didn't know how long she'd been a vampire, and couldn't tell what her age was when she became one, but she could have been anywhere between 45 and 60. From Aylash's journals, it was proposed that a vampire ages physically one year for every thirty or forty, depending on the individual. She clearly had some seniority over a good amount of the Gray Bear's membership; otherwise, she wouldn't be allowed such a hall pass. Even though it wasn't necessarily proper vampire etiquette, I chose to engage her directly.

"I've heard *so many* wonderful things about you." I couldn't tell if her bullshit detector was at max power.

"Bullshit, my young friend. You'll hear no such lies in these walls. Where is your human girlfriend, Mr. McCarty?"

"How do you know my name, or that I have a human girlfriend?"

"Word travels fast."

"I think the more accurate statement is that someone here fed her that information" Reginald countered. "Let me guess: Antoinette?"

"A lady never tells, Mr. Duplante."

Before I got completely lost in their soap opera, I tried to keep up the best I could.

"Who's Antoinette, and really, what is she doing here?"

"I'm here to pledge my assistance, and my vampires, to your cause, Mr. McCarty."

"My cause?"

"Your doomed and ill-advised trek to the House of the Winged God, of course."

Just then, the wrinkled, coarse natured woman who accompanied Edsel at Dorian's Pub appeared, standing behind Lenora, uncomfortably close, in my opinion. Reginald shook his head and slapped his thigh.

"Just as I suspected; Antoinette."

"Are you surprised? Should you be surprised?" Antoinette questioned Reginald. 'As soon as I saw this incompetent child in the pub, I could foretell that his presence here would end in The Gray Bear resuming its war with Aylash. To that end, I contacted Lenora. She did not disappoint in her assurance to help us defeat him once and for all."

"Surely, you don't expect me to believe that Lenora is agreeing to help us out of loyalty or the goodness of her heart. She is a cancer that has sewn seeds of decay for far too long. So long in fact that I cannot remember a time without her dissonance and meddling. She helped drive a deep wedge between the members of this House, which weakened us when we needed to be the most unified. I should have her thrown out, since I've vowed not to kill any vampires without provocation."

Lenora wore a smug smile on her mouth, as if she'd received the reaction from Reginald that she hoped for. She crossed her arms, and tapped her red-fingernailed digits on her arm.

"Don't be that way, Reg. We can co-exist like we used to. The English and the French together. Just imagine how fruitful the coalition could be."

"I do not wish to imagine; I wish to remember. To remember you and your English cowards saying yes when I asked you to support us in our grievance, whatever the result was. Unfortunately, I *would* have to use my imagination to remember that, as your answer was no, followed by silence, followed by ambivalence, followed by avoidance."

"If we were not permitted to form and maintain an official British House, then why would we entertain an official House's business, much less participate in an official House's eventual war?"

"How very Switzerland of you. Civilized and neutral while we were attacked by the largest order of vampires, and then defeated by the strongest when we were so close to victory and justice."

As thrilling as this back and forth was, I was anxious

to get back to my room and check on my girlfriend. But first, I had to go into the House's bowels and feed. My legs were starting to shake, and my hands were fidgeting uncontrollably. Apparently, my situation was a little too obvious for the people gathered.

"Jesus CHRIST! Can you please dismiss the boy so he can feed?!" Lenora screamed.

"I am not his owner! Davis, you are free to go and take care of your hunger. I know that it is I who interrupted your earlier attempt... Although it looked like you were to engage in something else altogether."

"That's none of your business, friend."

"Everything that happens in my House is my business... I'm curious, Davis. Are we? Are we... friends?"

"We're sure as shit gonna have to be, if we're going to face Aylash Revall."

"Spoken like a true optimist. Please do not appear too shocked if the age of the menu tonight is slightly younger than you're used to... The orphanage and I made an... arrangement."

Before I could voice my displeasure and my nausea at Reginald's words, I had to stifle that urge and get downstairs before I acted like a human version of Ballou. I made it to the old, English castle-style door with the slot in it, and was met by the same bored gatekeeper, who let me in and instructed me to take my pick.

"Do you have anyone over 18 years old?" He smiled,

and I could tell that he found me pathetic and thin skinned. It was the same smile my foreman flashed when I told him I was there to work on the oil rigs. And, incidentally, it was the same smile he flashed a few weeks later when I told him I was quitting and heading back to Abilene.

"That girl there is eighteen." He pointed to a frightened young lady, huddling in an unstoppable shiver in the corner of the cell. "All the younger ones have already been drained and piled up for The Abomination. The early bird here gets the youngest blood."

I was both relieved and disgusted. I didn't know the age of the youngest locked in here, and I didn't *want* to know. I wanted to pound my fist through the gatekeeper's face and let those who remained locked up go free. But I knew that would be a mistake that would end in all of our deaths, me and Annie included. Instead, I reluctantly sat next to the shivering 18-year-old, and asked her, her name.

"Mina", was her reply.

"I'm sorry, Mina, but I have to do this. You have to die, so that I may live. I will never forget you, and I will try to do something better with my life, to honor you and your sacrifice."

"You don't have to lie to me, vampire. You've been cursed, and you'll continue to *be* a curse, until the day you finally succumb to its violence. So get on with it and put me out of my misery."

She wore a white gold cross around her neck on a thin chain. After I fed, I took it, planning to fashion it into something of a charm bracelet for Annie. I went up to check on her, and surprisingly found her sitting in conversation with Magdalena.

“Wow. I didn’t expect to see this. To what do I owe the pleasure?”

“Unfortunately, no pleasure will be held. I saw Annie departing for the room and followed after, first to apologize. Then, I offered her the idea of a threesome, which she very quickly declined. I have to say, I was a little disappointed, but she is an intelligent woman, who knows what will and will not work in her relationship.”

“That’s one reason I love her... I’m a little shocked, babe. You’re not trying to rip her head off.” Annie shot me a quirky, agitated expression.

“Well, my love; that might be because I was alone in a room with someone who could quite literally rip off mine.” I giggled a little at this true statement. ‘Also, not only was Magdalena apologetic, as advertised, she was also sincere... We’re not gonna be besties and go shopping together, but I believe our truce will last.”

“I’m glad to hear it.”

“Did you feed?”

“I did. Now we just wait for the wisemen to vote on the nature of our visit to Aylash.”

Magdalena did a small doubletake. I noticed her

puzzled face, and asked what she knew that I didn't.

"You did not hear? The decision's been made. Reginald is taking Ballou out of the Gray Bear and with him to Serbia. An announcement like that can only mean that we – they – plan to go to war. Even some of the people who voted yes are angry with Reginald now. This could get rather ugly." *Holy Shit.*

Chapter Eighteen: The Great Hall's Final Bow

"Annie, I hate to ask you this, but---"

"Nope. Not a chance. I'm coming downstairs with you. You and I were taking this trip to Serbia before we ever met any of these old ass vampires, and we're still taking it. Together. There's nothing they're going to say that I can't hear."

"I understand. Really. But---"

"Oh," Annie asked Magdalena. "By the way, I thought vampires ended up losing their eyesight, within less than fifty years. How is it that vampires hundreds of years old are still walking around here without bifocals or seeing eye dogs?"

Magdalena laughed out loud at this inquiry. "You are such a funny, insightful woman. That unfortunate side effect is only relegated to a certain subset of the population. Your body, your genetics, have to come with certain blood sugar issues. This is mostly a problem for American vampires, and their processed, make-believe foods."

"Good enough for me. Come on, Davis. Let's go hear some more about how we fucked up everything for these French night drinkers."

The attitude was just oozing off of Annie as we made our way, once again, down to the great hall of the Gray Bear. I started to pry as to why she was sharp all of a sudden, but was shut down quickly.

"I don't want to talk about it, right now, Davis. Please, respect that. Just until we're alone."

"OK. Whatever you say, my love."

Before we even got to the door, we could hear a myriad of individual shouting matches all going on at once. Annie's demeanor and stance, which got more hunched over and surly looking as we approached suddenly softened, and she maybe thought twice about walking in.

"Are you sure you want to do this, Annie? You don't have to go in there."

"You're my man. I stand by my man."

I opened the door, and stepped inside first, holding Annie's hand, halfway shielding her behind me. The congregated all turned their heads to eye us, and Paul Lajoie cut through the noise with venom.

“There! There he is! We were still only halfway to picking up the pieces of our tragic grievance, and now you’ve all let this boy – this child – set it all aflame again. All because Le Fuckface says we should.”

Le Bouffon leapt at Lajoie, and for the second time in as many nights, Paul had someone’s hands on his throat. And not in a good way.

“Everything that’s been prophesized by Revall is coming true, even his own undoing at the hands of an unlikely foe. What does it call him? The Chosen Anomaly? The Foreign Savior? Something to that effect. It’s been at least a couple hundred years since I read it.”

“Wait” I interjected. “I read those words in all three journals. Aylash’s, Sartep’s, and Tulonus’. You don’t think those words were about me, do you? I can assure you, I’m no savior.”

“You SEE!?” Paul continued, swiping Le Bouffon’s loosened hands away. “He doesn’t even think of *himself* as a savior. How can we consider him one? Even labeling him a secret weapon, or the ace up our sleeves, would be a grave mistake.”

“Davis’ arrival, whether you like it or not, is a sign. The sign we’ve been looking for. And yes, the ace up our sleeves. Our defeat did not mean the end of our conflict; it just meant a temporary pause to it. Aylash wouldn’t have left for America if he didn’t fear he was already close to his downfall. He had to hide, and to rebuild, before he returned.”

"And rebuild he did, I can assure you that. Our ranks did not replenish here in France, but I know his did. I'm sure he's actively created an army of new vampires. Infants in this timeline, with their cell phones, video games, and YouTube culture. They couldn't give two shits about the ways of the vampire, Revall included."

"All the more reason we can win this time," Reginald reasoned. "You said yourself, Revall's army, at least half of it, are babies. Infants. They wouldn't stand a chance against seasoned, experienced ancients like us. And with Davis and his Luminastra, we could finally attain justice for the unacceptable wrong that befell the Gray Bear."

As that last sentence fell off Reginald's lips, I couldn't help but get this aching, nagging feeling that something had been left out of the Gray Bear/Blood Fountain story. It gripped my stomach like morning nausea when your parents are forcing you to eat breakfast before school. Annie and I locked eyes, and I could tell she got the same impression. I'd noticed that our brainwaves were more and more in sync with every passing day. I wasn't going to let the conversation go on any longer until I knew the full details.

"What exactly happened between the two Houses? "What was the final straw?"

Silence cast a dark shadow over the whole room. It's funny how one question can put out the wildest fire. Everyone must have suddenly had large weights draped around their necks, because their heads all pointed down at the floor. Of course, the only person qualified to answer my question would be Reginald, so I waited his silence out, and kept my eyes fixed on his body language.

"You see, that is... a delicate... situation."

Le Bouffon, short of answering for him, prodded Reginald a little.

"If he is the one who is to lead us and destroy Aylash Revall after 4,500 years, don't you think he is qualified to at least hear a memory's sad tale?"

Reginald looked at The Jester long and hard, and then, scratching at his psychology professor beard, turned his head to face me.

"The short answer is, I had been non-monogamous---"

"UNFAITHFUL!" Magdalena corrected him.

"Yes, Maggie. Unfaithful... to Magdalena. I was having an affair with a vampire named Breanna, who was also known in certain circles as Rose Marie. Unfortunately, she was also in a relationship with Le Bouffon, who had finally felt some kind of love for another woman, after over a hundred years without any real significant romance. Breanna unexpectedly had started to feel odd pains, uncharacteristic for a vampire. Very human pain. We don't know for sure, but we believe that she may have been the first vampire to ever conceive a child. We also do not know for sure who the father of that proposed child may have been. It was either mine, or it was Mart---, or it was Le Bouffon's. Long before this, Antonio Medici had begun planting his infectious words in Aylash's ears, and gaining cheap, unwarranted favoritism from the Winged God. He also planted seeds of discontent and betrayal in Aylash, in regard to the other Houses. How Revall didn't see through any of Medici's lies, I will never know... One thing Medici was particularly interested in, though, was Breanna. He'd made seemingly harmless advances on previous occasions, but those advances became more egregious and uncomfortable. I had warned him to refrain from su---"

"And so had I," Le Bouffon chimed in.

"Yes. The point is that Medici knew not to bother my lo---, not to bother Breanna. Once we distributed our grievance to the Houses, and heard no immediate response, we took a trip to visit Aylash, requesting that Antonio also attend. On a crisp and beautiful April 7th sunset, we descended upon Nis, hopeful for a logical and peaceful resolution. Instead..."

Reginald's hands began shaking. Going through the memories in his head produced some traumatic effects.

"I had asked that Breanna accompany us to Nis, excited about revealing the news of a possible vampire pregnancy. In hindsight, I don't know why. It's not like raising a vampire child would be anything other than an abomination, no pun intended. There was no proof that the fetus actually existed, or was viable. Regardless, I thought the news was earth shattering, especially for Revall, who'd been trying to conceive at least a half-vampire for virtually his entire existence... We were met on the steps of the Winged God, and Revall took Breanna's hand to kiss it..."

Again, Reginald had to pause and shake some horrific ghosts from within his brain. The Jester decided to take over.

"Then he grabbed *Rose Marie* and spun her around to face Reginald and me. We were shocked, but moved quickly to retrieve her. Aylash, with a swarming ambush of fifty followers now surrounding us, warned that if we moved one step closer to them, we would all be slaughtered right then. He took a handful of her hair and gripped it tight, and grabbed one of her arms, and started to pull. In opposite directions. Reginald called out in horror for Aylash to stop. He yelled 'She is pregnant.' Aylash then ripped Rose Marie in two uneven, jagged pieces, and then ripped those two halves into quarters."

Now it was Le Bouffon's turn to get choked up and halt his story. He peered out from his permanent mask, the whites of his eyes almost luminescent. His face was expressionless and mentally he was an ocean away. Reginald tagged back in.

"I screamed out in a futile, pathetic agony and dropped to my knees, tears pouring wildly out of my face. Le Bouffon attempted to attack Aylash, but was backhanded a good thirty feet away and subsequently held down by Revall's mob. Aylash slowly and cockily shuffled his feet over to my grieving slump and placed his hand on my head. For a brief moment, I thought he was going to end my life as well. His words were as cold as they were biting. He said, 'The House of the Gray Bear has no respect for their master, and no inkling of self-preservation. More importantly, it has no standing, no authority, and no representation at my table. If I want, I could destroy and then devour all of its vampires in one sitting. I will expect you to fall in line and follow your master as you were taught to. It will take a millennia to earn my admiration again. Go back to your weak House in your weak nation. While I still allow it.' With that, Aylash Revall and his gang of inbred cretins dipped back into the House of the Winged God, but not before I caught Antonio Giordano Medici standing at its doors, aloof and smiling ear to ear. As he closed the large stone doors to the Winged God, he whispered on the wind, 'She should have said yes.' Le Bouffon and I rushed to Breanna's desecrated corpse and attempted to gather her up, but as we did, the sky grew even darker, blacked out by Aylash's army of pet vultures and ravens. They dive bombed the two of us, tore into Breana's carcass, and flew away into the night with whatever was left of her. I still remember pieces of her silhouette as it fell scattered across the wooded mountains.

'Le Bouffon and I travelled home the next evening, and recounted the meeting to the others. Much to Aylash's surprise, we didn't sit tight and wait for his next command like some obedient lap dog. Those of us with the courage to fight..." Reginald stopped to look at Magdalena... "surrounded the House of the Blood Fountain in Rome four days later. We killed every single vampire inside, and burned them all to ash as we set the Blood Fountain ablaze. I took a disgusting portrait of Medici and Revall that hung in the foyer, tore it down, and pissed on it before tossing it into the actual decorative fountain that precedes the House's entrance. Medici's head soon landed atop it, and they both sunk down to its bottom. We moved on to the Winged God, confident and determined, and just for a blink of an eye, I thought we were actually going to pull it off. We didn't know the full extent of Aylash's powers. He combined the Luminastra Namtudari, the Spectralis Reptilios, and something I have no name for, and obliterated us in mere seconds. It is more than a small miracle that those of us who survived made it out of the House's vicinity or out of Nis at all. He has just as many humans doing his bidding as vampires. The only saving grace of that entire dismal chapter is that he was weakened, even if only slightly, and realized he was not invincible or immortal."

For a good ten seconds, no one moved an inch or spoke a sound. Finally, Reginald, seeking to conclude the evening's discussions, asked if I had any more questions. Unfortunately, Annie rose her hand.

"I have one."

Oh no.

"Do you? What would you like to ask?"

"Why the hell are you taking the bear?"

Sylvain Montreux shook his head and stood at attention, before addressing the room.

"It appears that we got sidetracked without resolving

that topic. I, too, asked the same question, Ms. Moore. I don't know if I've received a proper answer."

"Ballou deserves to face Aylash as much as any of us do," Reginald opined. 'His sacrilegious origin predates any of ours, no? His torturous existence predates ours, some of you by a thousand years. His is a one of a kind tale, as he himself is one of a kind. I don't have any preconceived notions of us surviving The Winged God a second time. We have to use every resource at our disposal, and if we perish, then we fought and perished together. If Ballou ever had his own chance at revenge, this is it. If we didn't take him, and he was left here alone with all of us dead in Serbia, is letting him starve in madness humane? What if humans snooping around the place discovered him? What if a young child discovers him? Are your souls ready to be responsible for what he does?"

"You're sending him to die!" Annie growled.

"No, I'm sending him to kill! To be avenged! He deserves that. He craves it!"

Sylvain was not convinced.

"If you try to take him, I will stop you. He *is* the Gray Bear. He must be its symbol and its resident until this House ceases." Several other high ranking members of the group sided with him, stoking his sense of righteousness.

"Well, try if you wish. I will be taking him. I've already secured two stolen military aircraft big enough to transport us all. One of them will house Ballou securely."

“I’m not joking with you. I will meet you with force if you proceed with this plan.”

“Well, tomorrow night, just after sundown, you will have to kill me... if you can.”

Chapter Nineteen: Civil War

Annie sat motionless in a chair, staring at the floor with a scowl chiseled into her face. I spoke diplomatically with a few of the people who agreed with Reginald or were still on the fence. I had to assure them that I would take their side during any confrontation. In turn, I made them assure me that there would *be* no confrontation until after I got to meet Aylash Revall one on one, and find out if there was a way to give me back my humanity. Eventually, the temperature of the evening cooled down, and the vampires who remained in the House professed their loyalty to Reginald. Unfortunately, almost a third of the vampires left with Sylvain, vowing only to return to prevent Reginald and the others from taking Ballou, The Abomination, to Serbia. As the night drug on, an unhealthy amount more followed suit, guilty about contradicting the wishes of their captain, but steadfast in their belief that Sylvain was right. I couldn't help but feel partly responsible for everything that had occurred since our arrival in Paris. I also had to find out if Annie was going to muddy the situation tomorrow.

"You might have really fucked things up, asking about the bear."

"Is that how you see it?"

"Well, I do think the night was about to end. At least that tense argumentative part of it."

"Sylvain said himself that he had asked about Ballou and didn't get an answer."

"He didn't get the answer he *wanted.*"

"Exactly, so the topic was not dead. It required more discussion, so I'm *glad* I asked."

"I'm NOT!" Annie was startled by the tone and increased volume in my voice. She wasn't deterred by it, however.

"Look, Davis. He's an animal. He's not a human. Even if he is a vampire. He's not able to make choices, and he's never experienced freedom. It'd be no different than if it was a Pitbull in a dog fighting ring, or a chicken forced to kill another."

"I respect your opinion, but I don't agree with it. And more to the point, this is vampire business, Annie. It's not student government on campus, or some domestic issue back home to be an activist or journalist about. We're fucking vampires, for God's sake. We're killing people to live. Your conscience or soft spot for The Abomination---"

“Don’t call him that! He has a name. He has feelings! He---”

“He would fucking eat you, *AFTER* ripping your jugular out to consume as much blood as possible in as quick a time frame as possible!”

“Goddamnit, Davis!”

“What?! It’s the truth, Annie. Ballou is a killer. Not unlike any of us. No different than The Jester, or Magdalena, or me. Except for the minor detail that he’s much more powerful, unstoppable, and hungry than we are.”

“I’m... I’m going to go down to the bar and have a drink. Or eight. I’ll be up later. Don’t come down looking for me.”

“Why not? Is Henri in tonight?”

Annie’s face told me that I made the wrong comment... at the wrong time. She didn’t say anything; she just grabbed her sweater and purse, and started for the door.

‘Wait. Annie, I’m sorry. I mess---” She slammed the door behind her. ‘---ed up.”

I knew it would be a mistake to follow after her. I couldn’t do anything now but make things worse, so I stayed back in the room and showered, hoping that my bloodlust had been satiated for the night. I did make a call down to the bar first, asking nicely for Roland the bartender to keep a watchful eye on Annie, and let me know immediately if she was in any trouble. Annie saddled up to the bar, and sat two seats down from Tamlyn Bernard and Magnus Olruud, who were engaged in a very heated debate... over what the best American sitcom of all time was. Overhearing them caused her to laugh, her first time to do so in a couple of days, and she injected herself into their conversation.

"I don't know whether to be more shocked that two vampires are arguing about Friends, Seinfeld, The Simpsons, and The Office, or that you have the time and energy to discuss anything other than what just happened here."

Tamlyn, eternally a teenager, but on this earth for some 50 years, was surprised in her own right, that Annie would be so close minded and unafraid to approach a vampire.

"Why would you assume that we don't speak about human things? I was turned when most of these shows were popular. They were the pop culture of the time. I didn't turn my back on humanity. Everything vampire is not orgies and blood baths."

"No. Of course not. I apologize."

Magnus changed the subject, since he could tell there were apparently more important things on Annie's mind.

"What do *you* think of what occurred here tonight?"

"I think it's unfortunate, and that maybe it might not have happened if not for our arrival."

"I have to agree." His lungs filled up with air and exhaled a large roar of laughter, while Tamlyn gave a smaller, more reserved giggle. His laugh was infectious, causing others who hadn't even heard the comment to also cackle aloud. "But arrive you did, and what's done is done. The pot was simmering for far too long. You just landed in time to heat it to a boil---"

"And then drop it all over the floor," Tamlyn added, with a shy smile.

"The whole reason we came here first was to learn about what led to your House's grievance, and then to get intel on Aylash before heading to meet him. Alone. We didn't expect it to turn into all of this."

"That's the beautiful accident of life, isn't it?" Magnus offered. "You plan and you plan, and then something comes along and ruins it. Then you make a new plan. I wouldn't feel so guilty about this conflict between Reginald and Sylvain. They respect each other, but the tensions between them have been growing and festering far before you were even born, much less showing up at the Gray Bear's door."

"Why did Magdalena and Edsel not get a vote on what the Gray Bear would do? Why are they not 'official' members?"

"Easy. Fuggerton is English, so fuck him, and Magdalena intentionally relinquished her rights and standing as a member. Reginald's betrayal was a bitter pill for her to swallow, as was the possibility that Reginald may have conceived a child with someone other than her.

She was envious of Breanna's stature here among us, and jealous of Reginald's infatuation with her. So she---"

"Wait. Why the attitude toward Fuggerton? Aren't you a foreigner too?"

"Yes, but I'm *Danish*. So *fuck* him." Again, Magnus' loud joyous bellow filled the bar, and everyone else joined in. Annie, confused, but too tired to continue, left the subject dead, and switched gears.

"Do you think Reginald and Sylvain will actually come to blows or worse tomorrow night?"

"Honestly, I do not know. I hope not, but Reginald is stubborn and hot tempered, and Sylvain is no pushover. He's commanded the respect and love of many within these walls. Whatever direction the two-headed snake splits into, some will land on one side of it, and some will land on the other. It's been less than four years since the war. We've tasted the death of our kind. Why not taste some more?"

"You don't seem too broken up about that."

"I just want one more time to see Aylash Revall, and to try and end him, forever. Wouldn't that be glorious?"

"Tamlyn, did you fight in the war?"

"No. Not overtly. I did play a small, deceptive part, but these battles called for strength and power. If I was fighting humans, I would have been very effective. Against older, bigger vampires, though... It was not my strong suit."

"How do you feel about Ballou being taken to another country and made to fight?"

"I don't care one way or the other. I've only ever seen The Abomination twice in the last eight years, so I don't have an emotional connection to him. We do not parade him around like a hero or a ridiculous mascot. I do know that he would follow Reginald into battle. Would he be able to be controlled? That's another story."

"You don't think he's being exploited?"

"I think he was exploited by being merged of, at a minimum, two different creatures and then turned into a vampire. I think he was exploited by the former members of this House by being celebrated on one hand and held captive in darkness on the other. If he is able to eat the one who did this to him, then his life has come full circle, and the irony is like a poetic justice." That explanation is exactly what Annie needed to shut her up on the subject of Ballou, The Abomination, and his transportation to Nis, Serbia and the House of the Winged God.

I was resting on a cushy sofa in our room, trying to relax, but running many future scenarios in my head, when I heard the door start to open. Annie was tipsy but not wasted, and she carried a shy, girlish, expression on her face. Our eyes met, and even though I don't think either of us needed to say it, we both muttered an "I'm sorry" before meeting in the center of the room, forehead to forehead.

"I'm going to support you on this journey, Davis, but that doesn't mean I can agree with everything you and the

Vampire Coalition of Europe do while you're on it. I'm a normal person, and this year has been the absolute opposite of normal. But I'm trying. God knows, I am trying."

"And I'm trying to not forget how different this world is from yours. It's not necessarily meant for you. So, thank you, for helping me to this point. Thank you for loving me. I can't promise that you'll approve of everything the rest of the way, and I can't promise I won't ask you to get somewhere safe when the time comes. Because part of my job, for as long as we're together, is to protect you, and that might include our paths diverging in Serbia. Hell, it might include our paths diverging tomorrow night."

Late the next morning, around 11:00, Annie awoke, showered, and went down for breakfast. Again, she'd startled the human staff, and again, the chef had to scramble to create a delicious breakfast out of the ingredients supplied by Henri's of Paris. The building and the grounds were both even more still and silent than the day before. The head of staff told Annie that the Gray Bear would be closed to human clientele, and that many a vampire had voiced that they would *not* be in attendance tonight.

Restless or nervous, or both, I woke from a troubled sleep at 5:00pm France time, and opened my eyes to find Annie at the foot of the bed staring at me. Her expression was full of love and lament.

"The House of the Gray Bear is a ghost town" she relayed to me.

"For now, maybe. I think that might change come sundown."

"Do you think they'll really fight about Ballou?"

"I think this fight is about more than Ballou. I think it's about what should have, or might have happened with the Blood Fountain and Aylash. I sense the tensions are long built up."

"So then we're the straw that broke the Gray Bear's back?"

"It appears that way... We're the Texas Straw."

As the beautiful red/orange/yellow/purple, and blue sky that Annie described to me as blissfully peaceful grew darker and darker, the sounds downstairs became louder and more erratic. I could hear voices, but also the crash of metal and stone. I could hear activity – frustrated activity.

"You stay here" I demanded from Annie. "I don't know a whole bunch about vampire protocol, but I know you're not welcome in this type of situation. It would be taken as an insult and an intrusion if you just waltzed your happy Abilene ass downstairs expecting to see the festivities like you were front row at a UFC fight."

I could tell she wanted to argue, but she weighed our last few conversations and the previous events in the great hall in her head, and relented.

"OK. If you think it's best."

"Thank you. God, thank you."

I kissed her goodbye and left the room, instructing her to lock the door behind me. At first, I took my time walking down a winding stone staircase to the first floor, but ended up in almost a sprint by the time I reached the bottom. I was... enthusiastic, about what lay ahead tonight. I was met at the bottom of the stairs by Paul Lajoie.

"Are you a spectator, tonight, or a participant?"

"Well, I guess I'm not decided yet, Paul. We don't even know what's *going* to happen... But once I figure it out, if you want, I'll make you the first to know." I looked him dead in the eye with a steely, emotionless glare.

"I look forward to it."

We walked shoulder to shoulder onto the large dancefloor of the Gray Bear, where some sixty or so vampires were already standing, on one side of its center or the other, in an apparent show of solidarity with either Reginald Duplante or Sylvain Montreux. The number of those behind Sylvain clearly outnumbered Reginald's contingent, but I couldn't accurately provide a percentage. They both looked at me curiously, as if trying to deduce where my loyalty lie.

"Are we really doing this?" Sylvain asked Reginald, with a clear exasperation in his voice.

"Are you really going to oppose taking Ballou to Nis?"

"Yes."

"Then we have no choice. Davis McCarty, who's side are you on?"

"I don't think I reall---"

Before I could announce my position aloud, Paul Lajoie was all over me with clawed scratches and closed fists to my face. His spark led to a fire of conflict, as vampire attacked vampire on and around the dancefloor, the fight even spilling outside onto the grounds. This was an all-out bar fight, or a rumble.

Paul was insanely fast and unnerving with his strikes, and my face was gashed open on either cheek rather impressively. However, his power was less than stunning, and at the first chance, I grabbed his right wrist and tore his arm completely from his body. He didn't know who he was fucking with, or what. His eyes virtually stretched an inch larger than they were, and he screamed out more in shock than pain. I took that right arm and swung it upside his head, causing him to somersault sideways and land like a life-size wooden marionette on the floor. He was immediately trying to crawl away, but I grabbed him by the foot, and was about to end him when a kick from behind went sailing into my back, and propelled me forward into a melee of battling vampires. We all fell to the floor, and I looked up to see a tall, handsome, but evil-looking vampire I hadn't yet met staring me down and picking up speed in my direction. *Who the fuck is that?* I thought.

"I will not let a foreign child kill an esteemed member of the Gray Bear... even if it is Paul Lajoie."

I kicked away a couple of others and stood up to face Handsome one on one. We traded punches and defense, kicks and hand fighting, before he was able to grab me just under both arms, and toss me in some amateur wrestling way that caused my back and head to pulverize the floor. I went into a daze, as he covered me with his weight. Before I knew what was happening, he was trying to choke me out. *Out* in this case, meant squeezing my throat until my head popped off of it. That would be no way for Annie to find me, so I reached between his legs, grabbed the back of his jeans, and pulled him down enough for him to lose a little leverage. I then took my left thumb and dug deep into his left eye socket, causing a wince and a yell from my new sparring partner. He got off of me, and we both jumped to our feet in time for me to land a crushing side kick to his abdomen. He sailed backward, and then disappeared abruptly.

I set my sights on finding Paul, and watched him slinking his way behind the bar to lick his wounds and hopefully wait out the rest of the fight. I didn't intend to let him do that, but I was interrupted by two vampires attacking me at once. They were apparently used to fighting as one, and they choreographed and telegraphed their strikes and lunges, always keeping me at bay with one of them while the other loaded up.

"Not bad at all" I called out to them. "You guys are pretty good." They responded in French, so I have no idea what was said.

Unfortunately for them, one missed a left hook, and I spun him around and held him in front of me like a human shield. I then punched him repeatedly in the back of the head while keeping the other guy from being able to get around his partner to me. Eventually, I landed one punch too many, and my fist plunged through his head and out his mouth, causing his partner to cease fighting. Horrified at the sight, his brief pause gave me the chance to grab him by both arms and kick him straight in the face, removing his head from his neck and sending it flailing through the air. I swung his headless corpse in a circle a few times to gain some momentum, and then threw it at a group of fighting vampires, not really caring who it hit.

I stopped and caught my breath, surveying the battlefield. Aside from watching Magnus obliterate about five guys at once, I couldn't tell what side was winning, and I couldn't locate Reginald or Sylvain in the crowd. Thinking they must be outside, I hurried out there to find out. Almost to the door, a female vampire flew through the air to engage me, but I caught her mid-flight and flung her through a window. Once outside, she thought better of continuing the battle with me, and chose to take her fight elsewhere.

In looking for Reginald, I found Le Bouffon, who was caught up with the same handsome guy who stopped me from killing Paul. They were really going at it, and even managed to deflect the blows of others trying to enter their fray. Le Bouffon stiff armed Handsome to the face, causing him to backflip onto his belly. Before The Jester could finish him, though, three others jumped on him from behind, and the mysterious and capable opponent once again disappeared in the blink of an eye. Le Bouffon shrugged them all off and killed one by sticking him with a dagger and lifting it the length of his torso before ripping through the slit and forcing his fist out the poor victim's back.

I couldn't help but think how savage and insane this all was. These vampires had just been sitting at the same tables and drinking and partying together just a few nights before. Now they were literally killing each other. Some of these vampires had been surviving as night drinkers for hundreds of years. And for what... because some of them wanted to use a rabid, grotesque vampire bear in their battle and some didn't. I could only shake my head, and then...

Then Thomas Richard attacked me verbally before throwing a well-timed left cross right into my mouth. His knuckles crashed against my teeth, and I don't know who would end up more damaged. Richard's vote in the great room was Yes, leading me to believe that he had been swayed to my side. Now it appears that was a mistake. I think.

"None of this would have happened if not for you. I blame you. I've killed my brothers on this hallowed ground tonight, because of *you*! That is why you must die. And that is why I will kill you."

Not so fast.

"I don't want to do this, Thomas. I think you'll be an asset in Serb---"

He swung wildly, which I've learned to counter well in

the last six months. I let him taking a particularly overarching swing, and as I ducked under him, I came up off the balls of my feet with possibly the best uppercut I've thrown thus far in my young life, and it connected so well, Richard was unconscious before he even met the peak of his flight backward to the ground. I thought about stomping his head to a flat pulp, but knew that he was defeated and still a possible asset in Serbia. There was no reason to add injury to insult. That's when I saw Sylvain and Reginald, battling one another while a circle of exhausted, spent vampires watched. They fought methodically, gentlemanly, and calculated. Neither man wanted to make a mistake, and give the other an advantage. Reginald landed a right/left combination to Sylvain's face, but Sylvain quickly bounced back with a hook to the ribs, another to the opposite side, and a straight left to Reginald's chin. This punch watered Reg's eyes and left him a little worse for wear. Sylvain then jumped and caught Reginald in a human body scissor that expelled all the air from Duplante's abdomen and lungs, and left him scratching and pushing at Sylvain's legs from a beaten, horizontal position. To further incapacitate Duplante, Sylvain brought down his dominant hand down like a hammer on Reginald's prone chest and abdomen. All individual fights across the property closed in on this centered conflict, and Sylvain's group appeared victorious, backing those loyal to Reginald into the circle and enveloping them.

"Reginald, there are only ten of you left. We've outnumbered you two to one. Do not be so proud and foolish that you're willing to die for this ill-conceived notion, and take your subjects down with you."

"Our fight is not yet over" an indignant Reginald Duplante replied, his face now turning red, and his ribs close to giving way and fracturing under the grip of Sylvian Montreux's strong thighs. Suddenly, a British lady's voice called out. It was Lenora Jeffries.

"He is quite right, my charismatic friend; this fight is not yet over." Without anyone noticing, Lenora and approximately forty of her best and most seasoned vampires from north of the Chunnel had surrounded the whole of the Gray Bear's combatants. Sylvain was perplexed, and quite angry.

"Lenora, what do you think you're doing!?"

"Making sure that the correct action is taken, and the right side wins. Aylash must pay for his arrogance."

"This is not your fight. You have no say here, and no reason to intervene."

"Oh, but I disagree. The outcome of tonight's unfortunate chapter in the Gray Bear's history will no doubt affect the future of all the vampires in Europe and its neighbors. Either quickly or slowly, tonight might lead to the end of this House or the end of our kind. My British brethren are now your allies, and we will not let the opportunity to end Aylash's reign fall away before it begins." Reginald cracked a slight smile of relief, and turned to view Sylvain's disgusted, wide-eyed face.

"You heard her, my friend. What choice do you have? It is now you who would take your followers down with you."

"Then so be it. We will not go quietly."

Sylvain leapt some twenty feet in the air, and came down with two fists pointing downward at Reginald's head, which Duplante craftily, and luckily, dodged. They continued their confrontation, with Reginald ordering Lenora's vampires to disarm and neutralize the opposing vampires *without* killing any more of them. Within minutes, Sylvain's outnumbered group had surrendered, only two more dying in the process. The sole battle raging on was between Sylvain and Reginald, and it went back and forth alone for ten more minutes, while everyone else stood and watched. At one point, I noticed Annie watching the battle from our room's window, clutching the drapes with tight, worried fists. Both men's attacks and reaction times were slowing, and they both stumbled along, at the point of exhaustion. Sylvain attempted something of a roundhouse kick, but it wasn't nearly swift enough, and Reginald caught it and wrapped Sylvain in his arms. He lifted him in the air, and brought Montreux down across his knee. Sylvain cried out in agony, and then Reginald ended the fight between them with two clutched fists, fingers intertwined, to the face. Obviously triumphant, Reginald stood to his feet, called out for an available blade, and grabbed Sylvain by the hair. He put the blade to Sylvain's throat, and leaned down to whisper in his ear.

"The battle is over. I need you at my side in Nis.

Please, my friend. Agree to help me. Let us finally avenge our unjust defeat and subsequent wound licking these past four years. Look into the eyes of your fellow vampires. Into their tortured souls. You're not letting them down by joining me. You'd let them down by dying tonight, foolishly. I would most likely have to make them join you in the afterlife, unsure if I could fully trust them. You taking my hand right now would ease their internal conflict... I haven't trusted anyone as much as I trusted you, basically from the first time you walked through these doors almost two hundred years ago... What else do---"

"Please. Shut up. Just shut up for a second, and let me rise to my feet, so I can either surrender or die standing proud."

Hesitant at first, thinking that Montreux might be planning to resume fighting, Reginald carefully removed the blade and backed away, allowing his humbled opponent to stand. Addressing the whole of the crowd, Sylvain spoke in a garish, proud voice, as if he was the victor.

"My friends. Thank you for following me into battle with our brothers, our sisters. Thank you for killing, and for dying, to protect our tormented creature, Ballou. Certain, unexpected circumstances shifted the tides of victory to the other side, or I am sure we would have won. Be that as it may, my loyalty to the House of the Gray Bear and to Reginald Duplante has never been called into question, nor should it ever. He is the captain of this fine House, and he has won the right to command us into the mouth of despair once more. Into the mouth of Aylash Revall. To defeat Aylash, we may very well need The Abomination, as well as this anomaly from Texas. Against my instincts, I will follow my captain to Serbia, and I am confident, whether I live or die on foreign soil, that we will succeed in ridding the world of its first, God forsaken atrocity."

Sylvain then stepped closer to Reginald, and they eyed each other silently for the smallest of eternities. I could feel the collective hairs stand on everyone's arms, as we waited to see if his words were just bullshit, or if there was indeed peace and contrition coming. Sylvain's lips parted slightly, and he gave a sly grin, extending his hand for Reginald to shake it. Duplante gazed at it for a second and then shook it thankfully. Placing his other hand on Sylvain's shoulder and raising their hands together triumphantly in the air, Reginald gave a quick summary of what must be done.

"Three nights from now, we will all load into two customized Antonov aircraft, Ballou included, and take flight for Serbia. We will land at Nikola Telsa Airport in Belgrade, and travel by motor vehicle to a village outside of Nis. The mountains will do well to keep us covered, but Revall has many human eyes watching out for him. The strategy of surprise would be our greatest ally, but tomorrow and the next day, leadership will put its heads together to devise second, third, and fourth alternatives to a primary plan of attack. All of you need to feed, rest, and tend to your wounds tonight, and sleep as much as you can until tomorrow night, when you will call, text, email, and knock on the doors of every vampire you know. You will instruct them to meet us here in two nights' time, and you will drive home the point that our very survival rests on the shoulders of every able-bodied vampire still bitter at, or afraid of Aylash Revall."

It wasn't a deafening ovation, but at least everyone still alive gave a positive reaction to his speech. People tearing each other apart a half hour ago were hugging, shaking hands, and making amends. I breathed a personal sigh of relief. Even though I still didn't know these Frenchmen enough to trust them with my life, I felt some comfort knowing I wouldn't be confronting Revall alone. I wondered what Annie was thinking about all thi--- wait. *Where's Annie?* She was no longer at the door. At almost the same time, the thought of Paul Lajoie entered my brain. I didn't see him again after he crawled to the bar. *Where could he have...*

Oh shit.

Chapter Twenty: Au Revoir

My legs had never moved so fast in all my life as they did charring the lawn of the Gray Bear, and barreling up that stone spiral staircase. I smashed open the bedroom door to find Paul Lajoie, minus one arm, sickly gray and near death, atop Annie, planted between her legs. Her pants were still on, but her shirt had been ripped open to expose her bra and body to Lajoie. Not quite porn, but way more than I was alright with letting him see. I believe he was...*dry humping* her.

"Time to say goodnight."

He turned his head to me, by which time I had already debated and chose against unveiling the growing Luminastra Namtudari within on him, afraid that it would destroy Annie in its path. Instead, I thrust my fingers through the skin covering his sharp, angled chin, grabbing him by the trachea, and yanked him off of my girlfriend. He tried to swing at me with his lone arm, but I blocked the punch, ripped that arm off, and tossed it through our window. I threw him right after it, and as he landed to the grounds of the Gray Bear like a javelin, I landed feet first on top of his head. It squished open like an over-ripe cantaloupe, and Paul Lajoie's attempt to rape or kill the love of my life – the only love of my life – had luckily dissolved. If I had been a second or two later, she might be dead, or a vampire. I made a mental note of that chilling, inconceivable fact, and waited for Reginald, Sylvain, and the rest of the group to wander frantically over to me.

"What is this?" Reginald questioned as he looked up to the window to find a crying wreck of an Annie standing there holding the curtain in front of her.

"Paul attacked Annie. If your speeches had gone on any longer, he would have either raped her or killed her, or both. Luckily, I got there in time to stop him."

"Oh, stop him you did, Monsieur. He won't be attacking anyone, ever again."

"I have to go check on Annie."

The threat seemingly over, this time I jogged up to the room, and found her sitting on the bed with her head down, sobbing. I walked over, took her hand gently, and sat down beside her. I didn't speak. I gave her the time she needed to just be in the moment, and waited until she was ready.

"The whole thing lasted maybe thirty seconds", she started. "But it felt like a lifetime. And that whole time, I just kept thinking over and over again in my head, *I know Davis is gonna burst through that door. I know Davis is gonna burst through that door...* And then, there you were."

"Did he hurt you?"

"He more scared me than anything. He did manhandle me, and he ripped my shirt open, but he didn't hit me, yet. And he didn't touch my... my privates... yet."

"Did he say anything?"

"Oh, he sure as fuck did, and that was probably his undoing. He took so much fucking time talking that he gave you the chance to make it up here." She started to cry harder, and had to stop from hyperventilating.

"What did he say?"

"I can't remember word for word, but he mentioned that he was going to make us pay for coming here and ruining everything. He said he was going to take his time with me, that he was going to feed on me enough to make his thing work, and that he was going to drain me dry of blood while he drilled me to death."

My muscles clinched and my veins protruded out of my skin as my anger reached peak level. Annie put her head in my chest and cried, both calming me and making me regretful for even putting her in this position.

"Damnit. I don't know what to do. If you're at my side, I think you're in danger. If I stash you somewhere safe, you're *still* in danger! I'm so sorry, Annie... Why do you lov---"

“Because I do! Because I love you. And, yes, it doesn’t make sense for a ‘smart’ girl like me to be in this predicament, but smart never had anything to do with love. I could have ignored you like everyone else did back in school, but your eyes, your shy smile, you... you just... You were meant for me, Davis. And I was meant for you, so... Fuck, man. Here we are.

It’s you and me, even if that gets me killed.”

“But I don’t want to get you killed, Annie.”

“And I don’t want to die! But I also don’t want to be anywhere without you. I might as well die, if you’re not by my side. If I’m not by yours.”

We sat there, cuddled up to one another, when Reginald and Le Bouffon knocked at the door.

“Is she alright?... I mean, are *you*, alright?”

“Yes, thank you. Did you win?”

“Yes, we did. We will be taking Ballou with us. I know that was a sore subject for you, but---”

“I’m over it. It’s fine. We appreciate the assistance, and the possible manpower, if things come to that.”

“I hate to disappoint you, but things most likely... will come to that.”

“Well, what better monster to have on your side than the biggest, meanest, sumbitch I’ve ever seen?”

“Yes. My thoughts, as well... Davis, when you wake

tomorrow evening, please feed quickly and meet us in the library."

"The library?"

"Yes, the great hall is... *tainted*, for me, at the moment. We lost 35 vampires tonight. The last place I spoke with half of them was in that room. The last words I spoke to them were words of anger and spite. I want to wipe the stench of that room off of me and adjourn to a more joyous location."

"Alright. Library, it is. See you at nightfall."

The next evening, I went down to the feeding room, selecting an older man, a criminal who the local jailer gave to the Gray Bear because he was tired of seeing him arrested and locked up every month. According to the gatekeeper's secondhand account, it was only a matter of time before the man progressed to more heinous crimes. I didn't care. I just needed to feed.

Afterward, as requested, I found the library, meeting up with a larger contingent of vampires than I left when I lay my head down in the morning. Many had already been contacted and made their way to the Gray Bear from all over France, England, and Spain, etc. One vampire, though, was absent, and I intended on finding out about him.

"Jester" I beckoned. "Last night, you and I both fought with a tall, handsome gentlem---"

"Valentis" he replied swiftly. "You're speaking of

Valentis."

"Who is he, and did he die, last night?"

"Oh, I doubt it. He's good at not dying. He's good at escaping after the tides turn against him."

"What's his story?"

"Just like you said. He's a tall, handsome vampire. The only other interesting part of his story is his skill at hand to hand combat, and his ability to half-warp."

"Half-warp? I read about this in Revall's journals. Can Valentis actually do this?"

"Indeed he can."

In Aylash Revall's journals, half-warping was the ability to vaporize oneself, for lack of a better explanation and re-emerge ten to fifty feet away. More like a small-scale teleportation where one is there one second, and gone the next. As far as Revall knew, he had been the only vampire to attain that gift. Another of his followers had tried, but reformed painfully halfway fused inside a wall, forcing Sartep to conduct a mercy killing. Now there was confirmation that this Valentis could also perform it, and that would explain his 'now you see me, now you don't' disappearing act. It's hard to tell with vampires; they're so fast to begin with, and many, like Le Bouffon for example, conduct themselves like modern day illusionists, very adept at slight-of-hand trickery.

"Where do you think Valentis is now, and will he help 'the cause' now that his side has lost and professed loyalty to Reginald?"

"I could only guess. He's not a man who sits in one place for long, and he's not necessarily loyal to anyone or anything. My impression is that he was actually here to settle a personal score, not honor Sylvain's position. Valentis is a complicated vampire, but his facade boils down to reveal a hyper narcissism and a need for self-preservation at his core."

"Great."

Reginald called the gathered to silence and displayed a map of Nis and its outlying region. His description of the House of the Winged God and the journey to reach it wreaked of a generic fantasy saga ripping off both modern hits and older classics that Annie would have read. He assured everyone in the room, however, that everything he said was true, and then gave some disheartening possibilities.

"There is a great chance that our plane will be detected and demolished as soon as we enter Belgrade. There's an even better chance that we're attacked, from all sides, along the road in route to our destination. If we actually make it to our rendezvous point and set up camp, we'll have to tread lightly through the forest, avoiding or confronting Revall's Serbian minions, and cross through a narrow valley where arrows can pierce us to death from above. If we make it out of the valley, we'll come to a clearing where the foliage and natural vegetation of the two mountains that sandwich The House of the Winged God has been completely sandblasted away by Revall's magic. This area has been renamed the Crystal Mountain, for the reflective, shard-like topography that Aylash left on its surface. To get to the House of the Winged God, you have to walk across the Bridge of Skulls, which is quite literally a bridge made of human skulls."

Reginald noticed the stomachs, mouths, and enthusiasm of everyone who hadn't yet visited this House drop onto the library's floor. This caused him to laugh and attempt to lighten the mood.

"Come on, everybody! It's only death!" he yelled throughout the room. "If we can't have a little fear, we're not really living, yes?" I thought I would ask a few questions, to set my mind at ease.

"How many people here, in this room, have seen the House of the Winged God?" Out of 170 people in the library, about 45 raised their hands. "How many of you have been inside it?" About 25. "How many fought in the battle that ended with Aylash blowing everybody up?" A few revolted looks preceded the answer of seventeen. I looked at Reginald, horrorstruck. "Seventeen people. Seventeen? That's all who've witnessed the power of the Luminastra Namtudari?"

"Correct. And don't forget the Spectralis Reptilios Invincibus. These seventeen saw Aylash reborn right before their very eyes. They saw him go from ancient, crumbling vampire on the verge of defeat to renewed, all-powerful conqueror setting his very creations ablaze before scattering their ashes to hell."

"And you're still here? Still prepared to face him

again?" Le Bouffon interrupted, as was his now infamous pattern.

"To a person, we're all devoted, dedicated to facing him once more. The former outcome will not happen again. I will gladly die if I can see him dead."

Everyone there stomped their feet in unison, beat their chests with clinched right fists, and yelled "Revall!" with the full force of their throats. It seems that even the people who were against this expedition were now apparently *very* on board. I thought that sentiments swayed far too quickly from one direction to the other, but I guess that's how things are done here. Super emotional, super adversarial, then you fight to the death and everything's fine after.

"So we fly two nights from now?"

"Correct," Reginald confirmed. "The final piece of the puzzle is getting Ballou into the travelling cage that will hopefully hold him the entirety of the trip."

"Have you thought about tranquilizing him?"

"It's actually been tried before. He only killed five vampires after being given three times the dose that would make a grizzly sleep for days. The main barrier is getting him to and into the cage. It's far too big to try and bring into the House, and even if we could, once he was in it, he would be far too heavy to move. We'll have to coax him out to the cage."

"Can I try?" Annie asked, walking into the library

uninvited.

Shit.

"And how would you do that?" Reginald was intrigued. "Become bait for him?"

"Kind of. I think I could talk to him."

"Can I show you something?"

"I guess."

"Perfect. Everybody, meeting's over. You know what we have to do and when to be here. Make sure everyone you know who is up to the task is here in two nights. We will leave regardless... Annie, please come with me."

Annie looked at me, knowing that I was not happy with her injection into the conversation. She just shrugged and mouthed, "Sorry" at me. Reginald led Annie by the hand to the feeding room, with me close behind. Opening the door, he instructed Annie to step inside, look over the potential vampire meals, and select the one she thought could appeal to Ballou's heart strings the most.

"What?" Annie asked, shocked.

"Just pick one. The one who looks the most like a... bear whisperer."

"I can't do---"

"You can and you will. We're going to test your hypothesis. Either you will prove yourself right, or you will prove yourself wrong. In either case, do not feel bad for the person you choose. They were going to die, anyway. This way, if they can stop Ballou one way or another, I will release them, and they will be free to go."

I knew in my heart of hearts that Reginald would never let anyone leave the Gray Bear alive, for fear that they might expose the more nefarious parts of its existence, but I also felt that this experiment was only going to end one way, anyhow. Annie walked into the feeding room, and slowly walked around in a circle, getting to look everyone in the eye. She was aghast at what she saw, and tears started running down her cheeks. She came upon a poor, tired woman, and knelt down in front of her.

"Are you afraid of bears?" she asked.

"Je peux te comprende," the woman replied. "Je ne parle pas anglais".

Annie, knowing rudimentary French from high school classes, and her annual trips to Paris, switched languages, and tried the best she could. Every word after this was in French, so I had to ask later what all was said.

"I'm giving you the chance to try and reason with an animal, and if you're able to sto---"

"You're going to throw me to The Abomination!" the woman screamed.

They went back and forth for a little before Reginald interjected himself, comforting the woman. This was something I could tell he never did, but he was good at it.

He got the woman to understand the gravity of the situation, and the supposed chance at freedom it provided her. This time, I was the one who knew better, while Annie was naïve. He unchained the woman, and the four of us walked to the room which held Ballou's cave.

"What's your name, child?" Reginald asked her.

"Rosalie."

"Rosalie, I'm going to give you a basket of meat. You're going to try and get Ballou to eat the basket instead of you, understand?"

"No! No, please! Do not do this to me!" Rosalie tried to back away, but was restrained by Reginald's grasp on her wrist.

"You can do this. I have confidence in you. We just need to see if this gentle American is correct in her assumption of our dear friend, Ballou. Please, take this basket and walk through that door, right there."

Rosalie stepped through the door, and inched step by step toward the damaged gate holding Ballou inside. She was terrified beyond words. We all watched from a safe distance, still inside the room, but above the floor and in close proximity to the exit. Reginald ordered the gate opened, and Rosalie started to scream as she heard the rumbled awakening of Ballou, The Abomination. His front paws shown themselves first, and then his enormous head, sniffing the meat, revealed itself from the darkness of the cave. He turned to the woman, who held the basket in her arms, and lifted it up to Ballou.

"H-H-Here, little bear. This is for y---"

Ballou had reared up on all four legs, giving a big stretch with his butt in the air, then galloped toward the woman, biting her head off like he was opening a condiment packet, and then he drank her blood from her headless neck. The whole scene resembled a baby drinking from a sippy cup. Annie yelled out and then threw up all over the floor and her shoes. Ballou turned his attention toward us for a second, made a face that seemed to say, 'I'll get to you in a second", and then returned to the basket of meat. Reginald had seen enough.

"So, now, Miss Annie, do you see why it might be a small miracle to get Ballout to the cage and into the aircraft? Do you see why it may not be the best use of your time to engage him? Your blood is his first priority. It would be his only objective. You cannot reason with him, you can't appeal to him with your girlish looks and your charm. He is a killer. And you... you are but a snack."

Annie put her head in my arms, crying in my chest, as I rubbed the back of her head.

"Don't feel bad about her, Annie. That wasn't your fault. She was going to get fed on, no matter what. Either by Ballou, or by a human vampire. Her fate was sealed when she entered the Gray Bear's feeding room."

"Did I really just see that? What the fuck are we doing here? How did we get to this point?"

"I think it all started when my mom told me she wasn't really my mom."

"This is all just a bad, bad dream. Right? This can't be real." I could sense that Annie was close to really losing it, and I had to get out her of the current environment.

"What if you got a room in Paris, and stayed there tonight? You could wake up tomorrow morning, have one of those croissants you like, and do Paris tourist stuff until it was time to come back and get on the plane." She lifted her head from my chest, and stared at me.

"Are you trying to get rid of me? Are you going to have me drugged again, and when I wake up, you're long gone on the way to Serbia?"

"No, no" I laughed. "Those days are over, my love. I'm just trying to give you some sanity, a semblance of normalcy before what might be the last chance at..."

"The last chance at what?"

"At anything, I reckon."

Annie agreed, and by midnight, she was in a private car, being driven back to Paris. I stayed behind, and worked out an agreement with Reginald that everyone would refrain from any action until after I met with Aylash Revall. Nothing would take place beforehand. It was a fragile, tentative agreement at best, and I could tell that there were several other strategies going on inside his head.

Much later, after we'd touched down in Belgrade and gotten to our camp in the village outside Nis, would Annie tell me about that last day in Paris, and how she ran into her mother out of all the people shuffling around the city half a world away from Abilene, and how they'd had coffee at Henri's. She told me about explaining away my absence in Paris, and that they talked about her relationship with me, and how we were a happy couple. She would tell me how much she'd forgotten about being human in everyday society, and how, even though it was simpler and safer, she would never go back. Not now that she had me.

I really did want to believe her.

The afternoon of September 1st, before we woke and loaded up the two large Antonov's to head to The House of the Winged God, a letter arrived at the Gray Bear. It was addressed to Reginald Duplante and one Martin Dupuis. Reginald, not waiting for whoever Martin Dupuis was, opened the letter, and was stunned by the following:

"Before you begin your onslaught of the Winged God, please give me 24 hours with the boy. I hear he possesses some very intriguing gifts, and I would like to see for myself, in private. He may very well be the one I've prophesized about, and we need to discuss some very important matters. After 24 hours, you are more than welcome to come try to destroy me. Send your reply at once.

Regards, Aylash Revall"

As the rest of us woke or arrived at the Gray Bear, he gathered us on the dancefloor of the main ballroom and told us of Aylash's letter.

"We'll have no element of surprise, as someone here has spoken to the wrong people. Whether it was someone you tried to recruit, or perhaps someone here who alerted Revall out of fear, or some ill-conceived sense of honor or loyalty to him, we must act as though all of our plans have been prematurely foiled. This may include the inclusion of Ballou and assistance from various other vampire groups. No doubt, he knows our method of transportation, and will be waiting gleefully. The only choice, in my opinion, is to comply with his request, and arrange a meeting between him and Davis... Do you have any problem with this, McCarty?"

"Problem? It's what I wanted to begin with. Maybe I can stop any war from---"

"Don't fool yourself!" Le Bouffon roared at me. It was then that I realized he was the Martin Dupuis Revall's letter was addressed to. "There will be no peaceful resolution if we step foot on his soil. The only question is, will we be fighting him, or *you* and him."

"What the hell does *that* me---"

"It means he might manipulate you and bring you over to his side, with promises of greatness and immortality. He's not only the most powerful being on earth, but he is probably the most cunning and enticing, with that cursed tongue of his... I think it's too much of a risk to send him Davis." Reginald tried to counter that thought.

"If we do not agree, as soon as we enter his airspace, he'll have us shot down and the aircraft burnt to a crisp, with all of us inside."

"He wouldn't risk killing Davis without speaking to him, first."

"If the alternative is another battle inside the Winged God, one he's worried he might not win this time, you don't think he would?"

"I think he's regrouped, and restrengthened, and reinforced his fortress and his manpower. I think he's back to being his otherworldly, arrogant self. It will be his downfall. But only if we have Davis with us. The two of them together, we're all but dead right now."

"We have to comply. Doing anything else will result in annihilation."

"Doing so will be playing into his hands!"

"We do not have a choice! It's clear that his eyes and ears see and hear all. It's evident that maybe even someone in this room is that all-seeing, all-hearing vessel that seeps into Aylash. We have to play the hand we're dealt, and see it through to the end. Maybe we might even get lucky, and Davis can dispatch and dispose of him without our help."

"He wouldn't be able to dispatch a dozen different vampires in this room."

Hey. It was time I spoke up.

"Why don't we go back to asking me what *I* want to do?" The room stopped and eyed me. All of a sudden, I had no follow-up.

"Fair enough, Davis" Reginald relented. "What *do* you want to do?"

"I want to speak with him alone. If it takes 24 hours, then so be it, but I have questions of him that no one *but* him can answer. I've experienced changes that no one but him has undergone. And since all his journals in my possession have him dying over 4,000 years ago, I need to know why the hell he faked his death and still managed to continue building this fucked up subhuman race up to the present day. I would like to know how and why he ended up at a rest home beside the House of the Black Moon... I want his secrets, and I want this word that he'll let---"

"You won't get his word, on anything" Le Bouffon assured me. "That would be too much of a capitulation. He will not negotiate with you, or anybody. He is the lord of this underbelly. This dark universe. If one hand is lifted against him, he'll try to impale and evaporate every single one of us."

"Well, we better start loading up, then."

Load up is what we did. Annie returned around 11:00pm, in time to help with the second plane. It was odd but pleasurable watching her side by side with my new race of people. It almost didn't seem out of place anymore. Eventually, she had to get out sight, though, as it was time to load the final piece of cargo. Ballou, The Abomination. Reginald thought he had the best possible scenario figured out, and it would involve him placing large cuts of meat every 10 feet or so, interspersed with live humans staked and chained to the ground, in a trail leading to the aircraft. From time to time, the sounds of those unfortunate souls' screams still crawl their way out of my head, through my ears, and down my spine to the floor. Inside the large, heavily fortified container that would hold him awaited four humans and enough hidden sedatives to put King Kong to sleep for an international flight. The plan worked, and some 300 vampires, one knocked out hybrid freak of nature, and one Annie Moore set off on a flight to Serbia.

No one in those aircraft would ever see the House of the Gray Bear again.

Part II: The House of The Winged God

Chapter Twenty-One: Shenanigans in Belgrade

When I was nine years old, I had this dream. It was so vivid, though, so lucid, that I thought it was real. I had woken up illogically early in the morning and walked outside, for no discernable reason whatsoever. It was hours before I normally arose for school. The sky was a purple, red, orange, and yellow amalgam of bright, contrasting beauty. The grass smelled of honeysuckle and dripped of dew. Cool but humid, everyone came out of their houses on this imaginary street block where every single house was new and beautiful, something to be proud of, all with white picket fences. I locked eyes with the neighbors on each side of me, and we all nodded our heads in amazement as we gazed upon the wonderment of the sky and its warm, mesmerizing hues.

This was the same sky I flew into over Belgrade, Serbia, at almost the same time of morning I had in my dream. Just after 3:15am. So bright the vampires thought we were all going to die, but there was no sun to kill them. Just the deceptive, mischievous phenomenon of night, reflection, gas, and atmosphere. I peered out the window of the aircraft's cockpit before we landed to find that etched-in image, and tears welled up in my eyes. After we landed and came to a stop, I ignored both my girlfriend and my aching, nervous counterparts still unbuckling their seatbelts, and stepped out the rear of the plane as it opened its large hatch door, to embrace the memory of my childhood dream. As far as I was concerned, this was as close to innocence as I would ever return. As close to the sun.

And then the gunshots came.

The first shot sailed past me and into the aircraft. The second hit the side of the plane. The vampires within the plane stuck their heads out, and then dove back inside it. Two to three more shots rang out, missing me, hitting someone in the plane. I used my heat signature detection, and located our assailants, two men, located atop what looked like a small house just east of the airport's runway. Ballou and Reginald's plane was in front of ours, still sealed up and in no danger, but depending on what type of firepower was being utilized, it could possibly pose a fatal problem for the rest of us in the second aircraft. So, angered by the interruption of my nostalgic interaction with the beautiful sky, and concerned for Annie and the other vampires along for the ride, I took off after the two. They immediately recognized the threat in my advance, and started to flee the scene. The first shooter had jumped off the roof and was heading to a parked vehicle, but the second one hyperextended his knee as he landed. This delayed his escape, and sealed his fate, as I caught up to him and plunged my open hand through his back and out his chest. I then stuck my other hand in, military pressed him above me, and ripped him in half. His hips and legs were in my right hand and everything from the spine upward was in my left. I tossed this remains aside and gave chase after the man in the car as he sped away down the road. I was able to move diagonally in a straight line to cut off his route, and as he turned left onto a slightly larger road, I sailed down upon his windshield feet first, bursting into the passenger seat. I grabbed him by the throat, and drug him into the backseat, the car swerving wildly with no driver controlling it and still enough momentum to prevent coming to a standstill. My right index and middle fingers infiltrated the man's eyeballs and drove them deep into his sockets. His screams made me giggle to myself, but I can't fully understand or explain why. With him still screaming and now blind, I leaned all the way to one side of the back seat, lifted my leg, measuring my kick, and then stiffened it straight across the side of his face. The right side of his face caved into his left, and his skull imploded, causing brains to ooze out of his ears and eye sockets. The car veered off the road and hit a dip, causing it to jump a few feet in the air before landing forcefully in front of someone else' property. I got out of the vehicle, and ran back to the runway at Nikola Tesla Airport. The supporting cast was now out and about, awaiting my return. Annie was in front of them all, standing with one hand on her hip and a scornful look on her face.

"What the fuck, McCarty?! Can you wait for someone to assist you before you go running off to fight enemies in a foreign country? I assume that whoever fired those shots is dead?"

"You assume correctly, and I didn't see anyone running to help me. All these people can run just as fast as I can."

"I had confidence in you" Reginald stated, a little on the patronizing side. 'Two humans is no match for an enlightened vampire. Unfortunately, for them, their aim leaves a little to be desired."

"I don't know a damn thing about Serbian military or Serbian hitmen, but something tells me that those two were just supposed to instill a warning. A skilled marksmen would have been able to blow my head off from four times as far away."

"Keen insight. I'm not denying your theory. We should gather our people and make our way into the transport vehicles immediately. I'll check on who was struck while Sylvain coordinates everyone else."

Annie moved forward toward me with a disgusted expression.

"What is it?" I asked, perplexed.

"Your hands and your... everything. You're covered in blood and... other stuff. Again."

"Babe. I had to. They were shooting at us. Real bullets. Not fake ones."

“And why did you completely ignore me when you left the plane?”

“I’m... I’m sorry. I can explain it later. I just got caught up in a memory. I won’t do that again.”

“Sure you won’t. Let’s get our shit, Killer.”

The sky remained the same purple, red, orange, and yellow masterpiece as we caravaned in four large travel buses from Belgrade to Nis, towing Ballou in his enormous metal container behind us. What would have normally taken just under two and a half hours to get there took us well over three, as we diverted from the easiest path and took some out of the way, side roads. We didn’t want our steps to be so predictable, and so easy to ambush. Since the sun would be out before we made it to our destination, all the windows had to be meticulously blacked out, preventing any sun from breaking through. Annie and I sat together, her head on my shoulder and our hands locked together. Edsel Antony Fuggerton sat in the seat next to mine, separated only by the aisle, and he took that time to get acquainted.

“A year ago, could you have fathomed any of this?”

“A year ago, I was wondering why the hell I was such a loser, unable to keep a job, even at a gas station.”

“And where was Annie in this equation?”

“She wasn’t in the equation. She was at college in Kansas, and we had just started to communicate again, after a misunderstanding slowed our friendship for a tad.”

Annie decided to assist me in my storytelling.

"He's referring to the time I told him I was willing to move back home for him, and he royally fucked that up."

"Thank you, dear," I uttered through a wincing, half-hurt expression.

"No problem. If things had gone differently in that conversation, he probably wouldn't have become a vampire, and we most certainly would not be on this bus right now headed to certain doom in Serbia."

Edsel was astounded. "Well, it seems like you royally fucked things up for all of us then."

"Yes, it would appear so," I replied with just a little hint of guilt in my words. Annie wasn't done yet.

"Not so fast, my English friend. You guys managed to get in a vampire war and get blown to shit all without Davis' help, or us even knowing that vampires existed."

"Touche, Annie." And with that, Fuggerton rested his chin on his chest and decided he'd attempt to nap for the rest of the ride.

"Davis, do you ever think of how things might have been if we just did 'this', or said 'that'?"

"Shit. Think about those things is *all* I did, from May 20th, 2020, all the way to last night. I wish I'd have told you to move closer, and that I loved you, and blah blah blah, but I was still so oblivious, so completely in denial that *you* could ever fall for *me*, and so afraid of scaring you away, that I didn't know what the fuck to do... Hey, it doesn't matter anymore, right? I mean, what's happened has happened, and what's done is done. Neither one of us can change it, so... Let's move on. Let's move forward."

We looked at each other for about ten seconds. Her eyes were so gentle. So fragile. And her smile was so sweet and loving. I leaned down and planted a tender kiss on her forehead and one on her cheek.

And then the gunshots came.

Five shots ripped through the windows and blackout tarps in our bus, inviting our nemesis, the sun, inside. Its exposure resembled a 'flashlights in the dark' effect I'd seen at my very first Unholy Saint concert. Luckily, the vampires in its reach moved quickly away, for fear of being an insect under its metaphorical microscope. Three more shots, followed by six more in quick succession, and our bus was starting to look like an after effect from an action film. I could only assume that the same assault had befallen the other two buses. Several bullets had found their way into the flesh of our traveling party, but the Serbian assassins apparently underestimated the ability of vampires to outlive a simple... *oh shit*! *The bullets are explosive*!

Vampires sitting and bleeding from their wounds all of a sudden had limbs or torsos blown apart by the hidden surprise encased in their bodies. This was a problem, and anyone hit would have just under five seconds to try and rip the bullets out of themselves before it was too late. The bus went into a collective panic, everyone yelling and either rushing to the wounded, or rushing *away* from them, not wanting to be the shrapnel's collateral damage. I knew for sure that three of us had perished from the blasts. I started going up and down the aisle, tending to anyone who might be wounded and/or about to transition into a hundred different pieces. Some bullets had gone straight through a victim, and were resting on the floor of the bus. Those had to get jettisoned from the bus, if possible. As I turned toward the back of the bus, I saw Tamlyn Bernard standing in the center of the aisle, a look of shock on her face, and her remaining blood pouring out of a hole in her shoulder. I ran to her, completely ready to rip a detonating bullet fragment out of her arm.

"It's OK", she assured me. 'The bullet went through the back of my shou---"

And then it blew her arm off.

Tamlyn was rocketed to the right, landing on another vampire. The explosive part of the bullet must have remained lodged inside her. I went and cupped her by the head, grabbed onto her right hand, and sat her upright. The look of shock was still on her face, but she made no sound. She didn't scream. She didn't cry. She just sat there looking straight ahead.

"Are you alright?" I asked, worriedly. Annie was now right behind me, and she was balling her eyes out. Instinctively, I pulled her next to me, put my arms around her, and acted as a human shield. Tamlyn turned her head and looked up at me. She finally replied, in a monotone, almost lobotomized voice.

“I’m fine. I don’t think I’m going to die from this wound... Why are we doing this? Why do we exist? Now I feel rage, and want to avenge this attack, but we’re actually the ones who came to a foreign country looking for a fight. It is we who are at fault. Isn’t this all for nothing? Do you know I’ve never even kissed a boy?”

I got the sense that she was starting to unravel. Annie got the same feeling, and as a single tear fell out of Tamlyn’s eye, followed by another, Annie grabbed her and held her, and vowed to stay with her until we got to our lodging. I secretly worried that her being so close to a vampire so “close to the edge” might be dangerous. If Tamlyn felt the urge to replenish her blood, Annie would be the perfect meal, already on a platter. I decided to keep my eye on them, while trying not to look too much like a suspicious father.

The bullets stopped coming, and we continued on our way. Reginald called people in the other buses, and they suffered similar results. Thankfully, the number of casualties compared to the number of bullets entering our vehicles was minor. Reginald, Sylvain, and Le Bouffon convened at the front of the bus near the driver, and had a private, quiet meeting before Reginald addressed us all publicly.

“We have suffered a surprising act of aggression here in Serbia. Or *is it* surprising, considering the demon behind it? We will all have to be on high alert from here on in, our senses sharp, and our eyes open wide. When we get to the village, we must all get some sleep. Humans will stand guard throughout the camp, and will make sure we are not disturbed." This last sentence made everyone shift around and fidget uneasily. No one could logically see how our human guides wouldn't actually be loyal to Revall. Reginald sensed this suspicion. "I assure you, everyone in this village southeast of the city is sympathetic to and aligned with our cause. They have suffered a great deal at the hands of Aylash Revall, as well, and are grateful that his reign may finally be ending."

I really did want to believe him.

Chapter Twenty-Two: Forgotten by Time

I didn't know what to expect of Nis. But I sure as hell didn't expect it to be so... modern. We'd finally gotten to the village southeast of the city, where we were lucky enough to be housed and hidden from Nis and from Aylash. After carefully unloading our luggage and other cargo under strategically erected tents, we all fed on some unfortunate humans we'd brought along from Versailles, and then we slept. Once night fell, and our body clocks lit us up like old fashioned alarms on the nightstand, everyone who hadn't been to Serbia before, or been anywhere for that matter, wanted to explore. And explore we did, like we were Amish teenagers on our free pass week from religious oppression, or rambunctious summer campers sneaking away from our assigned cabins. The city was so beautiful, surprisingly modern, and unsurprisingly ancient at the same time. Many monuments and relics of a city that had overcome a lot to become the cherished and valuable possession it was.

And almost a hundred vampires were set loose on it.

A good portion of us checked out the Chester British Pub, while another big group visited the Irish Pub Crazy Horse, which Annie and I chose because of our recent history with its namesake burlesque show in Paris. The contrast between vampires who wanted to see something completely different, and those more comfortable with finding small pieces from home, was clear-cut. I felt that the native citizens of Nis were already well acquainted with the vampire, and were obedient observers of its subculture, norms, and values. I couldn't say the same for the foreign vampires invading the city like drunken Vikings. The next day, the local news media would report some 11 mysterious deaths and 26 missing persons, all seemingly unrelated. Both statistics were easily peacetime records for the city. There was clearly an understanding of, and fragile coexistence with, the House of the Winged God and its occupancy, but such abnormal infamy would have to be extinguished by the members of the Gray Bear if we were even going to make it to meeting Aylash Revall. We would have to figure out the logistics of how Revall and his army fed that avoided a large-scale pushback by Nis and its government, and we would have to model our intake on that example.

We returned to the small village outside the city, and it wasn't until then that I completely identified and took in the differences between the two. More to the point, I think the village is what I pictured the city being. It was primitive in comparison to Nis' city limits, almost intentionally forgotten by time. Minimal electricity, minimal technology, no space or time for automobiles. No rich tenants, and no rich landlords for that matter. The buildings are all simple and old. The median age appears close to sixty. Just northeast of the village is the valley that Reginald described to us back in France, and at the end of that valley we can see a large mountain called Suva Planina. On the other side of that mountain lies the Bridge of Skulls, the Crystal Mountain, and the House of the Winged God. Annie had stayed behind so she could get some sleep, and so that the vampires could "bond". I tried my hardest not to wake her upon my arrival, but she was a light sleeper *before* being thrust into the world of vampires; she slept even lighter, nowadays.

"How was it? Did you kill anybody?" She was half asleep when she asked, but her ambivalence was stark and haunting. I didn't know if she was half joking or not.

"I... I prefer not to answer. Is that OK?"

"I don't see why it matters. I know you have to kill on occasion, so I wish you would just answer honestly when I ask. Is it a big deal?"

"It is to me. I don't like being asked if I killed someone, and more importantly, I don't *like* killing someone. For me, for most vampires, actually, the more appropriate term is feeding."

"Appropriate?" She was instantly 60% more awake. 'Are you and your kind politically correct, all of a sudden? *Appropriate*? Give me a fucking br---"

"Annie, why is this conversation devolving into a

fight?" Thankfully, she stopped and gave that question some thought.

"I don't know. I think I'm just exhausted, and shook up from what happened earlier. I don't have anything left in the tank, and I'm grumpy. I apologize."

"You don't have to apologize. This trip was a lot to take in, and you could have been killed this morning. Speaking of, and not to change the subject, but how's Tamlyn?"

"She's also shook up, but her stoic, Michael Myers-like silence doesn't really allow for further penetration. She is disappointed, though. She thought at this battle, she would finally get to fight. To really avenge her House for what had been done. But how's she going to do that now, with a dainty teenage girl's body and one arm?"

"I'm sure she could do something, be useful some other way."

"She was useful some other way, last time."

"It's unfortunate, but I can't help the situation. I can't rewind it... You should go back to sleep."

"What about you?"

"I have to meet with Reginald and some of the locals. We need to discuss... logistics. Feeding logistics."

"Got it. I love you, but I have to go back to bed."

I left our small, one-bedroom lodging and walked out into the center of the village, where two dozen vampires had congregated. Reginald introduced us to the "spokespeople" of the village, since there was no mayor or official government in place. This place was not under the jurisdiction of Nis proper. Igor and Isabel Petrovic were a married couple in their early fifties, who'd moved to the village from the city about thirty years prior. The main reason for the move: Isabel wanted to be closer to the House of the Winged God. She wanted to know the vampire lifestyle. *How disturbing*. Igor had the shortest, gray and black hair I'd seen on someone who still had a full head of it, hard lines on his cheeks and forehead, and piercing, steely black eyes. He was rail thin, but in shape. You could tell he worked hard his entire life, and was worn out. You could also tell he didn't know any other way to live. Isabel had long, full gray and black hair down to her shoulder blades, a more than ample bosom that couldn't help but draw one's eyes to it, and an intruding, intimidating stare. You could tell that she was always thinking, and always trying to get to the bottom of everyone's secrets. The two of them whispered back and forth to each other before their volume increased and their conversation got heated. Igor threw his hands up in the air in a way that signaled frustration and defeat, and he walked off with his head down. Isabel then addressed those still milling about.

"We are glad to have you, but you need to know that it is our kindness and need for such barbarism from the house on the mountain to stop that allows it. You cannot go about feeding on the people of Nis randomly. Just the scent of the wind and the tension of the atmosphere tells me that you've brought with you much suffering and death tonight. This will not be acceptable, and it will get your protections revoked. Aylash Revall and his vampires have various agreements in place with several local jurisdictions, as well as international trafficking networks, and I have made similar agreements to have certain "delicacies" stopped and delivered here before they move on to the Winged God. You will feed here and only here. I will not have our simple way of life destroyed by the city because of your disrespectful behavior, or because you killed the wrong person."

The vampires gathered in the center of the village eyed each other, skeptically. Half of us felt that it was *she* who was disrespectful, talking to vampires as if she was the superior of the two species. The other half felt like ashamed little children being chastised by their teacher or parents. Heads down, hands behind backs, and proverbial tails between legs. I was a little confused as to the argument between the couple, and thought I'd inquire aloud.

"Why is your husband frustrated?"

"He thought I should begin this conversation much more gently."

Edsel took a few steps toward me, and gave me a little tap on the shoulder. As I looked at him, he shook his head and mouthed "I'll tell you, later."

"And where do these delicacies come from?"

"Why do you care?"

"I'm curious."

"They come from all over. Bosnia, Croatia, Russia, Albania, Turkey. Not all human trafficking is sexual, or labor related. This operation is comparable to the cattle trade."

I looked back at Edsel and mouthed "What the fuck?" when Isabel gave us a quick summary of what the next day would look like.

"Tomorrow, sometime mid-morning, I will speak with Aylash's human consultant, and we will establish a meeting time for him and the Texan. The Texan's human lady will accompany me into the city, and help me with my errands."

"The *Texan* is me. My *name* is Davis."

"If you say so. Are you OK with your lady coming with me into Nis?"

"She was already going to visit Nis anyway, but I'm sure she can help you with your... errands."

"Perfect. I'm sure we will have much to speak about... I will meet Reginald and whoever he chooses to join him at sundown here in the square. The number of people present will determine where we sit down and discuss the details provided by Aylash's consultant."

"And who is this consultant?" I asked.

"Miko. My brother."

Everyone shuffled around, and our collective skepticism grew exponentially. The possibility of everyone in Nis and the village being on Aylash's side was very real to us. Reginald stepped in to dissuade our concerns.

"My friends, for the second time today, I can assure you, with total confidence, that Isabel and her associates here in Nis are fully compliant with aiding us in our mission, and that her relationship to Aylash's consultant is a benefit. It should not be a distraction or a point of worry."

Somehow his words didn't comfort me. I could tell by the expressions on many others that their doubts were also high. As we dispersed, Edsel and I nodded at each other and walked off together down an empty corridor between homes.

"What was that head shake about?" I asked him.

"What Isabel said about her argument with Igor, it was a lie."

"What do you mean?"

"Isabel intimated that Igor wished she'd talk 'gentler' to us, but in reality, he was telling her that they never should have agreed to host us at all, and was trying to get her to cut our time here short. She refused, and he walked off."

"Why didn't she tell us the truth?"

"We're already suspicious because of what she *did* say. Imagine if she added that her husband and co-leader of this village wanted us gone. Would you feel better about our accommodations or worse?"

"Point taken. What do think his deal is?"

"I've no idea, but I do plan on finding out. How do you *really* feel about Annie heading into the city with Isabel?"

"I'm 50-50. Reginald seems to believe that Isabel and this whole village is on our side, but I think getting to know them better will be important in gaining my trust. What about you?"

"Same here. We should either feed or get to bed. I believe there's less than an hour before sunrise."

I chose bed, and returned to the room I shared with Annie. She was knocked out, and I quietly crept over to my side of the bed, undressed, and slid under the covers, spooning my girlfriend. I could feel her heartbeat, and hear her pulse as it pumped blood throughout her body. I no longer felt the urge to insert my teeth into her neck. I noticed this change in my instincts a few weeks before our trip. One night, we'd been out in the middle of nowhere, hanging out on the tailgate of my truck, watching the stars and listening to the silence as it crashed against the random rustling of the wind or a random coyote call. We laid back and cuddled on a blanket in the truck bed, and even though I hadn't fed but a few drops since waking that evening, her warm and fresh life's liquid didn't cause me to panic or hunger. I was disciplined and at peace, knowing that she would bleed for me when I absolutely needed it. I was happy to say that this new phenomenon inside me had kept up its good behavior.

The next day, Annie got up, showered, and deftly left the room. I hadn't had a chance to say goodbye, or tell her about Isabel and the plan to go into Nis. I should have known she'd figure things out swiftly enough. Annie met Isabel at a bench under a covered gazebo.

"You are the Texan's lady?" she asked somewhat frankly.

"I suppose. I'm also a Texan, but that's neither here nor there. What's your name?"

"I am Isabel. Are you ready to go into Nis?"

"Are you asking, just in general, or are you asking because you're going and you want me to come along?"

"The second one."

"Of course. Let's go to Nis, then."

"Did you sleep well?"

"Not really. There was a lot on my mind."

"Did you see anything?"

"What do you mean?"

"Did you see anything, or anyone in your room?"

"Uhhh. Mmmm, no. Why?"

"Oh. Maybe he's not ready to come out yet?"

"Who?"

"You'll see."

Chapter Twenty-Three: Miko & Sergei

Isabel and Annie walked for over an hour to get to the town of Dushnik, deciding to rent bicycles there instead of walking over another hour to the city. While there they met *two* men, which pissed me off a little, because I was told that they would speak with Miko, Isabel's brother, not this other man, Sergei. The two parties met at the Holy Trinity Cathedral, Isabel and Annie arriving first.

"Miko is not here, yet. You can go in, if you like. It is very beautiful."

"Sure. Why not?" Annie shrugged as she nervously entered. About 15 minutes later, Isabel called to her from the door, and Annie came out to meet Miko, a look of shock and awe on her face. "Holy Shit! That place *is* beautiful." Her words didn't sit well with the two gentlemen.

“Who is this who speaks such blasphemy in my church?” the unexpected guest, Sergei, would question angrily.

“I’m sorry. I didn’t mean any disrespect. My name is Annie. Annie Mo---”

“She is an *American*? Is she with the Texan?”

“Yes, she – I – am. You can speak to me, unless you have some sort of problem with that.”

Isabel thought it best to intervene and make official introductions.

“Annie Moore, this quiet, handsome fellow is Miko. He is my little brother. This ugly, old, individual is Sergei. He is not my brother.” The look on Sergei’s face was one of extreme displeasure.

“I’m not old, and many women find me to be quite attractive.”

“I doubt it,” Isabel replied, staring a blank, deadpan laser through Sergei’s face. “Miko, what news do you have from Aylash?” Miko’s eyebrows raised, and he started explaining Aylash’s demands, carefully. Methodically.

“Mr. Revall wants to meet Davis in two days. As requested previously, he wants assurance that they will be alone for 24 hours before anyone else – anyone – arrives at the Winged God... He also wants Davis’ arrival to happen right after the first rays of dawn.”

Isabel knew that this would be problematic. Three

hundred vampires would find it hard to attack any stronghold, vampire or human, at dawn. So they would have to: 1) configure some sort of shade or cover that would protect them, which would be cumbersome, bulky, and antithetical to the element of surprise; or 2) wait longer to mobilize, giving Aylash approximately fourteen more hours alone with Davis. This second option would no doubt put me in danger, or put *them* in danger, afraid that any length of time might result in me being swayed by Revall to join his side, or struck down before they could assist. That second scenario would also spell certain doom for them, without my Namtudari as an asset to use in battle. It didn't take long for Annie to realize the implications herself.

"That's bullshit. Dawn is off the table."

"Why are you talking?" Sergei chimed in, dismissively, causing Isabel to come to Annie's defense.

"And why are *you* talking? I was here to speak to my brother, not some psychotic, sycophant." Now Sergei was really pissed.

"I don't know all the words you're using, but I know that I DON'T LIKE THEM! You should be more respectful."

Miko was starting to get very uncomfortable, caught between his de-facto co-worker and his (maybe) beloved sibling. "Please. Please. Let's calm down. We can work these details out, which is one reason why Aylash has asked for two days between now and Davis' visit. We can negotiate. But, seriously, Isa, why is this American talking?"

"Because I'm representing Davis, as his closest, longest friend, and his girlfriend." Her tone was stern and combative.

Sergei and Miko looked at each other, curiously, and then with odd smiles.

"You know that such a relation---" Sergei started, but was stopped quickly.

"Such a relationship between a vampire and a human won't work," Annie said through rolling eyes. 'Yes, I've heard. Trust me, I've heard. I don't give a shit what you think, or what the previous success rate is. We're going to be the exception, or I'm going to die trying."

"So at least you know the ending" Sergei finished.

"We'll see. I'm telling you that dawn is out of the question. Isabel, do you agree?" Miko developed a smirk, and a more serious tone.

"Isabel knows that some things are *non*... negotiable. She knows that I'm being diplomatic in my approach, but that Aylash Revall is not providing suggestions; he's dictating terms. Any disagreement or deviation from these terms will result in... less favorable destinies for everyone in your party." Annie wasn't deterred.

"I thought we were negotiating. You said we can *negotiate*. What happened to that?"

"You were too firm, Annie. Your attitude has affected the situation. It has changed the direction of this meeting."

Miko paused, while Isabel looked down at the floor regretfully and rang her hands together in a nervous, repetitive rhythm.

"*My* attitude? *My* attitude? That's funny. Isabel, are you going to try and help me out here, or not?"

"Can you please take a walk for a bit? I need to talk to Miko alone?"

Annie all of a sudden felt a wave of suspicion and unsafe conditions wash over her, causing a nauseas pit to form in her abdomen. She was unsure of how much more to push things, and of whether Isabel was on her side, or Miko's.

"And what about him?" Annie pointed to Sergei. 'Is he going to take a walk, too?" Isabel motioned over to an eatery near the church.

"Sergei, give us some time alone. It will not take long."

Sergei's eyes enlarged, and he was about to blow his lid when Miko placed his hand on his chest, and locked eyes with him.

"It's alright", Miko said calmy, elongating his sentence into a peaceful hiss. "I'll talk to her, but it will not change anything about Aylash's demands."

"It mustn't, or Aylash could very well kill the two of us

where we stand if we deliver anything but cooperation from Reginald Duplante's group."

Isabel waited for Sergei and Annie to both be out of hearing distance, and then she and Miko resumed their talk.

"Aylash is being unreasonable, with his timing. Dawn? These are all vampires."

"He's using everything in his power to gain an advantage."

"We're here in Nis. In his home. He *has* the advantage!"

"He's being invaded, and he's allowing it. He has to counterbalance that, somehow."

"Like he did by having assassins attack the French group in the daylight?"

"He had to show them that whatever safety they thought they had by arriving while he was asleep is just wishful thinking. Now, they will be on edge no matter what time of day, or where they are. It's pretty brilliant, really."

"It's an act of a coward, attacking them before they've done anything."

"He has it on good authority that they've come to fight him. To kill him. Hundreds wouldn't have boarded a private and secret flight to Serbia if there was any other intention... Have you given any more thought to what we talked about? About coming to work for Aylash?"

"I have not."

"Liar. I know you have." Isabel looked long and hard into her brother's eyes before speaking again.

"OK, so I've thought about it. I cannot do it. Igor would not allow it. And it would leave our home in peril."

"The village? Isn't it time they've learned to fend for themselves? And enter the 21st century?"

"It's not that easy. That's our home. Those are our people, and they've trusted us with leading them; with protecting them from the likes of Aylash Revall."

"*Protecting* them? If anything, *I'm* protecting them by being your brother, and by continuously pleading with Aylash not to consume the whole village, one by one."

"It's not like he hasn't poached people from the village, either to enslave them or to feed on them. Your "protection" is not 100%."

"And yet, you can still sleep safely at night."

"I've come close many times to accepting the same opportunity you were thrust into, but there was something always holding me back."

"Fear."

"No. Humanity. Decency. Common sense. I was so attracted to what might be behind Revall's doors, and to discovering the secrets he may have unlocked. But in the last ten years, especially, I've only found a hollow, decaying demon bent on destroying humanity, not evolving it. Not saving it... I will be glad when he is gone."

"Do you think this Texan and the Gray Bear are actually going to RID THE WORLD OF AYLASH REVALL?!" Isabel waved her hand up and down in a "Lower your damn volume!" motion.

"I have no idea, but I know there is something different about the Texan that made the Gray Bear agree to come here with him. Do you think they would have come if there was no hope of defeating Revall, especially considering what he's already done to them?" Before Miko could reply, Isabel was not finished. "And I need to make it clear that you are not to divulge anything other than the details of our meeting to Revall. I don't give you my innermost gossip, thoughts, or feelings, to have you run to him with them."

"I do not betray your trust, but it's obvious that you still do not know a thing about Aylash Revall. He can know what I'm thinking by looking in my eyes. He can know what's being said just by the body language of those around him. He knew of the Texan and the boy's obtaining of the Luminastra Namtudari before anyone else. He knows the thoughts, dreams, and breathing patterns of every single member of your pitiful little village. I won't have to tell him a thing... Do you know that he's watched you and Igor while you've slept?"

"What?"

“It’s true. He’s come into the village, and every now and then, he watches your people. He’s watched you and Igor. He can tell who will join him up on Crystal Mountain. That’s how he selected Sergei. Sergei’s behavior during his slumber was one of torment and unrest. Aylash knew he would be perfect.”

Isabel grew cold with fear and disgust. She could see the smile starting to form on Miko’s face, and she realized that he wasn’t just Aylash’s employee; he was his protégé. She knew that she wanted to be done with this conversation.

“Davis will meet Aylash two days from now, but I will not agree to dawn until he agrees to dawn. Until the House of the Gray Bear agrees. I will send the answer tomorrow morning. I have to go now.”

“Fair enough. You know there will be “complications”, if Aylash’s terms are not met.”

Isabel turned and looked for Annie as Miko slowly walked away, but she had just stepped foot in the Art5 Gallery, unsure of why it had beckoned to her in an advertisement along the way. Isabel then realized that she didn’t have a cell phone for Annie if they got separated.

Annie looked at the amazing works from all over the world that this gallery had managed to obtain, and an overwhelming grip of heaviness and longing overcame her. She mourned the fact that she and Davis wouldn’t be able to just walk into an art gallery, hand in hand, in the middle of the day and enjoy the creativity another human brought forth into the world. She felt sorry for him, and sorry for all the vampires in their party. She saw the vampires of France as faking their superiority and their adaptation as evolved and enlightened vampires. They all claimed to be otherwise happy in their situations, the civil war with the Blood Fountain and Winged God notwithstanding. She knew it was all bullshit. She knew that a large group of them had heard Davis and taken his words with a glimmer of hope. Hope that they might all return to human if Aylash was dead. While Isabel waited impatiently, Annie took one last look at the gallery, and thought she might buy a little trinket from Nis for Davis.

And that's when the gunshots came.

Six or seven shots crashed through the glass windows of Art5 Gallery and whizzed through the building, one sailing within two feet of Annie Moore. The scattered patrons of the gallery all hit the floor with surprising speed, and a small, crotch rocket type of motorcycle sped away through the city before anyone could even catch their thoughts, much less catch a glimpse of the perpetrator(s). Annie lay on the floor, making sure to stay there until she was sure there was no further threat. The commotion caused by the various sounds of yelling, running, and focused traffic told Isabel exactly what direction she needed to go to find her. As Isabel made a right turn onto the gallery's street, she caught a quick glimpse of Sergei standing coolly against a light pole. He gave her a nod and a wink as she ran toward the growing crowd of people standing shocked outside the gallery. She was enraged.

Feeling that the shots were indeed over with, Annie stood up, dusted herself off, and attempted to stop her body from convulsing. She was clearly suffering from trauma related to the now-constant barrage of murder attempts. This one, however, was much different; it was meant solely for her. She delicately exited the gallery as Isabel ran to her, pulling her from the scene.

"What? What just happened?" Annie called out, more to the sky than to Isabel.

"That was going to be my question for you."

"I think... I think someone just tried to... kill me? They shot right into a gallery of innocent people. Why would someone do that?"

"I don't think they were trying to kill you. I think they were trying to send a message. I think they were trying to scare you."

"Well, mission fucking accomplished!"

Chapter Twenty-Four: A Better Understanding

Finding out about Sergei and of the attempt to either kill or frighten Annie sent me into a rage that resulted in some damage to a small building that had existed for hundreds of years with not so much as a blemish. Furthermore, I was angry with Annie for not waking me as soon as she and Isabel returned. This wasn't trivial 'I spilled spaghetti sauce on my shirt today' type news; this was a third attempt to gun down my only love in just over twenty-four hours. Someone knew who Annie was, and they had been following her. *Was it Sergei? Had Miko known or directed this action? Was Isabel in on it?* The already palpable tension mixed with an already toxic level suspicion, and the majority of the Gray Bear was ready to pick up and fly back to France. Little did they know that Reginald had sent the two Antonov's away. Annie relayed that secret to me after Isabel told her in confidence, but I kept it to myself, not wanting to stir the pot even more. It did speak apparent volumes, though, about Reginald's perception of our chances. *If he thought we would be successful, why turn the planes around?*

I surmised that to feel completely free of having to look over our shoulders or listen in on every single conversation, we would need to gain a better understanding of our hosts, our location, and the culture of Nis and its satellite village. Therefore, at dinner, I planned to have a long conversation with Isabel and Igor. First, everyone involved had to agree on Aylash's demands or submit an alternative set of options. Reginald, as the leader of the Gray Bear, understandably spoke first.

"I'm torn between wanting to push back on that miserable bastard, and wanting to be so amenable it makes him uncomfortable."

"If we agree to have Davis meet him right before dawn," Sylvain countered, "We'll either have to deny his request for twenty-four hours alone with him, or extend that time."

"What if we agree, but then attack at nightfall anyway?" This made me raise my eyebrows and interject.

"Wouldn't that be against the rules of engagement or whatever chivalrous vampire shit you guys have adhered to forever?"

"What rules, Davis? What rules has Aylash not created and then broken himself? This... this is strategy. Make him think we're knocking on his door at one time, but kicking it in at another."

"If you say so. So, then is it settled?"

"I would say not," Le Bouffon chimed in.

"And why not?" Reginald questioned with more than a hint of frustration in his voice.

"I either want to comply with the request and follow it honorably, or tell Aylash Revall to fuck off!"

"Of course, you do. But we need to make the best decision, not the one that makes us look fearless, or *honorable*. And the best decision may be to appear agreeable while keeping Aylash unsure."

"Oh, captain, my captain. I am but your humble servant, and I will follow you int---"

"Please, Martin! No more games!"

There was a gasp followed by a silence that could pick up a feather falling onto a bed of cotton. Uttering Le Bouffon's real name in public hadn't been done since the early twentieth century, and now Reginald had just done so. He was no doubt "poking the bear", so to speak. Big time. Le Bouffon said nothing. He turned and walked out the door of the community dining room in the center of the village.

"Perhaps we should get some fresh air," I offered.

"And some fresh meat." Annie tacked on, causing another pause before everyone erupted in laughter. I realized that no one had laughed since before we stepped onto the aircraft in Versailles. Finally letting all that tension out was exactly what we needed. I could sense that Le Bouffon was perched on a roof somewhere believing the uproar was at his expense.

As Annie suggested, we decided to feed, and an abandoned house at the southernmost point of the village was the destination for such endeavors. Thankfully, or tragically, depending on your view, more than half of these houses were abandoned, as the village had become somewhat of a ghost town. I wanted to know more, so I stopped Isabel before she could tend to other things.

"Tell me about this place, Izzy."

"Izzy? Are you referring to me?"

"I am."

"Then you will call me Isabel."

"Fair enough. Tell me about this place, Isabel."

"I came here thirty years ago, to what was left of a village called Selo Semce. All the youth of the village had left, and all the older people had stayed. They didn't want any part of the new world with its modern "improvements", couldn't stomach returning to the place where so much suffering had occurred under Hitler's regime of terror, and didn't want any part of the larger conflict between Catholics and Orthodox."

"Yet you were only in your early twenties and *came here*. Why do that?"

"My older brother, Reiko, had *befriended* Aylash

Revall, for lack of a better word, and moved here to be a liaison between the House of the Winged God and Revall's operatives in Nis. He made working for a vampire sound so romantic, and so magical. Aylash had him wrapped around his finger."

"So you followed?"

"I followed... I had just married Igor a year earlier, and even though he wasn't happy about it, he wasn't going to stop me. He loved me too much. And he was already a hard manual labor type of guy, so working the land, growing tobacco, and corn, and popika all seemed to be simple and satisfying for him."

"Where is Reiko? How come we haven't met him, and why wasn't he there this afternoon, instead of your younger brother, Miko?"

"Reiko... Reiko is dead."

"Oh. Sorry. I didn't know."

"Of course you didn't know. I just told you about him."

"Can I ask what happened?"

Isabel looked at me long and hard. I didn't know if asking was wrong, or if her emotions about it were still too strong. Either way, her eyes flittered rapidly while she debated continuing her story. Decision made, she opened her mouth.

"Aylash killed him."

"What?"

"Aylash killed him. For stealing."

"What did he---"

"Some jewels. Aylash had brought back a small treasure from a visit to Morocco. Reiko thought he wouldn't miss a few jewels. And if he wouldn't miss a few, then maybe he wouldn't miss a few more. He was ambitious, and greedy, and foolish. He'd gotten comfortable in his role, and underestimated Aylash's attention to detail, or his *own* greed. Revall noticed the jewels missing and traced them back to Reiko and his brand new clothes and Rolex watch instantly. He entered Reiko's room in the village late one night, the same room you and your bride sleep in now, and drained him of every drop of blood. He also took Miko as repayment for losing a valued employee. Miko has worked for him ever since. This was close to twenty years ago."

"Me and Annie aren't... So, Miko has worked for Aylash ever since he was a child?"

"Since he was eleven. Aylash pulled him right out of his bedroom in Nis. My mother could do nothing... You and Annabella didn't marry before you became a vampire? Or afterward?"

"Who's Annabella? Oh, Annie! No, we never got married. We've only been together for a little while, actually."

"Annabella loves you very much. I can't even fathom

what she's sacrificed to be with you. And the two of you don't have an inkling what she still *has* to sacrifice to stay with you."

"Why do you keep calling her Annabella?"

"Is a better name."

"Sure... Did you ever try to get Miko freed?"

"No. I am not stupid."

"Did you try to take his place?"

"I thought about it. Igor put his foot down. He would not allow it. Nor would he try and speak with Aylash about Miko. He is also not stupid."

"And yet, after what happened, you stayed?"

"Yes. Stayed. I have to admit, being so close to the Winged God was exhilarating, and remaining in contact with Miko was important. Sometimes, I considered going to work for Aylash anyway. But the people here ended up making me a... a leadership role. I care about the old people here. You can look at them and see the stains of tobacco on their hands. Stains that won't come out. What good would I be to them if I put myself in that castle and did nothing but the devil's work?"

"So you agree that he's a devil and not a savior?"

"He's... changed. Not the same Revall. The last six years have been quite difficult. I sometimes wake in the morning hoping it's all just been a dream. And that this is still 2014, before Antonio Medici made himself at home here in Revall's fortress. That changed everything."

I was about to prod her for more details regarding that statement when Edsel Fuggerton and Igor interrupted us.

"Mr. Davis, Miko is here from the Winged God, and he has a message for you. Would you please join us up on Suva Planina? I've got a bottle of Slivovitz." I looked at Isabel, and she shrugged her shoulders, as if to say, "I don't know." I agreed to join them, but made sure to tell Annie first.

"What the hell is Slivovitz?" I asked Annie.

"Beats the shit out of me. What the hell are you going up on a mountain with Miko for?"

"It's not just him. I'll have Edsel and Igor with me."

"Yeah. That makes me feel a *lot* better."

I could see the scorn in her eyes and hear the bitterest sarcasm in her words.

Chapter Twenty-Five: On the Mountain

Suva Planina was such a beautiful mountain, what I could see of it in the pitch-black darkness. We hiked upward to a relatively safe plateau of a spot, hunkered down, and built a campfire. Even in the summer, the nights could get a little cold, and vampires are constantly looking to get warm anyhow. Miko was appreciative, as he also gets cold easily. He was eager to get business out of the way.

"Aylash Revall wants to make it clear how excited he is to meet you, knowing that you've come a very long way meet him. He's not as excited about the fact that you brought all of France and England with you."

"How did he know the English vampires were here?"

"It does not take long to find out such a thing. He has eyes and ears everywhere. He also wanted me to pass on that he first heard of you when Alister Amaranth sent word of a new vampire with an unbelievable gift only bestowed on vampires in fairytales."

"And Revall, himself."

"Precisely. In fairy tales." Miko turned to Edsel. 'My lord will not be merciful if the Gray Bear attacks. He will be... the opposite."

"I wouldn't expect anything less."

Igor reached into a burlap sack, and pulled out a glass bottle. Round belly with a long, thin neck. Dark liquid inside. He handed it to me first.

"Drink this." The gleam in his eye told me I was in for something. I put it to my lips and poured it back into my throat. I spit it out, choking and burning. They all laughed madly.

"What the *FUCK* IS THAT?!" I exclaimed.

"That's Slivovitz, little boy!" Igor yelled, unable to hide his giddiness at my rite of passage. 'Americans can't handle it."

"Elephants can't handle it!," Fuggerton laughed.

"I'm not a drinker anyway. I mean, I wasn't one when I was human, or regular human, I mean. Damn. Am I already drunk?"

"No, but give it a couple more shots," was Igor's reply.

“Is that all you needed to tell me, from Revall’s camp? Did we come all the way up here for that?”

Before Miko could answer, Igor put his finger to his lips, like ‘shoosh’, and explained.

“This is bonding. Getting know each other before die.”

“Wonderful. I applaud your resounding vote of confidence. How is Isabel’s English so much better than yours? No offense.”

“Isabel cares to know things. I don’t care. I get up and go work at 5:00. I come home at 7:00, eat, bathe, and go to sleep at 9:00. I have no time for care, or English, or vampire.”

“OK. I see you.” I turned my attention to: “Miko...” I looked at his shoes, his clothes, his skin, and his eyes, hoping to find a piece of his soul I could relate to. Hoping to gather some unspoken intel that I could use in my meeting with Revall. ‘Why work for Revall? Haven’t you paid the debt incurred by your brother?”

“Maybe my sister has a big mouth, yes?” Miko shot a glance at Igor, as if to also say, “no offense.” ‘I am a younger Serbian. I have a need for the finer things. Here, those finer things come with a price. But they also come with adventure. I could have never dreamed of a weirder, more amazing story than the one I can tell my children one day.”

“Why the hell would you even think of bringing children into this world? Not just this ordinary world, but this underworld? This darkness. Also, do you actually think Aylash Revall would permit---"

"This is exactly what we tell him!" Igor erupted in justification, and in better English. *I wonder if he's putting on the 'can't speak English' as a front.* 'No place for children. No place for baby here. Vampire eat them." *So much for the good accent.*

The bottle got passed around again and when it got to me, everyone's eyes were steadily fixed on my reaction. I felt a well of anxiety build within my esophagus, which was still burning from my first drink of this concoction.

"Uhhh---"

"Drink! Is national drink of Serbia. You like soon. Drink. Be warm." Igor was adamant.

"Soon, we'll be so inebriated that we'll forget the desire to feed on these two." Edsel jested. Maybe half joking.

"I'll do... one more shot. I'm serious, though. I didn't really drink beforehand, and this liquor is *WAY* outta my league." I took the bottle and downed another swig, wincing and trying not to hack up. 'But, seriously, though. Miko. Talk of children? Are you planning on going into another line of work?"

"I've got a five-year plan, although you might make it a five-day plan." We all shared a small, stifled laugh.

"And you, Igor. You and Isabel thought better of having kids?" Dead silence. Edsel and I looked at each other, and it was evident that I fucked up.

"Isabel and I did have kid," Igor spit out somberly. 'Beautiful boy kid. Luka was name. He die. Ghost of Reiko kill him." Any fire or humor or life that was in Igor's eyes got extinguished pretty fucking quick. 'Same room you and Annabella in now. Reiko's room. Luka's room. Room of Death." *Then why the hell would you let someone sleep in it?*

"Igor!" Miko shouted. Then they got into a back and forth tirade in Serbian that Edsel could translate maybe 75% of, because of the speed and local dialect with which they tore into each other. After they let up, Igor apologized, which I wouldn't accept.

"No, Igor. It's me who's sorry. I didn't know. But what were you saying about 'ghost of Reiko'?"

"He's being superstitious." Miko interjected, which amused Edsel to no end.

"You're the one working for a bloody vampire, mate," he sniped. That's when I reached out and grabbed the bottle of Slivovitz to pass around.

"Drink," I ordered, appropriating Igor's accent to add some humor to the atmosphere. He took a swig, passed it back to me, and continued answering my question.

"Many times we see Reiko, or feel him. Mostly a cold chill running up the spine or along the feet at night. He walks in and out of doors; opens windows and leaves them open. He cannot leave village, or doesn't want leave village. He die there. He stay there." Once again, Edsel and I looked at each other, neither of us knowing exactly what to say. 'But worst of is, we see and feel Luka. Luka only three when die. Now Luka three forever." Miko lowered his head, shaking it indignantly. I just knew he was going to rain on Igor's paranormal parade.

"Reiko didn't kill your son, you lunatic. Reiko isn't walking the rooms of your village. He's dead because he was stupid, and I'm an indentured servant because of his stupidity. But I'm alive, and making the most of it, and Luka's death was an accident. Nothing more. Do you understand, you stupid, superstiti---" Igor spit a mouthful of Slivovitz on the fire, and it bellowed upward angrily.

"You know nothing. You haven't seen. You don't live in Selo Semce."

"*NOBODY* lives in Selo Semce! You're all just zombies. Labor zombies. Agricultural zombies. Same thing every day. Every night. It's pathetic...................................... And the worst part is, you're no safer from Aylash than the victims that get delivered to him on a platter. You're no safer than the unmentionable experiments in his dungeon." *What was that?* 'If he wants to end this village, he'll end it. If he survives Davis and Reginald's tandem onslaught, you can guarantee Selo Semce is the first visit he'll make afterward. How do you think that makes me feel, knowing there's nothing I can do to stop him?"

Again. Silence. It was then that Miko stood and made his farewell. He nodded at each of us, and silently started to make his way down the mountain, aided by the flashlight of his cell phone, a stark ornament of the difference between this village and the rest of the civilized world. But before he could...

"Wait. Where is Reginald?," I asked. 'Didn't you have anything to share with him?"

"It's been shared. He was not to be a part of this "bonding" experience." And Miko travelled downward, eventually out of sight.

"I feel Luka." Igor reinforced. "I feel Reiko, too. And Miko is right; Reiko stupid. Igor sleeps now. Same thing every day, just like Miko say. I'm proud of my work. I'm free in a different way than Miko." He stood up, gave an awkward, forced smile, and now there were just two.

"Igor left us the bottle, my young Texas friend. We shouldn't disappoint him by leaving it less than completely empty."

The thought of drinking more Slivovitz made me a little nauseous and I wanted to dry heave the sweet, heavy, moonshiny taste of it out of my mouth. I *also* didn't want to disappoint Igor, though. "Well, hand it over, then... What do you think our chances are?"

"Of what, exactly?"

"Well... of me not getting suckered into a trap and killed. Of you and the rest of your Gray Bear attacking and defeating Aylash Revall."

"Does defeating mean killing Aylash?"

“I would think it’d have to.”

“Well, then. I’d say our chances of the latter all depend on the former. You have to stay alive long enough to help us defeat him. If he kills you in that first twenty-four, thirty, thirty-six whatever hour time frame, the rest of us are buggered, my friend.”

“Buggered is a bad thing?”

“Fucked in the ass.”

“Oh. Buggered.”

“Indeed... Let me ask you something,” Edsel proclaimed before taking a huge swig of the bottle. ‘Are you afraid of meeting him?”

“I don’t know. Were you afraid to meet him?”

“Not the first few times, but maybe the last time. They were under very different circumstances. It’s one thing to have a cordial meeting with someone, and something different altogether when you’re showing up at their front door with a dagger in your hand, to kill them.”

“How did you get caught up in this? You’re British. Why weren’t you with Lenora Jeffries and all the other Brits who steered clear of this confrontation?”

“You want the real answer?” The final scene from A Few Good Men popped in my head, and I was playing it behind my eyes when Fuggerton snapped his fingers, dumbstruck by my complete zone out. ‘McCarty. Do you want to know the answer?”

“Yes, sorry. I want the real answer.”

“Jim Morrison.”

“Who?”

Edsel looked at me as if he’d asked me who the President of the United States was, and I couldn’t answer. He took off his spectacles, cleaning them with a handkerchief he pulled out of his dress shirt’s chest pocket, and just... stared. He stared like we were speaking in two different languages while piling bricks on the tower of Babel.

“Jim Morrison. Of the Doors?”

“Oh. I’ve heard of them. Is he the guy with the wavy hair in a black and white poster?”

“Not that you’ve narrowed it down at all, but I’m going to say yes?”

“I saw a poster of him in this record store back home. I want to say it’s a pretty iconic image. I think.” Fuggerton shook his head, hanging it lower and lower.

“The youth of today. I mean, it should be forbidden for anyone under the age of forty-five to become a vampire... So, Jim Morrison moved to Paris around...” Edsel checked his watch. ‘... March of 1971. Magdalena, who I was already close with, befriended his pseudo wife Pam, and their relationship blossomed into a “something” between her and Jim. Maggie told me I just HAD to meet the world famous ‘Jeem Morreesone’, so I stopped in from London for a weekend. I was invited to their apartment for dinner one night, and we all ended up at Bacchanal, which, incidentally, later became Henri's."

"And so...?"

"I loved hanging out here so much that I ended up staying. I'd known Reginald and several members of the Gray Bear for quite some time, but this weekend was just *special.* I didn't want to leave. It wasn't as if I had a day job and a family back home. Nomadic life is normal for a vampire. It's definitely required once people start noticing that you don't age. Not like them at least. That might be the only thing the Twilight films got right."

"So you're here because of Jim Morrison?"

"In a roundabout way, yes. I think that's the shortest answer... Another drink, and then another question." We both downed another sickening shot of Slivo, and my stomach was starting to burn from the foreign invasion. 'If you do survive, what are you going to do? That is, if you survive Aylash, but remain a vampire?"

"I don't know."

"Brilliant."

"I hadn't given it much thought, because the variables are such that survival isn't a foregone conclusion. In fact, in my opinion it's closer to 60-40 that we *don't* make it out alive."

"I'm going out on a limb by saying you don't realize the connection between that last sentence and Jim Morrison?"

"Sorry, don't know what the fuck yer talking about."

"Understood. Continue."

I'm more of a 'seat of my pants, take it as it comes' sort of guy, so---"

"Davis, if that were true, you wouldn't have gone through everything you went through to get here. All the reading, all the research, all the planni---"

"That was mostly Annie."

"She didn't do it for *her*! She did it for *you*! God knows why."

"What does that mean?"

"It means her love for you is not normal. Even the most romantic, written-in-the-stars, dedicated stories of love pale in comparison to a woman with everything to live for sacrificing her most wonderful years for a man she can only die for. If she wasn't so transparent and honest, I would think she was just in it for the thrill. Or the story. But she truly loves you, and it doesn't matter to her that the man she loved became the monster that could end her... in one way or another."

"I don't know if it's the liquor talking, but I really do want to punch you right now." Edsel cracked a smile and tried to clarify.

"By no means am I trying to dissuade you from continuing your relationship. I'm sure you've already dealt with your fair share of that, and you will no doubt face more of it. If you do make it out of here with your true love intact, I might think of settling down. Far from big cities, or far enough that you can feed in the shadows and return to your quiet compound somewhere in the woods. I've been to Texas before, and there are still thousands of acres of untouched land."

"When have *you* been to Texas?"

"Three times. 1925, 1961, and 1990. They were trips to see America, to be clear. But Texas was on the itinerary. It holds a mysterious, adventurous place in the hearts and minds of many Europeans."

"Well, I'll be damned. How did you like it?"

"I was quite fond of central Texas; Austin and San Antonio. I found the entire state so rich in history for such a relatively young place."

"We used to be our own country."

"Yes, I am aware of those brief nine years. The suit I wore today has lasted fifty years longer than the Republic of Texas, but that *is* something to be proud of, I suppose."

"Wanting to punch you again, so we should probably make our way back to the village."

"Yes, I suppose we should. If you make it back home, maybe south is where you should take your love."

Upon entering the room Annie and I shared, I thought I saw something in the corner, but didn't know if I was letting my mind play tricks on me after hearing Igor's story. Annie half woke up and turned to face me as I slid into bed.

"Hi, baby," she snored out drowsily. 'Oooh, your breath smells like shit."

"Thank you... Do you know who Jim Morrison is?"

"Duh. Why? Do you want to go back to Paris and visit Pere Lachaise?"

"What?"

"Where he's buried."

"Good night, babe," I sighed, feeling considerably less knowledgeable than my girlfriend. 'I'll try not to breathe on you."

Chapter Twenty-Six: Final Offer

"Take me to it."

While I snored away until sundown, Annie had woken with not only a pep in her step, but with a purpose. She was out the door faster than a cartoon character blasting through a wall, and up Isabel's ass.

"Take you to what?" Isabel replied, frustrated at this abrupt conversation.

"Take me to the House of the Winged God, or as close to it as we can get."

"You are insane. You have a crazy look on you. I will not help you."

"OK. I'll go myself."

Annie bolted out of the kitchen where Isabel stood preparing their daily meal of beans and cabbage soup, and headed straight for the valley that led to Suva Planina. Isabel hastily tore off her apron, patted down her dress, and gave chase.

"Wait. Wait. You can't go there. You don't know what's in the woods. Many eyes watch the valley, even in the daylight. I'll have to go with you... Stop, you crazy girl!"

Annie kept right on trucking, smiling a mile wide; she knew that Isabel would come after her.

"I guess you'll have to stop me from getting eaten or shot... or eaten *and* shot. Whatever comes first."

Isabel yelled out some random girl's name, directing her to take over on the soup, and she and Annie made their way to the valley. Isabel took the time to inform Annie of a few things.

"Look, you don't really know what you're getting yourself into. For someone who's been shot at multiple times in the last few days, you haven't seen anything dangerous yet."

"I saw vampires blow up in front of me. I got their insides on me."

"Like I said, nothing dangerous yet."

The two of them stalked angrily down to the mouth of the valley, suddenly trailed by Igor and three other older gentlemen. He seemed rather agitated.

"Why you doing this? This is stupid. Go back!"

"I'm going to see this place. I know for a damn fact that Davis isn't going to let me come with him, nor will Reginald if and when the shit hits the fan. So, therefore, the only chance I have to see this place is in the daytime, before Davis goes to get notes for his book report." Igor looked at Annie with a sunken, sullen expression, and then he looked at Isabel, who sank her head to her right shoulder, and shrugged her shoulders, before waving her arms in a "let's go" motion. The six headed into the valley, and soon they were deep on the path, with thick, lush wooded green trees covering the mountains that rose like a Japanese movie monster on each side.

And that's when the arrows came.

A barrage of long, black, silver-tipped arrows sailed at them from both sides, one collapsing the jaw of an older chaperone as it penetrated his face and stopped, stuck halfway through him. His muffled scream was hindered by the placement of the arrow. Another arrow struck Igor in the leg just below the knee, and one landed in the bun of pulled back hair Isabel had fashioned on her head. She was the luckiest woman on Earth that morning.

"RUN!" Igor yelled out, and everyone who could did so, picking up their pace. It wouldn't be an overstatement to say that they all ran faster than they ever had in their lives. 'The woods will hide us from the arrows!" The valley narrowed and narrowed and then disappeared, covered now by heavily crowded trees. So crowded that the sunlight could barely infiltrate it. So crowded in fact that a vampire might even be able to...

"No! This won't work. We're dead if we go in there!" Isabel cried out. She knew the benefit of this topography for Aylash's minions. Annie figured it out, as well, right around the time that she realized they were surrounded.

"What the fuck do you think you're doing?" Sergei stood arrogantly against a tree, as his men aimed their crossbows at Igor's men and fired into them, wounding them fatally but not instantly. Three vampires, ravenous and ready, came out of the shaded darkness and pounced on the men, devouring them by the throats.

"Please let us go!" Annie shouted, now terribly aware of Isabel's forewarnings.

"Why should I? Why would you enter this valley, these woods? You should not be here."

"I wanted to see where... I don't have to *explain* myself to you."

Annie took a step forward like she was going to confront Sergei, when she took an abrupt left turn and fled into the trees. Isabel screamed for her to stop, and Sergei gave Isabel a sad grin before he ordered the vampires and human soldiers to track her down. Annie put her thighs and hamstrings to the test, stomping down hard and swift with her feet. The low-slung tree branches and sprouted, uncut bushes cut and scraped against her skin, and the vampires grew joyous in inhaling her blood on the air. Sergei, still unmoved from his spot against the tree, called out, attempting to appeal to her intelligence.

"You know how pathetic this looks, yes? You'll never outrun a vampire, on his homeland, which he knows better than you with his eyes closed. Please stop, and maybe they will be merciful, and drain you quickly."

Annie kept at it, and cut back toward the entrance to the woods, hoping to clear the safety of sunlight in the valley. She would still have to tend with the archers and their arrows, of course, but at least she wouldn't have to deal with...

Vampires were now jogging idly on either side of her as she struggled to dodge the limbs and roots of the forested mountain. One lunged out and shoulder checked her, sending Annie crumbling rapidly to the ground. She cried out as her ribs crashed against a thick, thousand year old tree's roots. That vampire grabbed Annie by a head of hair and yanked her upright forcefully. He was just about to dig his nails in her chest and his teeth in her neck when a voice from deep in the woods commanded him to stop. This voice was French. Out of the shadows stepped a tall, handsome, machine of a man. Annie hadn't seen him before, but I would have recognized him instantly.

"Don't harm the woman. She's the Texan's woman, and she's far too valuable a jewel to steal or deface. She might end up bringing the Texan to Aylash's side." The vampires looked at the stranger with contempt, all wanting to drink Annie's sweet, uncontaminated blood. They all turned back to find Sergei, and read his face or lips for a verdict.

"Do as he says. He's correct. The girl is more valuable

alive. Also, leave Isabel and Igor to return home in peace. Their protection is granted. For now." Annie was unhanded and she gazed upon the handsome individual who, in this moment, acted as her savior.

"Bonjour," the stranger spoke. 'My name is Valentis."

"I don't remember you riding on either of the planes with us, or staying anywhere in the village."

"Your eyes are true. I was neither on a plane, nor part of the hunting party in the village. I tried to defeat Reginald and his ill-advised compatriots in Versailles before they could make the mistake of touching down on Nis and the ghost town village of Selo Semce."

"Why?"

"Because it's a losing battle, and I didn't want to see my brethren die unnecessarily. Mercilessly. Brutally... Eternally."

"So you're here with the enemy? That's pretty fucked up." Valentis looked at the ground, and shook his head. An abundance of words he wanted to say filled his brain. Instead, he spoke none of them.

"Let me show you something. Isabel and Igor, you come, too. You'll need to be able to show Annie the way back to your piss-poor village." Valentis, nodded at Sergei, who motioned for us to follow him. Isabel already knew the destination from the direction they were heading in, and she felt a chill permeate through her. She didn't know if Valentis would actually let them live.

“Wh-whe-re are we going?” Annie croaked out shakily, as they seemed to resume the journey they’d started out on.

“This is where you wanted to go, yes?” Sergei replied. ‘We’re going to let you see it.”

On the other side of the mountains, Valentis and the other vampires stopped short and cloaked themselves in large, dark garments as the trees and other greenery died away. Sergei and his archers kept forward, and what had been a lush, living mountain range was transfixed by a barren, sandblasted desolate mass adorned with shards of crystallized, glasslike terrain. Up ahead lay a bridge, and past that bridge lie a monolithic, stone and stucco fortress, lonely and imposing at the same time.

“Is that it?” Annie asked shyly. ‘Is that the House of the Winged God?”

“What else would it be?” was Sergei’s soft, deadpan response. ‘Come closer. I want to show you the bridge.”

They walked along one side of the Crystal Mountain, up to a beautifully ornate bridge built of aged wood and solemn stone, but as they got closer, Annie didn’t find it as beautiful anymore. The pavement of the bridge was composed entirely of human skulls. Annie stepped back and gasped. She’d been much more desensitized in the last few days, though, and she no longer gave in to her go-to urge to vomit. Internally, she also realized that doing so would be a clear sign of weakness among the gathered.

“Very nice. Can we go now?” Annie half-jokingly

blurted out.

"No, no. Not yet. I want you fully embrace the majesty of the Bridge of Skulls. Take it in."

"Yep. Very nice. I'm ready to head ba---"

"It only took Aylash Revall three hundred years to finish the bridge. There are roughly fourteen thousand souls represented on this bridge. It is over one hundred and fifty feet long. In 1809, the Turks slaughtered many Serbians. They built Cela-Kula, the tower of skulls, using close to a thousand Serbian skulls to decorate the tower. It is in Nis. Did Isabel show you? They got the idea for Cela-Kula from Aylash's Bridge of Skulls. They meant it as a tribute to their victory and a warning to Slavic people far and wide."

"Yes, they must be proud of their skull tower, as Aylash must be about his skull bridge. *WHY* are you showing me this?"

"Because I want you to get a glimpse of your lover's final resting place. Live or die, he will forever call the House of the Winged God home. Your new friends, from France. They will die here, and they will renovate the Bridge of Skulls with their own. You will only see it again if you've made peace with death, and come willing to become a blood payment." Sergei spread his left arm out proudly over the landscape. 'Aylash Revall will make you all pay for your transgressions, and he will make Davis his pupil, or his slave. Make sure he arrives here tomorrow at dawn. How he shrouds himself from the sun is his problem. No one is to come with him, and no one from the

Gray Bear is to be seen until twenty-four hours after Davis steps foot off of the Bridge of Skulls, and onto Aylash's estate. Go now, before the vampires get too hungry to heed my direction."

Annie looked to Isabel and Igor, like "what the fuck have you gotten us into?," and they in turn looked at her, like "what the fuck have you gotten *US* into?," and they helped a hobbled Igor through the woods, across the valley, and back to their village. As they walked along, as fast as they could, they could hear creaks and snaps of tree limbs, and see the isolated visages of salivating red and yellow eyes peering at them from the woods.

Annie felt a stone-like weight in her heart. She looked back in the direction of whence they came, and she felt that tonight would be her last night on earth with Davis McCarty. She sought to plan accordingly.

Chapter Twenty-Seven: A First Glimpse of the Devil

I awoke a few hours before sundown, and was still shaking the heavy cobwebs of slumber from my head and eyes, when Annie burst through the door of our room and launched herself into my arms. It took approximately four seconds for her unbridled tears to soak through my shirt. I was too shocked and startled to feel any kind of emotion; I just need to find out what the hell happened.

"Annie! Annie! What's wrong. What happened?!"

"I wanted to see the House of th---"

"You didn't!"

"I wanted to see it. So I had Isabel take me. Igor and some men from the village accompanied us. They're all dead. Everyone except for Igor and Isabel." I put my hand to my mouth and bit down. I was enraged and frightened all at once. Annie tried to regain her composure, I think more for my sake than hers.

"Annie, what were you thinking? And how did those men die?"

"Human henchmen. Assassins with crossbows, hidden away in the woods. But that's not the half of it. The wooded mountains are so dense and high with trees and foliage that vampires can protect themselves from the sun. Hence, there were vampires there, too. One you might know... Valentis."

"Valentis?! What the hell was he doing there?"

"Obviously siding with who he thinks will be victorious... He and Sergei took us to the Bridge of Skulls."

"You saw it? What did it look like?"

With the most deadpan and unimpressed look I've ever seen from Annie Moore, she replied, "It looked like a bridge of skulls."

"And the House of the Winged God?"

"It's not some fancy Black Moon or Gray Bear bullshit. This thing looks like if Vlad the Impaler was some Russian UFC fighter who only trained by fighting grizzlies and gorillas, and he built that shit. It's not for raving all night and fraternizing with drunk humans; it's for guarding against an invasion. It's to keep someone alive for 4,500 years. And 4,500 years after that."

"Well, then I'm going to check it out for myself."

"What? When?"

"As soon as nightfall comes."

"Do you think that's... Let me rephrase. *I* don't think that's a good idea."

"Regardless. I'm doi---"

"Davis, please! Don't go until it's time to go. Which reminds me: You're to be there tomorrow morning, right before dawn, and *no one* is supposed to be with you or seen approaching Aylash's castle until twenty-four hours after you step foot on his estate. Any deviation from that directive will result in some fucked up shit."

"That was the initial request."

"Well, it's not a request anymore."

"Did Reginald comply?"

"Isabel told him that it would be best. Take that for what it's worth." I took a breath and eased my shoulders down to my sides, attempting to reflect an air of calm and reason. Annie saw through my machinations instantly. 'You're still going to go look at it tonight, aren't you?"

"Annie, I have to. I don't want to be intimidated by it, and immediately found out as a scared fish out of water."

"Scared? You've proven in pretty short fucking order that you can take care of yourself! You drove your brand new baby vampire ass cross country, walked into a den of vipers alone, more than once, and came out alive. You flew across the world to meet, or confront, or kill this king of the vampires. You're not a baby anymore."

"Then why try to stop me from taking a stroll at night, and simply taking a glance at a building?" This question stumped her. She had to face some truths tingling her brain from deep within.

"Because *I'm* afraid. *I'm* a human. *I'm* walking prey, and this... this whatever it is you're walking into tomorrow morning... It's not with the 'king' of the vampires. That was an inaccurate description. It's with the God of the vampires. And I'm afraid I'm going to lose you." A lump filled Annie's throat, and the waterworks let loose from her tear ducts as she stared at me, remorsefully. 'I don't want to lose you. And all of a sudden, I wish we were back in Abilene, and I wish I had never *told you* Aylash Revall was still alive."

"I would have figured it out, eventually. Or someone would have told me. I think that, like it or not, I'm part of some unspoken vampire network now, forever tied to the night. Or to Sinjin, of all people... Either way, I'm sorry for adding to your fear, and I'm most grateful for your concern and your love. For me, I need to do this. I need to see it with my eyes, so I can align the picture in my mind with a reality, and form a plan."

"Can I come?"

"Hell no! You already went through that once, and if there are guards in the woods at night, or worse, then I won't have you go through it again." There was a silence in the room for what seemed like forever, and then...

"Oh, thank God!" Annie blurted out in relief, causing us both to chuckle like we weren't on some suicide vampire mission halfway across the world. ‘But promise me you’ll come back to me tonight. And promise you won’t feed on the locals. I have something special in mind.”

“OK. I Promise.”

An hour later it was dark, and I decided to exit the village and head through the valley. Isabel and Igor sat outside their home and watched silently as I walked by, their heads shaking like I was the biggest idiot they’d ever met. And maybe I was. They knew where I was going, and this time, they would not be following after. I walked along the valley floor and Annie's scent guided me along her earlier path. Once we got to the entrance to the woods, I could smell the blood of the villagers who lost their lives attempting to protect my girlfriend, and the humans whose arrows’ aims were true. I could also smell the putrid, vile scent of the vampires who devoured them. My vampire’s nose could also uncover something that at least Annie didn’t know. The vampires not only fed on Igor’s villagers, but on those human assassins that killed them. This may be something that Aylash directs every time he uses humans to carry out some death sentence. No witnesses. No loose lips.

Eventually, I came to the edge of the forest and discovered the stark contrast between one mountain’s end, and another’s beginning. Aylash Revall’s mountain reflected the loss of humanity and life within him. It was devoid of life, devoid of growth. A shattered, burnt surface resembling some cracked, parched desert in Africa more than the vibrant, fully alive city of Nis or the majesty of

Suva Planina. And then I came upon it. The Bridge of Skulls. Very impressive. I couldn't think of one human on earth who would choose to walk across it. Hell; I could only think of a select few night drinkers senseless enough to brave such a stroll. I came to the bridge's edge, ran my hand along its wood and stone sides, and pressed one foot down on the unfortunate first few heads of bone staring up at me, eyeless and smiling. I looked over the bridge to the shallow waterway below, and caught the House of the Winged God as it emerged from low-lying clouds and otherworldly mist.

And there he was.

Even in the darkness, from quite a distance, I could see the tall, rail-thin, winged creature as he crouched ominously atop a tower of his beloved fortress. He was hundreds of yards away, but the details of his skin and face were magnified a hundred fold in my eyes. I could see a sneer of a grin, and I swear I could make out his lips as he mouthed the words, "Soon, you will bow to me."

I... was afraid.

Chapter Twenty-Eight: Bliss, Finally

I backed up and swiveled on my heels to return to the village, and I could hear laughter hidden in the trees. My infrared vision couldn't pick up any heat signatures, but my ears picked up a hell of a lot of movement. I sped up the pace of my walk gradually until I was in a full sprint. I doubt anything could have caught me, save for a cheetah, but, incredibly, the sounds from the woods stayed on pace with me. Just as I made it to the border between trees and valley, a pair of eyes materialized in front of me, and a young, new vampire – maybe newer than me, even – leapt at me. I caught him in midair in a military press before slamming him unforgivingly to the earth. As he reached both hands up to scratch the flesh from my face, I swatted them away before grabbing his jaw and zigzagging his head from his body. I stood up and gave my back a good stretch, when I could smell a particularly hard stench behind me.

"You shouldn't be here, American," a handsome but ill-looking vampire stated with contempt. 'You won't be able to harm Aylash, but because of you, he's going to eliminate a large section of our kind from existence. I hope you're happy." Before I could ask him his name, he vanished. Not into thin air, but basically as quickly.

With no more apparent surprises along the path back to the village, I treaded lightly until I got to mine and Annie's possibly haunted room full of history and straw. To my very astonished eyes, I walked into a full, steaming bathtub in the center of the room, which didn't exist before I left it, over two dozen lit candles, and a very sexy looking Annie Moore. Her hair was down and full, and she wore an overgrown, comfy white robe opened up to display an articulately decorated beige bra and panties. Where she got these items, I didn't know and wouldn't ask. She looked at me both lovingly and seductively. She let me gaze upon her for a moment, then spoke, choosing her words carefully.

"I know that I can't predict the future, and I want to be as positive about the outcome of this journey... but just in case, I don't want you, or me, to never go another day without having finally made love to each other."

In case my mouth, gaping wide open, or my eyes, virtually bulging out of their compartments, weren't any indication, I was completely dumbfounded. Speechless for several seconds that stretched into their own eternity, I finally found the most clever reply.

"But I have to feed." I was *such* a ladies man.

"You will. From me. On me."

"We tried that before. It didn't go well... you passed out."

"Oh you don't have to remind *me*; I was there. I'm good, now. I promise." I eyed her skeptically.

"I don't... Are you sure?"

"Babe. Look around. I've done a lot to set the atmosphere. Please don't ruin it. Let me guide you."

Before I could say something that would indeed ruin it, she put her finger to my lips and took my hand, leading me to the tub. She lifted my shirt over my head and off, and unbuckled my belt. She knelt down, lifted my legs one by one, and took off my boots and socks before removing my jeans. With me still in my boxers, she stood and dropped her robe. Her eyes glimmered against the flames of the lit candles, and a cautious smile slid across her face as she took my hands and directed them in removing her bra and panties while she worked my boxers off of me, one alternating tug after another. She was about to direct me into the tub, but I stopped her.

"Wait. Wait... Let me... Let me look at you."

She was immaculate. Her breasts were not too big and not too small. She had a dark brown, precision-trimmed triangular wedge of pubic hair. Her body was unscarred, aside from the slits she'd put on it letting me drink. She looked different than the naked women I've seen at strip clubs. She was more... real. More natural. Just as perfect, but in a different way. After a while, I could sense a shy embarrassment crawl across her. She was ready to move on.

"Step in the tub and ease down into it," she commanded. 'I'll follow, and sit between your legs."

I did as requested, and opened my legs to allow her in. With her fully seated in the tub, I enveloped her in my arms, and held her tight to me. The water was hot and soothing. She grabbed a small bowl that sat on the edge of the tub and poured some wonderful smelling something or other into the water. Bubbles soon arose as she stirred the water with her hand. She took my right hand, and placed it on her breast, gently using my fingers to stroke her nipple. I took the shampoo and washed her hair gently and thoughtfully, running long, relaxing paths through her shoulder length locks with my fingers. She squeezed some body wash onto a sponge, and turned to face me. She pulled us both up to our knees, and she had me wash her body first. When it came time to wash her vagina, I stopped, giving her a look like, "Is this alright?" She gave a small hiccup of a laugh, and then nodded her head approvingly. After rinsing and wringing out the sponge, she reciprocated on my body. Internally, it was awkward for me, because my mind was thoroughly aroused, but my man parts, of course, didn't jump to attention. We knew I would need to consume for that to happen, and it was though she read my mind. She clutched a razor blade from the floor next to the tub, and handed it to me.

"I've noticed a little weight gain since we first started devising this plan to travel. And I noticed a substantial increase in that weight gain since we've been abroad. I'm not working out or doing yoga, and I've quite enjoyed my meals while you sleep away the day. As such, my breasts are fuller and hang a little more, which means you can make an incision just under my breast, and it will be naturally covered up." She lifted her left breast with her hand. 'You may do so now. Don't cut straight horizontally, but along the natural curve of my breast." I did so, causing her to bite her lip and make a high-pitched quiver like a mouse. The blood began to run. "Now drink," she commanded.

"You've had this planned for how long?" I asked as I licked the blood from her rib cage and abdomen.

"I guess for quite a while, now."

As I continued to lap up her blood, she took my hair in her hands and caressed it softly. Scooping up handfuls of water, she cleared the blood off her torso, and provided more instruction.

"Now lift me up and carry me to the bed." Done. 'Lay down on your back." Done.

My penis had finally gotten the memo Annie's blood had dictated, and was quickly at full length. She looked down at it, and seemed satisfied. She straddled my body, and closed my legs straight with her thighs. She knelt down and met my mouth with a passionate kiss that lasted several minutes, our hands fumbling and prodding and groping each other's bodies. Annie then grabbed my hands and held them over my head, like I was her prisoner, which in a way I was. She then planted soft kisses on my arms and neck and chest, before sitting up straight, lowering herself onto my penis. She was really warm, and wet. I couldn't hide the fear, or the smile, on my face.

"Ahhh. You're bigger than I thought you would be."

"Is that a good thing? Are you OK?"

"No, no. I'm good. I'm real good."

She began gyrating slowly up and down on top of me, and at first I didn't know if I felt the right... sensations. That momentary uncertainty quickly dissipated, and a rush of ecstasy radiated throughout my body and accumulated in my pelvic region. She would alternate her rhythm and speed, steadily starting to moan with pleasure, and in my head I was thanking her for knowing what to do and how to do it. I then secretly thought to myself, *How the hell does she know so much if she's only done it four times?* Annie noticed the distraction on my face, and sought to snap me back into the moment.

"Your turn." She hopped off and, while intertwining our fingers together, laid down on her back and pulled me atop her. She spread her legs wide and pulled her knees up, feet still flat on the bed, inviting me inside her. "Go slow."

I worked carefully to perfect my aim, and then I thrust my hips forward and upward, penetrating her. She gave a loud moan, and grabbed my shoulders.

"Is this good?" I asked.

"Very good. Oh, so good, baby. Keep going like that for a while, then vary your speed." I did as she asked, and about five minutes later, she threw me for a loop. 'Harder". *What?*

"What?"

"Harder. Give it to me harder."

I paused, unsure for a second, my hips and ass lifting to form a rounded point. Then I complied, re-entering her with a forceful thrust.

'Aaaahhh!" She moaned loudly. Louder than she had to this point, which made me repeat the action. 'Yes! More. Just like that." I was starting to feel a weird sensation emitting from my belly. It then surged toward the head of my penis. I started to moan loudly, myself.

"Annie. I think... I think I'm about to---"

"No! No. Not yet. Hold on, Davis. Hold on." She was panting and faint, but utterly delighted. 'And go faster. Give it to me harder and faster."

I complied, and we were both moaning and yelling. Annie gripped onto my back, and dug her nails into it, causing me to scream out in pain. That pain only resulted in heightening my pleasure, and Annie and I eventually succumbed to our bliss, finishing at the same time.

"Oh, Davis. Oh, baby. I love you so much. I love you so much."

I could just lay next to her, exhilarated, but exhausted.

I had finally lost my virginity, and it was spectacular! I couldn't wait to do it again. But first, rest. Annie lay on her side with her head on my chest, and she faded off to sleep for maybe half an hour. Waking up, she looked up at me with a goofy, beautiful smile, and we kissed.

"Hi, my love" I whispered.

"Did you like it?" she asked, as if there were any other answer.

"I loved it."

"Do you want some more?" *Oh, God yes.*

"If I say yes, does that make me completely greedy and selfish sounding?"

"No. It makes you a man."

"Then yes, please."

Annie stretched out to grab the blade from the side table, and then sat up on her legs, pulling her hair forward to give me a clear shot of her back.

"I want you to make about a three inch cut along the bottom of my shoulder blade, and let the blood run good and down my back before you start lapping it up."

"Annie... Are you sure? Your back looks so smooth and free of any blemish. I would hate to ruin that."

"It's OK. Trust me. It's only this one time." I did as asked, and sure enough, the blood came streaming down, like rain on a window. 'Now, drink me."

I took my tongue and extended it as far out of my mouth as possible, licking Annie's blood from the top of her right buttock to as near the incision as possible. I started weaving my tongue side to side, in sort of a snake's motion, alternating my speed. Once I licked her clean, I would start back at the small of her back, waiting for the blood to run down, and start over, now planting kisses along her skin as I drank of her.

"I think that's enough. I'm good."

"Are you sure? How do you know?"

I took her hand and placed it on my engorged tool.

"Is this proof enough?" She turned her head to see my face, a wicked smile formed on her lips.

"Kiss my neck and shoulders." Annie adopted a commanding, authoritarian tone. 'Then sprinkle kisses across my back." After doing exactly as she asked, while running my fingers through her hair, and caressing her breasts from behind, she took my hands and put them at my side. She then bent over, raising her ass in the air as her face leaned into the cotton pillowcase stuffed with straw. She parted her legs slightly, and tickled my right hip with her fingernails. 'Now... take me."

Chapter Twenty-Nine: The Long Walk Across the Bridge

As much as Annie and I wanted nothing more than to just stay in that room forever, repeating our newfound expression of love, the task at hand was inching ever closer, and we would soon have to shift focus to finalizing the strategy and plan of attack. I opened the door to go find Reginald just as Isabel was about to knock on it.

"Oh, I'm sorry to disturb you, but it looks like you're finish-, I mean, it looks like you were about to come out. Reginald would like to speak with you. Time is short."

"Yes, I was... coming out to find him."

"He is in the covered dining pavilion in the village center. The odd vampire with the mask and a few others, they are there, too." Peaking her head in the room to find Annie, Isabel's expression grew satisfied and mischievous. 'Ahhh, Annabella. You finally made a man of the monster, no?"

Annie's face grew red with embarrassment. She stammered, trying to find a suitable reply. "I... I don't... I don't know what you're talking about, Isabel."

"It's OK. I could hear everything by the window. Davis is lucky to have his Annabella, for one more night, at least."

Her words threw a somber wrench into the playful and loving gears of our night together. Annie's face switched instantly to having to think about my possible death.

"I'm going to get dressed, and I'll meet you out there, OK, babe?" Her eyes told me not to argue, and just go ahead. My intuition told me that she was going to have a cry, and needed to be alone for that.

"Sure, Annie. Just come out when you're ready."

I made my way to the center of the village, finding Reginald and his cast of characters waiting for me, anxiously. Impatiently. It dawned on me that during these few days here in the village, we were largely separated from each other. For as important as this trip was, we didn't really spend any time together. Instead of bring that up, I kept it buried, hoping that I would get to discuss it and other things after a victorious visit to the House of the Winged God.

"How was your potentially final night with your loved one?" Reginald asked, provocatively. 'I hope you said all that needed to be said."

“We actually didn’t do much talking,” I quipped, proving I could be as clever and innuendo spewing as he could.

“No doubt. Are you ready to take your walk to Aylash’s castle?”

“I am. Are you settled on waiting the twenty-four hours to come after me, and at dawn?”

“We haven’t decided yet,” was his response, which both shocked and angered me.

“What do you *mean*, you haven’t *decided* yet?”

“He means he’s not going to tell you.” Le Bouffon interjected, the first time I’d actually heard his voice or seen him since we arrived at the village.

“And why the hell not?”

“Because if *you* don’t know, then Aylash won’t know; nor will he be able to torture it out of you.” Annie just *had* to show in time to hear those words fall from The Jester’s lips. She grabbed ahold of my waist tight, and rested her head on my arm.

“So this is for my own good, then?”

Reginald regained his control of the conversation. “It’s for the best, Davis. For you and for everybody. Also, because, truly, I have not decided yet.” I looked at Edsel, who could only lift his eyebrows and throw his hands upward in an “I don’t know” type of gesture. ‘I can tell you that we will not have a change of heart. We’re not here to negotiate terms of surrender, or a peace talk of any kind. When we arrive, it will be to see bloodshed, and it will be to rid the world of Aylash Revall, no matter the cost, no matter the result."

"Well, I guess I better get going, then."

A sizable contingent of vampires and humans set out to see me on my way. Annie and I walked hand in hand to the edge of the valley, right before it narrowed into the woods, and it was difficult for us to separate our clasp. Isabel was equipped to get me on to my mission; her hardness and ability to be devoid of emotion must come in handy during many situations in this region of the world.

"Davis, let me pray for you. I will take care of your Annabella while you are gone. My patron saint will protect you on your journey."

Annie looked into my eyes, and made me swear to return.

"Annie, I can't promise anything. But I will do everything in my power to come back and hold you in my arms again." Isabel was ready for a one-liner.

"You'll do more than *that*, judging from last night." We both just turned and stared at her, our expressions asking for a little privacy. "Oh, yes. Say goodbye to your Annabella. I'm sure you will see each other again."

"Make sure you come back to me, Davis." Annie's eyes were droopy and morose. "I don't want to live without you. And, if you die, I'm pretty sure Uber-Dracula is going to come for us here and finish the job."

"I won't let him hurt you, Annie." We embraced, kissing each other softly, when Reginald and Edsel interrupted.

"Davis, it's time," Reginald declared solemnly. 'You need to go now if you're going to beat the daylight."

Annie stepped back several feet to allow for important discussion, and Edsel chimed in. "Remember, you're there to ask your questions, find out what you can, and keep him occupied. He won't be able to get our plan of attack out of you, because you won't know what it is, yourself. Do not engage him in battle alone. You're at an overwhelming disadvantage by yourself. And, if you die, *we're all* at an overwhelming disadvantage, surprise attack or not."

"Understood. I'll do what I need to do... Thank you. For coming along. I don't know if I'd said that yet."

"No need, but you're welcome, Davis." Reginald replied, shaking my hand firmly. 'Good luck. Now get going."

I went through the woods, listening for every creak and snap beneath my feet, and every other sound that may be lying in wait for me, but there was no disturbance. In fact, the stillness of the woods was far more unnerving than any would-be, tangible enemy. Eventually, I came upon the Crystal Mountain, and the Bridge of Skulls. There was a fog hovering low over the bridge, and some unidentified bird was singing a horrific morning hymn.

Just as I looked at the imposing monstrosity that was The House of the Winged God, its fortified front gate lifted vertically, and two large doors therein swung open to reveal my host. Aylash Revall was standing there, one hand leaning slightly against the wall, and the other on his hip. He wore a long, ancient-looking beige covering, similar to something that covered the privates in a Roman marble statue. His body was 70% or so uncovered, and he wore no shoes. He was smiling as I began my approach. I took a cautious first step onto the bridge, unsure if the skulls would all collapse, sending me falling some thirty feet below. They held firm, and emitted an aching, crunching groan as I trampled over them to Aylash.

"Don't be afraid," he called out to me, in accented, but good enough English. "The architecture is sound."

My right hand running along the smooth, worn surface of the wood, I made a mental note of the visual, not knowing if I would ever see the outside again.

Aylash's smile grew wider.

Chapter Thirty: Old Meets New

I stepped down onto solid ground, and gave an unexpected exhalation of relief. My nerves were at an all-time high of agitation, and my arms were covered in goosebumps. I could hear Aylash laugh to himself. He had to have experienced this from every single person, both friend and foe, that ever stepped over that bridge. It was truly a masterpiece... of terror. I had a short amount of silence to analyze him. He was tall and thin, gray skin turning almost white in some spots. Dark, horrid veins protruded from beneath that grayness, highly visible. I could not see his wings, but knew that they were folded just behind his torso. He was completely bald, with hard, narrow bones jutting from his face, almost black eyes, and sharp, jagged teeth penetrating through dark purple and blood red, infected gums. His body was almost completely hairless. As I inched closer, he took a black cape with a velvety, red satin interior, and looped it over his head and around his neck, via a stained, browning, golden yellow rope. If he was a normal human, I would guess him to be anywhere between seventy and eighty years old. "Davis! Come. Join me!" Aylash greeted me jovially, like we were old friends, and walked forward to embrace me, but I skidded back, instantly on guard. He paused his movement, a little taken aback and perhaps even a little disappointed. 'I promise, no harm will come to you. We've made an agreement, and more than that, I am anxious and curious to know about you." There was clearly a look of fascination in his eyes.

"Umm. Hello," I eeked out of my dry, bumbling mouth. I started moving toward him, carefully.

"I want to show you the entire castle, and provide you with as much of the history as you came to seek, but first, you will need to feed."

"I already fed. I'm f---"

"Nonsense!" Aylash snapped back. 'The minimal amount of blood your girlfriend siphoned off for you will not be sufficient if you're to stay alert for 24 hours. It will take some time to go through this experience."

"How did you know---"

"Do not insult me. My nose can smell the newness of sex on you, and no doubt your lover would have wanted to share herself in the chance that she may never see you again. For centuries, men and women have consecrated their relationships, or indulged in their abbreviated wedding nights right before the man goes off to battle.

Entire populations have sustained themselves on the explosion of pregnancy that comes from war. Vampires in love are no different, not that a newborn nine months from now will be your result. Trust me, I've been trying to conceive a child for thousands of years." We walked through the doors of his Winged God, and I had questions regarding that statement.

"Why would you want a child? *Ever*? Why would you want to bring a baby into a vampire's existence?"

"Succession, Davis. No different than any father. I want to leave a legacy."

"How would you leave a legacy for someone you're going to outlive? You're not thinking that---"

"Yes. I'm thinking that if my child wasn't already born part vampire, I would transform them... when the timing was right, of course."

"Timing? What the hell are you talking about?"

"We're getting ahead of ourselves. Please. You need to feed." He motioned to some unseen minion. "Afterward, I will give you the tour. Then, we can debate the philosophical and moral merits of vampirism and child-rearing... I do want to warn you that I may speak "over your head" at times. I've consumed millennia of education, after all."

"I'll try to keep up," I said sarcastically.

We exited the long, foreboding foyer and entered a large open epicenter of the fortress, which stretched up to the top of the entire thing. From it, I could see multiple, half-spiral, stone staircases that led to all sorts of rooms on many different levels. The memory of some piece of art with a three-dimensional staircase illusion shot its arrow through my brain. "This is what I refer to as the eye of the storm. From here, I can fly to the northernmost tower of the Winged God, and look down upon all of Nis and the countryside."

"So those wings are real?"

"Very. Very real and very functional."

"How? How did you---"

"In due time. Feast."

As I thought they would, said unseen minion appeared with a human meal in his grasp; an elderly man, completely nude, and frightened beyond belief. Aylash's man hurled him into the center of the open room, a few feet away from me.

"Please!" the man pleaded in his native tongue. I told him I didn't understand, and he switched to a very broken English, while clutching at my pants to pull himself up.

‘Please! Please help me! Don’t let them kill me!”

“I’m sorry; I have to do this.”

The man’s eyes bulged out of his sockets, and he tried to hit me with a terribly feeble punch that glanced off my shoulder. I gripped him like I would a dance partner I was dipping, and nudged his head out of my way with my chin. I injected my fangs into his soft, paper-like skin, and drank him for all he had. He didn’t scream or plead for his life once he was in my grasp. He just simply wept softly until he passed. I looked up at Revall with equal parts scorn and appreciation.

“See? Now we can continue on,” he said flatly. Out of my peripheral, I saw two men drag away my dinner.

“Where are Miko and Sergei? And where is Valentis?”

“You know of Valentis?”

“I battled with him back at the Gray Bear. Annie told me he was here, and helped kill a few of Igor’s villagers.”

“How unfortunate, that civil spat among the French. You won’t battle him tonight. The three of them had to represent me concerning business back in France.”

“Unfortunate, indeed. I was *really* hoping to see him again.”

We walked up one of the staircases on one side of the castle, and once on the second floor, Aylash opened a door to reveal three vampires sleeping peacefully in beds. "There are some twenty-four rooms just like this one on this wing of the castle. All with three vampires inside." *Mental note made: 24 x 3.* 'As we turn left and make our way to the other side of this wing, there are forty-eight more rooms, also with three vampires inside." *Mental note number two: 48 x 3. Shit, that's a lot of vampires. How big is this damn place?*

"Are they all from here? From Nis and Selo Semce?"

"No. Of course not." Aylash's expression told me he thought the question was silly. 'I couldn't take that many people from one area. Not without doing it at a tortoise's pace. I didn't have time to build back up slowly, so these vampires are from all over. Europe, the Middle East, America, England. I had to rebuild the army that Reginald Duplante and his whores subtracted from me."

"Why couldn't you have resolved their grievance diplomatically? Did it have to lead to bloodshed?"

"I'm sure Reginald has given you some self-pitying, self-victimizing story about how I became a monster, and how my relationship with Antonio Medici led to a change in me."

"Well... yeah."

"He doesn't explain that our tensions had been simmering for far longer than that, and how he began to challenge me as an authority figure, and a spokesman for all vampire-kind. Reginald could have taken his grievance up with me individually, but he published it – he broadcast it, across the earth, and there had to be consequences for such action."

"Why do you need all these vampires? Why do they have to be an army? And why does this place have so many goddamned rooms?!" This caused an uproarious laugh from Revall.

"Oh! You haven't seen anything yet, my young friend. I'm going to answer all your questions and give you food for thought that will lead to many more questions... if you've the aptitude."

"What's *that* supposed to mean?" Aylash slithered backwards to feign an apologetic stance.

"I do not mean to offend you. I just mean, you're still so... new to this. Things may still be... difficult."

"They weren't too difficult for me to kill the entire House of the Black Moon." I could tell that this statement raised Aylash's internal temperature some fifty degrees. He attempted to remain nonchalant, however.

"Yes. Maybe I shouldn't underestimate you. After all, you do possess the Luminastra Namtudari, you the first American to do so. Actually, you're only the third vampire in all of history to do so."

"Who's the second?"

“My former disciple, Isa. But that... that was a long time ago. You’re the only vampire in the last three thousand years to attain the Namtudari.”

“How did she---”

“That’s for another time. Are you ready to hear my story?”

“You’re goddamn right, I am.”

Chapter Thirty-One: Revelations

"I was born the illegitimate son of a nobleman and a peasant. As such, I was a peasant, but one with an inherited set of genes and intellect. I couldn't escape my destiny as a man of change. As I approached manhood, I was deemed a radical due to my beliefs and my musings, but just as much because of my integrity and defiance in the face of authority. Even in a time where saying the wrong things to, or in front of, the wrong people could lead to public beheading, I never wavered in my steadfast desire to attain – no, create – something new. I watched as the poorest of my people starved and crumbled to dust, forgotten footnotes among the highest citizens of Sumer. I was determined to reach an equality between rich and poor alike, but to also discover a way for all of humanity to improve upon itself."

"Pretty lofty goal for a peasant in ancient Iraq." I couldn't help myself.

"Perhaps, but I thought and saw the world in a way that maybe only a few others ever had. All those people were priests, or shaman, or philosophers. And just like me, the general public feared or ridiculed them. At best, these thinkers were taken with a grain of salt... I had to provide proof of my hypothesis. I had to... experiment. And I had to gain a trust among my people. I looked to lead, and needed to find the right followers."

"Sounds like a salesman to me." Again, I couldn't help myself.

"You're not wrong. In the beginning, as a teenager speaking in the market square, I must have sounded like a lunatic at first, and a slick snake charmer eventually. There was some fraud to my monologues, because the things I was claiming hadn't been proven yet. Most things I spoke of, I hadn't even *tried* yet. But I'd seen magic. I experienced occurrences and phenomena that I could not explain, and I realized that some of the sacred men near my dwelling had discovered some secrets to the universe. No one was willing to push forward, though. To push *through*. I wanted to take the magic I'd seen and elevate it in a way that humanity would be the beneficiary."

"How did you end up creating the potion, or whatever, that ended up transforming you into the world's first vampire?"

"Trial and error. Much failure... Don't you have that information in the journals you stole from the Black Moon? Or did you think I didn't know?"

“I don’t have everything. I took what I thought was relevant in the relatively short time I had to go through the material. And I believe that certain parts of your work was burned intentionally by your first followers.”

“This is true. My people were afraid of me, and afraid that they would also become what I had, if the recipe for that particular solution continued to exist. I could hardly blame them. The first two months as a vampire, not that my condition was named for over a thousand more years, were especially harsh. I felt trapped in a purgatory of sorts, all the while trying to navigate a heretofore unprecedented affliction.”

“Did you want to die at times?”

“The natural answer would be yes, right? However, as inexplicable as it sounds, I never felt the need to end my own life. I was suffering, yes, but I still felt that I was doing something right. Something necessary. I still feel that way, which is why I’ve been able to sustain and evolve.”

“Which brings me to a line of questions I’ve had for months now: why did Alister Amaranth tell me you died after only 150 years as a vampire? Why did you go to America, and why did you hide out in an old folks home? Wouldn’t you have been more comfortable and free to roam about at the Black Moon? And why Serbia? Why this part of Serbia?”

“These are all valid questions, and I will try to give

you thorough yet succinct answers to all. First, the world at large had to be kept as in the dark as possible about the existence of real vampires. This has been hard in the 21st century, with all the advances in speed of information and photographic evidence. So maybe the story of a real life vampire can float about in the cultures of the world, but if that story was tied to some finite, unremarkable reality, it could temper any concentrated interest in exposing us. I believe the quote is “the greatest trick the devil ever pulled was convincing the world he didn’t exist.” I had to remain in the shadows to continue operating as I needed. Eventually, my influence was enough that highly empowered people in this part of the world assisted me in doing so. Two, I traveled to America to heal. After the battle with the Gray Bear, I was wounded and spent, and it was harder on my body to renew itself after utilizing both the Spectralis Invincibus and the Luminastra Namtudari. America is farther than any vampires here would want to travel for revenge against me, and I knew I would be protected by Alister’s allegiance. Conversely, if there was any attempt to locate me in America, the Black Moon would be too easy a stone to turn over. I needed a more inconspicuous place. Unfortunately, my impulses and... appetites, were too strong to control. It wasn’t long before I’d overstayed my welcome at the Horizon Vista. By then, luckily, I was physically able to return to Serbia, but mentally damaged. Everything I’d given my life, over lifetimes, to build was evaporating around me like a drop of water in the desert. I knew my peace would be brief. So, upon returning to my home, I started rebuilding my ranks. The Winged God would no longer be a safe haven for vampires; it would be a training ground... I built the House of the Winged God, the first vampire House, just outside of Nis because at the time the world was a smaller place, and there weren't objects like airplanes and satellites in the sky to detect every single thing. It was secluded to an extent. The main reason I settled just this side of Suva Planina, though? The water. It is so clean, so pure, so unaltered by the outside. To this day, it is free from the contamination of the world. Water, just like it is for every other organism and nature, is the key to a vampire's life."

"Why are there exactly three vampires in every room?"

"That equation keeps a tension among the inhabitants. There is always one thinking that the other two are plotting against them. It also keeps the romantic factor ambiguous. If there were only two vampires to a room, they would eventually form a bond. Three makes it trickier. It keeps them somewhat guarded, the introverts at least."

"You're playing games with your own acolytes?'

"I'm keeping them sharp. Keeping them skeptical and calculating."

"You're playing God. You're manipulating."

"It's funny, this word God. I haven't seen the evidence of one. I seriously doubt my existence was in his plan."

“Why wouldn’t it be?”

“Any entity or being who would have pre-ordained vampirism and everything I believe *I’ve* instigated, *cannot* be good for the universe.”

“Did you ever meet Jesus?”

“Hahahaha!” I didn’t know this would sound so ridiculous to him. ‘You need to understand how isolated the world’s four corners once were. There was no printing press at the time of Jesus. Only royals, holy teachers, and wealthy citizens owned hand-written books. Most couldn’t even read. I’d never heard of Jesus until at least a century after his death, and he didn’t become the worldwide fixture he is now, until the seventh century, approximately two hundred years after Constantine made Christianity the official religion of Rome... Let me make things clear for you before we proceed any further; I have no proof, sign, or faint hint that a god created the universe, or that Jesus of Nazareth is God come to earth. I’ve seen and done too much on, and to, this world to believe that there is anything more than what we put into it.”

“I was afraid you’d say that.”

“And what of you? Are you a believer? In any religion?”

“I’m not completely sure. I didn’t think I ever would be, but certain things have happened to make me question. To make me *want* to believe.” Aylash’s face looked unimpressed, like he'd heard similar words from millions of others over the last few thousand years.

"Why don't we talk about why you're really here?"

"Excuse me?"

"You want to find out if you can become human again. And if you can, you want to know if you have to kill me for that to happen."

"I don't believe I---"

"You didn't have to. Not that I wouldn't have already guessed, but Alister mentioned it. Do you want the answer?"

"I do."

"You cannot. It is not a curable disease. It's not a disease at all, but a transformation. A degradation. A cruel wrinkle of de-evolution whose source refuses to perish. It is not reversable. To attain this cursed gift, I had to combine certain substances that should not have been combined, otherwise. Their potency was brutal and immediate, and everlasting. Their discovery did, in a way, lead to the evolution and limited immortality I was seeking. I just didn't... read the fine print, to use a more recent generation's phrase."

"So there's no chance?"

"None."

“But what else would you say? ‘Sure, just kill me and you’ll go back to normal. In fact, all of the vampires of the earth will just return to human if you just cut off my head’.”

“Trust me.”

“Would you trust me?”

“No.”

“Thank you for the honesty.”

“It’s the least I could do.”

“So, for 150 years, you played this game where you would move here and move there, and you and your band of gypsies would evade the law, but what were you afraid of? Couldn’t you kill anyone who tried to capture or execute you?”

“Perhaps. But what might be a dozen men one day might turn into a hundred the next. And if I somehow vanquish them, maybe that hundred becomes a thousand. I’m not omnipotent. As there were only a small number of my followers, and an even smaller number of vampires, we would have been discovered, overtaken, and slaughtered.”

“Would that have been a bad thing? For humanity, I mean.” Aylash looked long and hard at me, scanning me up and down. There were probably a few responses wrestling for priority in his head, but he chose the most honest.

"I have to admit, Davis. At some point, what was best for "humanity" became secondary to my own interests... And there you have it. My own self-righteousness, which I did truly believe in at one point, was dismissed by my need for power. For glory. In that respect, I am no different from most of the men in my position. I gues---"

"There've never been men in *your position*. You're a singular figure in human history."

"WAS a singular figure! After I created my first equal, that statement was no longer relevant. Even Sartep had small delusions of grandeur, where he would usurp me, and carry on my work."

"But did he actually try?"

"No. He ultimately remained loyal, as did all my closest creations. The point is not that I'm the first vampire; it's that I was and am still, just a man. Power corrupts us. Uniqueness corrupts us. It magnifies and enlarges the ego, to repulsive consequences. The goal was to transform all of humanity for the better. Unfortunately, what I transformed into could only be seen by the world as an abomination."

"Then why continue?"

"I do not like to see things *unfinished*, and I do not like to lose. More importantly, I eventually wanted my name to go down as the one who either improved humanity or destroyed it with *his* hands. Of *his* mind."

"So you're crazy, then?"

Aylash snapped his fingers, the chandeliers and torches automatically went out, and a sour, whistling, chirping sound infiltrated every nook of his fortress, causing a terrible, nauseous feeling deep in my gut. He snapped his fingers again, and vampires from all sides were now staring at me with evil, insensitive eyes and salivating mouths. As I gazed upon them, Aylash put his hand to my throat before I even knew he'd moved an inch, and he stared into my eyes.

"I would watch what I say in my master's house... Things have been so... cordial, up to this point. It would be a shame to disrupt that, breaking your Annie's heart." I didn't know if I should fight back, or bow down, but I knew the grip on my throat was more than just physical; it was a display of metaphorical power. Through choking and gurgling, I croaked out a...

"Yes... Yes, of course... So, you're *not* crazy."

After this, the mood turned stagnant and painfully awkward, in my opinion. Aylash's history lesson became more of an open house from an uninteresting realtor. There were high points, of course. His ballroom, where he claims to have danced with kings, queens, dictators, tyrants, and prime ministers; it was grandiose and elegant, really out of place compared to the drab, utilitarian, grayness of most of the castle. The artifacts he collected over thousands of years from all over the world, all just decorations in the building, would be seen as priceless to any art curator. As we descended, though, underneath the ground level of the Winged God, we entered a much darker, more evil feeling place. Aylash could sense the hairs stand up on my neck, and feel the chill grip my arms, as if I was some blond cheerleader being dragged through a haunted house at Halloween by her boyfriend.

"Are you afraid, Davis?"

"No. Hell no." I wasn't lying, but I wasn't exactly telling the truth, either. We reached a narrow, simple door, and I realized, I couldn't tell how far down we've gone, or how many levels of the castle there now were.

"Good. We're about to enter a room that will make you afraid. It will make you want to run out of this house and return to Texas. It might make you question reality and wish for the death of all mankind."

"Perfect. Can't wait." I had to play it cool, even if I, and Aylash, knew I was now scared shitless.

Chapter Thirty-Two: The Exhibition

The door opened slowly and loudly, its cobwebs being stretched and broken from their hold on the wall. I noticed the long, sharpened fingernails on Aylash's left hand as he pushed the door aside, and could make out some tattooed symbol on the back of his hand that I had somehow overlooked thus far. Even though we were far underground, the room we walked into had at least a twenty foot ceiling. I eyeballed it as 100' long x 80' wide, but could have been smaller. Could have been larger. It was big. One part laboratory, one part torture chamber, my quick scan concluded that it contained many tables, cages, instruments, and creatures. There was a large pool of water center right with a large platform overhanging it. My guess was that the platform was either used for dumping something into the water, or feeding something that lurked *inside* the water; perhaps both. On the opposite side of the room sat cages stacked upon each other three high, most containing some animal, or human, or dead carcass of one or the other. The alive ones were either close to starvation, or rabid with madness. The stench in the room was almost unbearable, but Aylash had probably gotten used to it ages ago. At the very opposite end of the door, a large, black tarp covered up something enormous, keeping its secret hidden from view. In the center of the room, tables, cabinets, and bookshelves sat assembled, forming Aylash's main experimentation hub. The expression on my face must have given off a sense of wonder, because Aylash saw it clearly.

"Are you curious about what's in those cabinets, and on those shelves?"

"Is it that obvious?"

"Just slightly." The ease with which he spoke English puzzled me.

"How many languages do you know?"

"Hmmm. At one time, maybe fifteen. Now, I'm fluent in maybe nine. Fluent enough. The less I traveled, the less I needed to remember certain languages."

"Were you sad when the number of vampire houses dwindled from twelve to just the two?"

"I wouldn't say "sad." I think disappointed is more accurate. Some houses needed to close. Some maybe should have never opened. To think that a creature so apt to destroy not only itself, but everything around it, could act almost like a government was wishful thinking at best... I think it might have been a mistake to not open one in England. Their population, as well as their unification, warranted a House, but politics led to their refusal, and, eventually, to the war we had four years ago. I did what I thought was best, at the time."

"Speaking of Engl---"

"I've gotten distracted. Let us resume the tour, unless you need to sleep for a bit. It is our natural bedtime, after all."

"No, no. No, I'm good." *I'm fucking exhausted.* 'Let's keep... Let's keep going."

"Very well. Where we stand now is where I've formed most of my hypotheses and conducted most of my experiments over the last three thousand years. It is where I sprouted these wings." *Which I still haven't seen.* 'And where I've created or modified several different animals. I wish I could say that number was in the thousands, or at least in the hundreds, but alas, I've found that nature is a more precise and patient cultivator."

"Maybe it's Go---"

"The ones that have continued breathing are a blessing... or a curse. Let's view them, shall we?"

Aylash scurried over to a marble slab of a worktable that had what must be freshly caught fish laying on it. He grabbed a large specimen of the table and walked just close enough to the pool to throw it in. The water became alive, sloshing around and overflowing onto the floor. Soon, the head of an alligator popped up out of the water with the fish in its mouth. Not just any gator; this thing's head was maybe five times as large as a normal alligator's. It was definitely geneticized. It became obvious that the "pool" was just the tip of the iceberg, an opening for which the gator made an appearance to snag food.

"What the fu---"

"That is Marcel. He likes to eat... As we come this way, our attractions become a little more... freakish, for lack of a more endearing term. I warn you in advance."

Aylash pushed some button, and the stacked cages began moving and shifting, causing animals and humans alike to shriek and howl; their sounds flew to the ceiling and pulsated throughout the room. The most agonizing of these sounds came from the large tarped-off structure at the back. As the cages played their game of musical chairs, they eventually came to rest, with a rather large, structurally reinforced cube of steel now sitting front and center. The wails of the congregated eased and went silent. What stood inside the cage on all fours, staring directly at me, was... *what is it*?

"What *is* that?" I asked of the enormous monstrosity in front of me. I'd never seen anything like it, ever. Not even in books or dreams. Yet, somehow, it recalled a *familiarity*. It's face was deformed. Eyes unsynchronized.

Only a few large, dull teeth emerging from its horrific muzzle like ivory trunks. Whatever it was, it was *strong*.

"Haha! That, my young Davis, is the hybrid marriage of a rhinoceros and a hippo. Strong, grumpy, *hungry*. Impenetrable. It took a painstakingly long time to find success; apparently the two species did not want to coexist. More accurately, they couldn't coexist without the right *coagulant*, if you will."

"And what was that?"

"Ahh. My secret."

"Is it a vampire?"

"No. I learned my lesson with Ballou. Adding another element of uncontrollability to an already out-of-control beast, a second time, would be criminally foolish. But I did want to manufacture an animal that would be able to hold its own against The Abomination, if I ever came across it again." Aylash's head was mostly turned away from me, but I could sense his eyes peripherally scanning me for a slight sign that would give away Ballou's inclusion here in Nis. I did not let on.

"Are you able to... is it friendly? To you?"

"Not exactly. It is... what it is. The next things are not... They are not right. That's the best way to put it."

Another button and some more movement, and then

HOLYWHATTHEFUCKINGSHIT!

"What the shit am I looking at?"

In two cages, side by side, sat a "man" with three heads, and a... I have no idea.

"You are looking at the consequence of curiosity. I'd always had a fascination with the mythological three-headed dog, Cerberus. This was my attempt at creating a human version. I envisioned him standing strong and imposing, a guard to the gates of the Winged God. Instead I ended up with an eyesore I cannot euthanize. Like a weakhearted human who can't say no to a stray dog or cat, I can't bring myself to put him – them – out of their misery. Henrick there took a turn for the worse after we spliced the third head. He's the one on the far right. He hasn't moved in some time, and I believe he's slowly decaying. The middle head, belonging to Elijah, he is the more subdued of the two active personas, but is still a miserable bastard. The far left head, though, Slaja, he retains all his faculties, all his hatred, and all his cunning. He was not a variable I forecasted when putting this idea into motion. If left unchained, the three of them... well, the two of them, at least, would try to kill me. They can barely move, mind you, but try nonetheless, they would."

Just then, the creature of a man grabbed the bars of the cage with his hands and shook at it, wildly. Slaja, the third head, muttered something in Serbian that I could not make out, even if it was in English. Aylash punched him through the cage in the chest, and all active heads gasped for air, unable to breathe. I was ready to leave that poor, pathetic creation alone and get to a true monster. As we turned our attention to the thing in the next cage, I was speechless and horrified.

"Please tell me that the vision you had for this thing is different from what I'm looking at."

"Indeed."

Try to picture the body of a normal human male, thin, sinewy, and muscular, but with no head. Instead, imagine a gaping hole where a neck would start, and from that hole, gyrating like some mechanized sex toy, is a ten-inch long, deep-veined tongue covered in boils and lacerations and a singular, five-inch long optic nerve with one yellowing, bloodshot eyeball attached to it. It was curved and protruding like a periscope from some unseen place in the chasm of the headless abyss. He would move slow like stubborn honey dribbling down a plastic bottle, and then make these sudden, lightning quick movements before returning back to slow motion. His nervous system was definitely affected by his... situation. I was actually nauseous, and I hadn't eaten food since El Paso, Texas last January.

"I don't have... I can't... Seriously, what the fuck is that thing?"

"This unfortunate soul... is Malcom. When you end up having more time on your hands than any one person was ever supposed to have, you tend to get bored at times. I would suppose that this is the case with the majority of my creations. If I had just stopped at vampires, maybe I would have perished myself ages ago. I don't know if that's a bad thing or a good thing."

"The fact that you can actually entertain your death possibly being a positive for the world is proof of hope that you're not completely delusional. The true madman sees all of his actions and behaviors as righteous, or virtuous."

"Young Davis. I didn't know you were capable of such philosophical profundity. Truly captivating."

"I've learned a lot the last seven months. I've read a lot. Not much else to do when my love is asleep in her home, and I'm stuck isolated in some abandoned building."

"You don't live together?" Aylash's face belied his puzzlement.

"No. Not yet. She lives with her... That's enough of my private life. You don't need to know anymore, especially if you plan on killing me."

"Kill you?! I am planning on just the opposite. I want you to succeed me." *He actually is crazy.*

"Succeed you? Are you completely insane? There is no fucking way I'm---"

"Never say never, my young friend. You are the one I've foretold of since before I built this house. Since before I started others across the world. You're the one I first envisioned some four thousand years ago, when I didn't know if each morning would result in my final mortal breath. You are the chosen o---."

"Let me stop you right there. I'm *not* the chos---."

Just then, a servant interrupted us with a message. There was a visitor approaching the gate.

"The visitor will have to wait. Davis, I can't show you my many wonders without giving you an eyeful of my newest, and possibly most disastrous, creations. Mr. McCarty, please follow me to the large, covered cell in the back of the laboratory. I want to show you the Soulless."

Chapter 32.5: The Soulless

As we approached the ominous black tarp covering whatever insidious, deranged attempt at science Aylash had dreamt up, tortured, ear-piercing wails rose to an eruptive boil from underneath it. Aylash Revall placed his hand on a drawstring, and while my mind was elsewhere, thinking who the visitor outside might be, he pulled back on it, parting the tarp in half. Inside a heavy-duty, reinforced cell stood over a hundred zombie-looking vampires, all bald, all gray-skinned, all without visible pupils. Thin and muscular, they all looked like clones of some unfortunate prototype, barely discernable by their facial features and varying heights. They appeared maniacal, unhinged, and overly eager to be freed from their confinement, screaming unintelligibly like some satanic black metal band my classmate Jeff Bedford would have been obsessed with. I put my hand over my mouth, and studied them from head to toe. They were unlike any vampire I'd ever seen.

"What, how, and why?"

"After undergoing the Spectralis Reptilios Invincibus, I got the idea to inject some of my fluids into other beings, human and vampire alike, to see if what was flowing through me could be replicated in another. This... This is the result."

"What are they?"

"Monsters? Animals? Your guess is as good as mine. Their humanity leaves almost immediately after the injection. I played with the formula many times over, analyzing what it is in my corrupted blood and flesh that is enhanced by the Invincibus, but transferring it to another person has only made them stronger, not cooperative."

"Why keep them around, and what do you plan to do with them?"

"Good question. First, I plan on using them to demolish the uprising that is mobilizing outside my front gate, and second, I plan on improving their condition, so that they may be controllable and able to do my bidding in the near future... Speaking of that uprising, it appears we'll have to finish this conversation a little later. Your friend, Mr. Fuggerton, is approaching. Let's attend to him, shall we?"

Chapter Thirty-Three: Dawn Comes Early

"Fuggerton?" I was perplexed. *It couldn't have been twenty-four hours, could it?* There was no way. I was more shocked that there would be no element of surprise. Wasn't that the point of keeping me in the dark about the plan?

"Yes. Edsel is nearing the gate. I do hope his visit is a pleasant one." Aylash's eyes and mouth exuded a devious intention.

"As do I."

We made our way back up the dizzying amalgam of staircases and entry ways until we were in the main part of the Winged God, and through a window I could see Edsel standing outside the outer gate waiting for approval to proceed further. He was alone. I felt that was a mistake.

There were no clocks inside, but Aylash didn't need

them.

“It is just shy of 3:30am. Why does your friend knock on my door this much before dawn? Reginald knew the directive.”

“You’ll have to ask Fuggerton, I’m afraid.”

“You *should* be afraid.” Aylash’s expression morphed from curious to downright demonic. He beckoned to his glorified doorman, who pulled a lever on the wall, and the outer gate lifted up while the two inner doors swung open steadily. Edsel Antony Fuggerton walked precariously towards us, being halted abruptly before stepping into the foyer. The double doors closed behind him, and I could visibly see his body language as fear and apprehension took hold of him.

“Hello, Davis,” Edsel called out. ‘I hope you’re doing well.”

“He’s completely safe, Mr. Fuggerton. Why have you disturbed our visit prematurely. You’re not authorized to arrive for another three hours.”

“As a matter of respect and decorum, I must inform you that Mr. Duplante has ultimately rejected the terms of your---”

“How unimaginative and predictable,” Aylash interrupted. ‘I must regretfully inform you that your services on earth are no longer required.”

Before Edsel could react one way or another, a rusty, latticed, iron gate closed in front of him from above, as did one from behind. He tried to pull it up and pry the bars open, but to no avail. They were too fortified, even for a vampire. The wooden front doors opened up to four individuals with spears, and four more appeared from within the castle. All advanced toward Fuggerton.

"You won't be able to stop us this time, Aylash. The end is here, finally. Your reign is over, and possibly the chance for all of us to be human again."

"You *are* human, my pet. You are all mortal, and you will *all* die."

All eight vampires thrust their spears through the iron gates, and while Edsel was deft enough to swat three away, five deeply penetrated his flesh, causing him to roar out in anguish. They then used those spears to pin him to the gate facing Revall. Aylash produced a shimmering, curved sword, similar to one I'd had in a collection of dollar store plastic Arab figures, and started to approach Edsel slowly. I rushed to help him, but Aylash met me with a backhand that sent me sailing into a wall, my impact placing a significant crack in it. I believe I lost consciousness for several seconds, if not longer.

"Coward," Fuggerton insulted, but the comment went ignored.

"This prize, one of my most cherished, came from the Persian Empire. It killed many a soldier, including the mighty Spartan. I will spill blood with it for the first time in over a thousand years. Consider yourself blessed."

Still dazed, possibly concussed, I yelled at Fuggerton with a hoarse throat. "Why?! Why did you come here?! Why did you come alone? Edsel, I will avenge you. The Gray Bear and I will avenge---"

"Damnit, Davis!" Fuggerton growled. With an exhaustion in his throat, a grin on his face, and a gleam in his eye, he uttered one last sentence. 'I told you, you could call me Mother!"

And with that, Aylash turned the sword upside down and stabbed it through Edsel Antony Fuggerton's head. His eyes rolled up into his lids, and his body went limp. Aylash removed his prized possession and ordered the gates raised and Fuggerton's body taken to the lab to be consumed by one or more of his creations. He then turned to me, prepared to mock my grief... but I was not there.

I sped as fast as I could, on wobbly legs, to the hellish exhibit in the dungeon-like bowels of Aylash's Winged God, intent on destroying everything inside it. Highly impressed by the force and lasting effect of Aylash's backhand to my jaw, I got to the door of the laboratory, and surprisingly still had enough strength to smash through it. I grabbed one of the torches that hung on the wall, and hurled it into Revall's potions and other assorted liquids, and the reaction of their merger caused an immediate, intensely flammable fireball to emerge. It started burning everything, and as I watched, Aylash's hand grabbed me by the collar and hurled me into the pool that held the alligator. Its water was murky and tepid, and I couldn't see more than a foot in front of me, when I saw teeth, lots of them, trying to bite down on my face. I managed to intercept his jaws just in time, holding them open long enough to turn his face away from me. I then let his mouth close, and gripped it shut. One of the only things I remembered from biology class was that a gator's jaw's opening muscles are nowhere near as strong as his closing ones. He thrashed from side to side trying to get free, and I took one hand and plunged it through his underbelly, ripping at meat and organs, and whatever else I could. He broke away from me angrily, but wounded and fearful, and swam to safety. I could no longer see him; just a trail of blood as it disappeared faintly in the muck. Almost out of oxygen, I sprang out of the water and gasped aggressively for air. A leather whip wrapped around my neck with the sting of a rattlesnake's bite, and pulled me out, once again depriving my of breath.

"I will kill you now, for your insolence," Aylash growled at me, heavily disappointed. He'd extinguished the fire while I fought with the steroid gator. 'All your travels and adventures, all for not. You're just a sniveling infant in my world, and you will not be remembered."

"Don't you want to end me in front of Reginald?" I asked through choked inhalations. I was grasping at any possible stay of execution I could think of. Revall's arrogance was just large enough to grant my wish.

"Hmmm. Reginald. I wonder how defeated he would seem if he watched you die in front of him and his compatriots. But first, I'm going to let you see the magic you've failed to comprehend."

Aylash began trembling rapidly, like he was being electrocuted. Then a powerfully blinding yellow-white light, not unlike the one produced by the Luminastra Namtudari, formed within and around Revall, levitating his body some six inches above the ground. A loud, aggravating sound bounced all through the walls of Aylash's underground lair, and I could neither see nor hear comfortably. A sudden burst of energy exploded from his body, and I was thrown backward, unable to control my destination. My back and head crashed against the stone floor, and when I sat up, a different Aylash Revall was hovering in the air in front of me. He went from weak and aging to young and muscular, his wrinkles and blemishes replaced by smooth, hydrated skin. I saw no pupils, only electric, white sockets. Back in France, Reginald had once likened the result of this change as Yul Brenner in *The King and I*, but a foot taller with more muscles. I just had to trust him and whatever that was a reference to. He aimed an open palm in my direction, and it radiated with a purple and white electricity. I knew what was coming, and took shelter quickly behind a stack of smoldering file cabinets before he could incinerate me. He struck anyway, the cabinets blew apart, two of them sandwiching me against the cages full of Aylash's atrocities. Those creatures were at first frightened, but then tried to tear at my clothes and flesh through the small openings of their imprisonment. My ribs weren't broken, but I could definitely tell that they'd been damaged. I hoped in vain that my own Namtudari would show up, but before anything emanated from within me, Aylash lifted me off the floor like I was an infant, stood me up straight, and leveled me with an uppercut that closed my eyes and put me to sleep.

A half mile away, Reginald, Sylvain, and their loyal subjects were marching toward the Bridge of Skulls, and they were dead set on vindication. The plan was to have the Gray Bear leading the way, Lenora and her English vampires falling closely behind, and Le Bouffon and Ballou bringing up the rear, batting clean-up, the grotesque bear monster held in his cage until the time was right to set him loose. The cobbled together army of vampires was less than half a football field from the bridge when Aylash emerged from its doors dragging my unconscious form alongside him. My knees and boots scraped the floor beneath me. My ears awoke before I did, and I could hear Reginald as he and Aylash began a back and forth full of cliché and melodrama that you'd hear in a really bad action movie. What I remember from that conversation went something like this:

"This is your last warning," Duplante called out. 'Let Davis go, and your demise might be more... *diplomatic*."

"Do you care for the boy so much that you're... willing to make demands? Of me?"

"I won't ask again."

"You didn't *ask* the first time. It's clear that he's useless. I doubt the myth of his Namtudari is even true. He was far too easy to defeat and render unconscious. Are you sure you want to attach your chances of survival to him?"

"Let him go."

"As you wish." Aylash's devilish grin grew several inches wider. I had just started to reach for his legs, unsuccessfully, when he clinched tight to the back of my shirt, and flung me twenty feet in the air, over the bridge, and right into the heart of Reginald's advancing throng. They were adept enough to hold their arms out and soften the blow, but I landed with a velocity that knocked them backward and toppled them over like bowling pins.

"Great job, Davis. You wore him down, and now we've got him right where we want him," Thomas Richard muttered sarcastically, one of the people unable to keep themselves upright once I crashed down upon him.

"Great to see you, too, Thomas. I was saving him for you."

Reginald stared a deep figurative hole into Aylash's soul, and then roared "ATTACK!" at the top of his lungs to the rest of the group. Revall's own vampires shuffled out of the castle from several entrances, and as they came to a stop in seemingly no uniformed positions, Aylash's smile would not go away. Something about his expression told me that we were fucked.

We just didn't know how much.

Chapter Thirty-Four: Betrayal

In row after row of strategically organized individuals, The Gray Bear's vampires, led by Reginald Duplante, Sylvain Montreux, and Magnus Olruud, marched as one toward Aylash and his unfortunate supporters. The collective look of pride and confidence shone, emblazoned, on the faces of the Gray Bear, and seeing Revall in person, some for the first time, made them all the more desperate and energized to end his time *in the sun*, no pun intended. Aylash, for all the spectacle, didn't seem impressed.

"Is this it?" he scoffed aloud quizzically at Reginald. '*This* is the group you've assembled to kill me, the world's oldest man, the world's most dangerous man? The world's most *powerful*... man? I do not know whether to laugh at the pathetic futility of it all, or cry at how insulted I am.

You did not prepare adequately, and it shows."

"Maybe I have something that will impress you," Reginald replied. 'Martin!" he yelled out to the sky, waving a burning rag as a signal. Le Bouffon came to a stop with Ballou's transportation cage in tow. He folded his arms triumphantly, and went to lift the door of Ballou's cage, sure that it would send shivers of doubt through Revall's veins. Unfortunately...

"Not so fast, my friend." It was Lenora Jeffries. She held one finger in front of her, as if to say "stop" to Le Bouffon, and her left arm was held high above her. As she dropped it down to her side, as if starting an old fashioned drag race, her gathered English vampires descended upon Le Bouffon, and he was swallowed up in a torrential rain of British teeth and claws. It was obvious he would not survive. Ballou roared and smashed his head against his confinement repeatedly, but it was no use. Reginald saw the commotion and realized instantly that he and the Gray Bear had been betrayed. He was mad at himself more than he was at Lenora. *I should have known, especially after Antoinette disappeared without a trace,* was the thought that would no doubt reverberate through his mind. His army turned to run to Le Bouffon's aid, but were simultaneously confronted by Aylash's vampires as they crossed the bridge in droves, trying to rip the French invaders apart. Reginald and his group were boxed in from both sides, his abominable weapon imprisoned, and one of his most lethal assets swarmed and probably in a hundred pieces. The battle had not started well at all. I came to in time to see one of my new friends devoured by Serbian teeth, and dismembered wildly. As three of Revall's creatures reached for me, I impaled one from the groin up with my left arm and tore out the throat of a second with my right. I ripped his dangling head from his body and used it to cave in the skull of the third vampire. The once tactical landscape quickly developed into savage, fast-paced, unceremonious warfare, and I would have to be on my toes. I don't know why Revall threw me back into the crowd instead of destroying me right away as a display of power, but I was thankful for his mercy, or his mistake.

"Davis, can you make your way to the front?" Reginald bellowed to me from over the rumble of the onslaught. 'I need your assistance up here."

"What about Le Bouffon and Ballou?"

"Sylvain and I will maneuver back and see to them. Please help Magnus. He's an impressive warrior, but not a one-man army."

At the rear of the conflict, Lenora Jeffries wore a proud smirk as her English brethren started thinning the ranks of the French from behind, closing in on the middle of the battlefield. We would soon be the meat of a vampire sandwich if we didn't do something drastic to gain a proper footing. As if God himself had heard those thoughts, something drastic indeed occurred.

"Lenora!... Lenora!" I could hear someone screaming Jeffries' name from somewhere, but couldn't pinpoint an exact location. It was muffled. The mass of vampires that overtook Le Bouffon hadn't stopped attacking him, but their movements did. Eventually, the entire pile came to a halt, and a single hand, its satiny, colorful sleeve now familiar, thrust itself out of the heap of motionless gray. It was Le Bouffon's hand. He was alive. 'Lenora! I'm coming for you!" The Jester proclaimed as he lifted himself up and out of the two dozen or so English men and women he'd just thwarted from assassination. That he managed to kill them all by himself from underneath their mountainous formation was bewildering to me. 'And... I'm bringing my furry pet with me!" Le Bouffon grabbed the large ring that attached to a steel bar, and pulled it from right to left, opening a cage door. Out bolted Ballou, The Abomination, and the entire atmosphere seemed to change dramatically. Lenora and the rest of her vampires ran for the opposite end of the fray as fast as they could, with Ballou giving chase with a ravenous look on his face and noodles of saliva dripping from his jowls. Reginald smiled at The Jester and then turned around to eye Revall.

Aylash was *not* pleased.

Chapter Thirty-Five: Cataclysmic

Miraculously, the tides had started to turn in our favor. Le Bouffon's reemergence under the stacked mass of Englishmen, and his successful unleashing of Ballou, had invigorated everyone into gaining their second wind. The fight was being won on both sides, half of us beating back Lenora's treacherous contingent while the other half advanced upon Aylash's front gate, disposing of his army of mutants and minions. Magnus and I stood back to back and allowed Revall's vampires to come to us. Even in my weakened state, these tortured followers were no match for the two of us, and we rotated clockwise, hammering, stabbing, and pulling apart anything that got within arms' reach.

Further behind us, Reginald and Sylvain fought through a litany of opponents, and the experience and wisdom they possessed was clearly on display, as the efficiency of their movements counteracted all the wild, flailing abandon of Revall's army. I noticed internally that all these vampires that Aylash had turned fought as though they were trying to slaughter humans. They seemed more hungry than trained, more insane than disciplined. It was like shooting fish in a barrel for two vampires that were almost a combined 1,300 years old, even with the cracks of age visible on their frames.

A rolling cannon of French vampires mowed their way through the defenses of vampires still attempting to hold the bridge, and Thomas Richard stood out high above them all. He fought and tore and killed like a rabid honey badger, and I actually felt a little sympathetic for those who got in his path. He ripped one teenage vampire's hands off and threw them over the bridge to the valley below, before palming the boy's face and head like a basketball, and crushing his skull against the ground like an over-ripe fruit. He scalped a female vampire with a single bare hand, separating her luscious, full locks from her once beautiful head. A spinning round house kick ended up reuniting her head with that hair, but separated it from her body. His mission was clear; his path was forward. He would not be denied.

Little Tamlyn proved to be the biggest surprise of all of my new comrades, walking in roughly a straight line, dodging a vampire here, blocking another's swing there, and then... then she half-warped. *Mother fuck*! I don't know if anyone of us knew she could do that, or if *she* even knew she could do that. But sure as shit, whenever it seemed that a vampire was closing in, and her luck was up, she'd half-warp and reappear just ahead of them. She was only able to transport basically five feet from her previous spot, so she was doing it a lot. In hindsight, it would appear that the energy required to perform this task took its toll on the body. But for now...

Even the bravest and most nihilistic, blood-thirsty vampire in Revall's corps tried its best to steer clear of Ballou, who was rampaging through Lenora's English bastards and even taking random bites of members of the Gray Bear. I knew that he would eventually have to come face to face with one or another of Revall's other hybrids, wondering which it would be. In his state of rage, I comfortably felt that it didn't matter who the opponent would be. The Abomination was living up to his name, vampires and other lesser abominations be damned.

Then another lead change.

Aylash set fire to the bridge of skulls. Where or whom the fire came from, directly, I cannot say, but he effectively managed to incinerate approximately fifty of us while cutting off the path for at least a hundred more. Magnus and I detached our strategic bond, and I ran to the bridge to try and rescue as many vampires as I could. It was futile; I grabbed limbs, but that was all that was useful or left of my new friends. They'd been burnt for all their worth. The fire was not normal. It carried the force of the sun. Or multiple suns. Mine and Magnus' distraction proved to be just what Aylash needed for him to finally enter the fray. Perhaps, that was his intention. He flew down from the platform that stood over the draw bridge of the House of the Winged God, and he made his way directly to Magnus Olruud.

“I’m finally going to rip your head off.” Magnus boasted. “I’m going to take your head to Denmark, and your ears to France. Your ears will be placed on a mantle at the House of the Gray Bear, so they can hear our victorious celebration day after day, night after glorious night.” Aylash just stood and stared silently. Mockingly.

Magnus swung a massive arm down like an ax handle, but Aylash sidestepped it nonchalantly. Magnus swung another, but Revall just stopped it in mid-air, throwing it back with a head nod that suggested ‘try again, try better’. Magnus did just this, attempting to connect with a swift and powerful right cross, which Aylash directed far to the other side of Magnus’ body. Then he finally spoke.

“All this time waiting and wishing for this moment to come again, and you’re not even remotely prepared for it? Don’t you find that to be just a little pathetic?”

Now enraged, Magnus clasped his hands together, intertwining his fingers, and swung his arms wildly like a possessed mace and chain. Aylash still had no trouble avoiding damage, but he underestimated Magnus’ strength, and even the blows he blocked were causing him imbalance and maximum effort to remain upright. Magnus finally landed a swinging ‘ax-handle’ left to Revall’s cheekbone, and you could see the saliva and sweat explode off of his face against the backdrop of the fire on the bridge. You could also see an anger form on Revall’s face, embarrassed by actually giving up a shot to a ‘lesser’ creature. Magnus’ joy at his breakthrough was short-lived, as he could see Revall’s anger as well.

"You've taken a journey, and taken your best chance at ending my existence. This will have been your last chance, and the end of the line for Magnus Olruud. I tried to raise examples of a race that I saw overtaking humanity, eventually. However, I see now that I should have been more selective with who I transformed, and who I discarded. You, Magnus. You should have been dis---"

Magnus interrupted Aylash's monologue with several consecutive attempts at his ax handle swings, but each was ducked or dodged, and his stamina and strength faltered significantly. Fighting and killing of this nature had been a rare occurrence, and Magnus was exhausted. Aylash was ready. Ready to move on. As Magnus lifted both clasped hands high above his head for one final blow, Revall grabbed him by the throat with his right hand, lifted an overgrown, 340 lb. mountain of a man in the air, and drove his left arm through Magnus' chest as if it was water. Magnus gurgled and spasmed, and blackened, decaying blood started to seep from his lips. His eyes were large and terrified. Aylash penetrated his arm into Magnus' body, and jostling slightly, freed Magnus' heart from its cavity. He stared deep into Olruud's eyes, and took a savage, jagged bite out of the heart before hurling both it and its lifeless owner to the ground. Some fifty yards away, still on the other side of the bridge, Tamlyn Bernard screamed out in agony.

"Nooooo!!!" Tamlyn's voice pierced the oxygen in the sky and shot its volume across the bridge to my ears, causing me to momentarily halt my death battle with an enemy and turn in her direction. She stood there, frozen in despair, fuming in flames. Then she disappeared.

"Nooooo!!!" she called out again, except this time on our side of the bridge, our side of the conflict. She had managed to half-warp farther than perhaps she ever had before, and confronted Aylash Revall, tearing at him with hard kicks to the knees and hips, her one good arm landing quick jabs and gouges. She was faster than most of his strikes, and began half-warping to evade his others. The repetition of this quickly drained her, though, and as I tried vehemently to fight through undead obstacles on my way to her aid, Aylash observed as her tornado of movement slowed to a faint dribble. He quickly grasped her head by the hair with one hand and her left ankle with his other, and he shaped her body into an accordion, collapsing her spine as if he was trying to break the Thanksgiving turkey's wishbone. Tamlyn turned into a crumpled, disgusting mess, and my heart sank to the earth as I watched her destruction. She was not dead yet, of course, and Aylash lifted her neck to his mouth and bit down on her throat, turning to face me as he drained the final bit of blood and life from her body. I was almost to them when Revall thrust her corpse into a melee of vampires where it was kicked and shuffled and otherwise ignored by those fighting to save their own lives.

"Are you finally ready t---" Aylash thought we were on speaking terms, but I instead threw all my might into spearing him in the abdomen. We melded our bodies together, and as we landed, he rolled backward acrobatically, him now on top of me. "Do you think you can defeat me, after everything I've shown you, and everything I've shared?" He went from being nose to nose with me, to getting right up in my ear, and lowering his register to a whisper. "Are you really that foolish? The American spirit; it completely baffles my mind. I don't know if it's arrogance or ignorance. If I could bottle it and sell it, I would truly be the richest man on earth."

"I *will* defeat you. And you know it. That's why you've taken such measures. That's why you prepared so hastily, and it won't change a thing. It won't stop m---"

Before I could finish my soliloquy, Revall stood up, with his arms holding tight to the breast of my shirt, and flung me forcefully back into a group of allies who were coming to join my fight. We all fell to the ground, and when I looked up, Aylash was crouched above me, pounding down on my face with a closed fist that rivaled a Greek god's. My lower jaw dislocated, and three teeth propelled out of my lips as if shot out of a cannon at the circus. My eyes watered, and cleared just in time for him to kick me in the ribs with enough force to lift me in the air. I crashed down hard roughly twenty feet in front of the Bridge of Skulls, and as I stood warily, Aylash sent a kick to my chest that threw me backwards into the flames. He wanted to see me burn alive.

Instead, as Aylash stood there, trying to peer through the flames, Thomas Richard emerged, smoking and blistering as he ran through them, sending a flying fist to Revall's face. Aylash's head snapped back, and Thomas landed several more blows to his head and body.

“Your wave of terror is over, Aylash. I’ve survived your worst, and I will end you, for my brother. And for the Gray Bear.”

“My worst? Dear boy, you couldn’t live long enough to see me at my worst. You don’t know of the entire villages and budding civilizations that fell to me at my ‘worst’. Entire family bloodlines, generations old, ended with a snap of a finger, due to me at my *worst*. You. You are about to see me at my most ambivalent. My most apathetic. And it’s still more than you can comprehend...” Thomas swung and kicked, elbowed and wrestled, but Aylash not surprised by an abrupt ambush is a different type of combatant. He continued to speak, while surely gaining the upper hand in their fight. “... More than you can overcome. You survived me at my most trivial, just to come right back here a few years later. You are fulfilling a self-made tragedy. You received a second chance, and you failed to capitalize on it. I’ve already proven tonight that I will show you all no mercy. You are my next victim, and I will piss on your body so when you reunite with your brother in Hell, you will arrive soaking wet and wreaking of failure. You will carry the scent of my waste into the afterlife.”

Thomas jumped up into the air, and grabbed Revall’s head in his hands, but almost as quickly as he did, Aylash clawed one sharp-nailed hand into Richard’s side, squeezing onto a long dilapidated kidney. He then ripped off Thomas’ left leg at the knee with his other. Thomas let go of his grip and fell to the ground, writhing in pain. Aylash then stomped triumphantly down on Richard’s other leg, fracturing its femur into a dozen pieces. He stomped on Thomas' abdomen, and blood spurted out of Richard's mouth like a fountain. He stomped on his chest, caving in his breast plate, and puncturing his lungs. Another member of the Gray Bear lunged onto Revall's back in an attempt to both sneak attack him and assist Thomas. He was met with Revall's fingers slipping into his throat and exploring his skull and nasal cavities from the inside out for his trouble. Revall's yanked him down by his jaw, and then kicked him aside so he could die alone, an afterthought on a battlefield. Thomas attempted feebly to stand, but could only hunch over on his hands and broken legs, allowing Aylash to crush down on him with a perfectly placed elbow, causing a cavernous dent in Richard's head. Thomas lay on his back and looked up to Aylash with surrender and shame in his eyes.

"Do it, please. Rid me of this world." Richard's plea was answered, but not without one more bit of insult.

"I will speak to the demons of the next world, and make sure they agree to rape you and your twin every day for eternity, while your eyes are pried open and forced to gaze upon each other's anguish. You've met me at my most... disappointed." And with that, he stomped his powerful foot down one last time on Thomas Richard's face, and no one would have been able to identify him afterward.

Aylash paused briefly and looked down upon his handy work before scanning the scene to get a report on how everyone was faring. The Gray Bear and its allies had briefly turned the tides, before Aylash's fire switched them upside down again. Now, while the members of our team seemed to be killing more of Aylash' vampires than they of us, the loss of two of the most valiant and talented killers on Reginald's team definitely caused an atmosphere of mourning and defeat to fall over the battlefield, felt even by those who didn't know that Thomas and Magnus were dead. Aylash smiled and grew happy with himself. He refocused his attention on seeing if I had burnt to death, when he got a surprising answer.

"Revall!" I yelled, back on solid ground, out of the fire, flames and embers still flickering bright on my clothes. "You wanted confirmation of the Luminastra Namtudari? You got it." I raised my hands at my side, slowly, while the energy locked up within finally decided to free itself from my prison of a home. I aimed both hands directly at Revall, and he spread his wings and flew above the target as I shot my blue and white weaponized electricity through his followers, through members of the Gray Bear even, and onto the front gate of the Winged God. Everything and everyone stopped what they were doing for a good four seconds and watched as I sent another wave of energy into the air, trying to fry Aylash Revall in the sky. He was clearly more advanced with his wings than anyone might have guessed, and he managed to evade the chasing electric death. I was visibly compromised by the side effects caused by using the Namtudari, and I dropped to one knee, trying to catch my breath as rapidly as I could. I felt eight sets of arms grab onto me, all attempting to rip my life from my body, and the Luminastra welled up inside me again, this time ejecting itself through whatever opening or pore it could, and the eight souls gripping onto me were now charred, frozen ash.

Reginald and Sylvain saw me scorch our opponents, and once again they were renewed in their purpose; in their drive.

"It's about time you unleashed yourself, McCarty." Reginald yelled out to me. "Better late than never, I suppose."

"I suppose. Now let's *kill* these motherfuckers."

I could feel a deep manifesting ball of electricity forming in my gut, and it rose through my veins and sat crackling with intensity on the palms of my hands. The whole of Aylash's minions just stared, unmoving, watching the process. Then, before they realized it, it was too late for them to escape its purpose. I aimed it, positioning my hands in front of me, and waved them in a spraying motion as the Luminastra Namtudari crippled and destroyed them all in an instant. What might have been hundreds were reduced to dozens, and somewhere above them all, Aylash Revall was flying, escaping, watching it all... like a coward.

Meanwhile, still trapped on the other side of the now weakening fire on the bridge, Le Bouffon, Ballou, and many of their friends continued battling the English betrayers who sought to align themselves with Aylash. They were clearly winning, but the balance was ever so fragile. I guess I hadn't expected Lenora Jeffries to be much of a fighter, but fight she could. She killed everyone in her path until an inevitable confrontation with the

Jester beckoned them ever closer to each other.

"How could you have done this to us? Couldn't you have simply stayed in England and left us to our devices, even our own demise, if that was to be our fate? Why go through the mechanism of such an elaborate deception?"

"Two reasons: one, I had to make sure that the surprise was such that it was too late to turn back; that it ruined your chances and swung things in one direction. Two, I despise you. I find the Gray Bear responsible for my never receiving a House in England. I wholeheartedly believe that Reginald's opposition to the idea was the biggest reason for its refusal. Why were we denied a House? We're bloody England for Christ's sake! Was France's sense of importance so delicate, so selfish, that the thought of an English House might spell a threat to the Gray Bear's membership? To its existence?"

"Nonsense!" Le Bouffon spit out of his mouth with wrath and contempt. "You didn't receive a House because you were undeserving; not honorable. You ARE not honorable. You've exemplified that tonight, this the last night of your life."

"I wouldn't bet on it, monsieur."

The two were now less than ten feet away from each other, and closing in. They stopped while the world around them kept moving in a monsoon toward the steps of the Winged God. Ballou was far ahead, carving a path of destruction, leaving nothing but fear and death in his wake. It was time for Lenora and Le Bouffon to face off and hold each other accountable for the decisions and shortcomings hundreds of years in the making.

Le Bouffon's strategy was to go low to match Lenora's diminutive frame, while hers was to go airborne, able to spring herself high in the air like a jack in the box. Michael Jordan and even Vince Carter would be envious. She hoped to land down hard on the Jester, but her airtime allowed for him to recalculate, and he speared her with a shoulder tackle mid-landing. No slouch at all, she took a breath and darted stiff finger jabs into his face and mask. As they landed, she grabbed his ingrained mask with both hands and tried to rip it off of the Jester's face. He yelled in pain, and fish-hooked Lenora's mouth with his thumbs, ripping the sides of her lips wide open. He then side swiped her hands off of his mask, and held them both down to one side while he elbowed and punched her head and face with his left.

"Owww, you fucking twat!" Lenora yelled at Le Bouffon.

"Such a lady," The Jester replied sarcastically. "You've been a thorn in this world for too long, and if we, the Gray Bear, die tonight, you can be honored to have been partly responsible. But now it is your time to face the reaper. It will be neither majestic nor merciful."

Le Bouffon brought down a hammer fist onto Lenora's face, caving in her nose and top teeth. As she gasped for air and tried to spit those teeth out of her throat, he lifted her and threw her by the back of the neck, some thirty or so yards in the air, just above Ballou's stride. The Abomination pulled her out of her flight, as if he and The

Jester planned a game of fetch, and chomped down heartily. She was gone in four bites. Forever disappeared, both literally and figuratively, into the belly of the beast.

Le Bouffon gazed proudly as Ballou charged over the Bridge of Skulls ready to face his maker. Unfortunately, his maker had landed right behind Le Bouffon, everyone else caught up in the battle nearer and nearer to the Winged God's doors.

"So it comes to this, eh, Jester?" Le Bouffon turned around dramatically, disillusioned by how off guard he was caught, but also secretly admiring Aylash Revall's approach.

"No one will ever underestimate how clever you are, Aylash. You've managed to welcome your truest rival to your home court, bring all of us here, determined to destroy you, and you've separated us into smaller and smaller sections you could pick off. You were able to have our fellow vampires deceive and betray us. And we walked right into it, heads and hearts held high, like idiots."

"That's a very good summation, my old friend. But not entir---"

"I'm not your friend, you twisted, megalomaniacal tyrant!"

"Call it what you will. I was just saying that your summation was not entirely accurate. You failed to identify the most egregious violation of trust in all of the Gray Bear. Margerie." Le Bouffon looked confused, not knowing right away who or what Aylash Revall was referring to. 'Margerie Duplante. She was the one who provided me with all of the information of your doings, your meetings, your carrying on after our civil war. She was a great help in knowing everything the Gray Bear was planning. She also let me know that Davis McCarty had come to visit, and what he possessed inside those veins of his."

Le Bouffon looked as though he'd seen Jesus Christ come down from heaven. The weight of a stone tugged his body downward, almost to his knees, and even though he wanted to deny the words he'd just heard, a pure, solid truth enlightened his brain. His only question was...

"Why?"

"Because even though she has been a vampire for over three hundred years, and been a loyal member of the Gray Bear ever since she became one, there was one thing she loved more than any of you, one thing she couldn't let go of. I used that to distort her. To corrupt her. She felt as if she had no choice, and to be fair, she didn't."

"Valentis," The Jester whispered, solemnly.

"That's right, my shattered disciple. Her son. Valentis."

"How?"

"I surprised her one night while she was on a 'stroll'. I just simply told her that I would make it my utmost important mission to seek out Valentis and apprehend him. Then I would torture him brutally for a minimum of one hundred years, and for up to a thousand. If she had only fed exclusively at the Gray Bear, I might have not reached her. I might have chosen someone else. Her thrill of the hunt was her weakness. You'd be surprised how quickly loyalty fades when a mother has to consider the well-being of her only child."

"How long?"

"I just told you; up to a thousand years."

"No. How long has Margerie been supplying you information?"

"Oh, yes. Since the Gray Bear reformed after the war, right before I made my way to America. When it became clear that you wouldn't be fading away to dust, I sought to have some semblance of control over your House's innerworkings, in case something like this ever happened. It was relatively quiet, with no correspondence from Margerie, until the Texan arrived in Paris."

"I've heard enough. I'm ready to kill you, now."

Aylash Revall threw his head back in laughter, both amused with, and inspired by, Le Bouffon's confidence.

"Come kill me, then. Since you're ready."

Le Bouffon started to run right at Aylash, but then stopped abruptly after seeing his defensive posture. He then walked sideways to the right, with a hop in his step, before zig zagging in front of Revall. He stopped abruptly again, and Revall started to jitter and bob up and down on his heels, a little confused and frustrated by Le Bouffon's abnormal strategy. The Jester then started taking long, sweeping steps in a circular motion, and it appeared he was performing some forgotten Victorian waltz.

"What is this mating ritual? Come and end me, little clown."

"Patience, my maker. I'll be there shortly. Breathe in the air one last time." But just as Le Bouffon ended that sentence, he sprinted directly for Aylash, tackling him to the ground. With one of Revall's arms pinned underneath him, Le Bouffon over-hooked the other, and then sent forearm after forearm into Revall's face. Instantly bloodied and bruised, Aylash was caught in a precarious disadvantage, when Le Bouffon... let go of him. He stood up and let Aylash start to rise to his feet, when he attacked him again, barreling over him, leaving Revall on his stomach. Once again chicken-winging an arm, Le Bouffon used his free arm to club Revall in the face with swinging left hooks, Aylash trying to shield his left side from the punishing blows. Even as the most powerful being on earth, against another capable, impressively strong vampire, he was still vulnerable to attack. His body knew this, and reacted in kind. Still on his belly, a rumbling energy started emitting from underneath him, and he began to hover a few inches over the ground. Le Bouffon could feel and hear the energy spreading out around them, knew what doom was impending, and he rose to his feet in an attempt to evacuate the immediate area. However, with one arm, Aylash Revall grabbed onto The Jester's wrist, and spun around on his back to face him. Le

Bouffon could not break free of his vice-like grip.

"Alas, I admit how unfair it is to combat such a formidable and unique weapon. But that's how the cards are dealt, is it not?" Le Bouffon knelt on Aylash's chest, and attempted to beat him to death before he could manifest his deadly creation out of his body, but the energy building within Revall caused The Jester's knee to burn and wobble, and forced his free hand to remain suspended feet above Aylash. The blue and white electricity was now frighteningly visible in Revall's eyes and mouth, and it began to hone itself into a ball as Le Bouffon struggled unsuccessfully to free himself of Aylash's grasp.

"You belong in hell, Revall! Do you hear me, you son of a bitch?! You belong in---"

The ball forming within Revall became a beam of all-powerful, all-consuming electric power, and it shot through Le Bouffon's chest, infiltrating his body upward and downward. With a basketball sized hole in his torso, Le Bouffon was dead before his knees hit the ground, but the energy that crept within him forced itself outward, and his head and upper body exploded, expelling Jester here and there all over the grounds of the Crystal Mountain. Aylash Revall laid on his back for another five seconds, looking up at the night sky as he wiped bits of Martin Dupuis off of his chest and cheeks. He then turned his face toward his fortress to view the ongoing action taking place. The Abomination had marched over the Bridge of Skulls and was now rampaging all over anyone and everyone it could get its paws or jaws on.

“Time to eradicate my overgrown, woolly creature from the Earth” Revall whispered to himself. He stood up and then unfurled his wings again, taking to the sky. As Ballou took two of Aylash’s men into his mouth and ground them into smaller pieces simultaneously, Revall landed some thirty feet behind him, just ahead of the bridge. Ballou immediately recalled the scent and site of his former owner, turned, and galloped on all fours toward the world’s first vampire. Revall started to harness the Luminastra building deep within him, but he underestimated Ballou’s speed. He focused it at The Abomination just in time to blast the creature’s shoulder, causing a cavernous gash, but not deadly enough to obliterate it. Ballou roared out in pain, and tumbled sideways three times, slipping off the bridge and falling into the pristine water below.

Having used the Luminastra Namtudari three times in quick succession caused Aylash to feel an exhaustion he hadn’t felt in hundreds, maybe thousands, of years. Even the transformative benefits of his recent Spectralis Invincibus, making him anew going into battle, took their own toll on his stamina and strength. He, like everyone else on the battlefield, hadn’t drank any blood in some time. This fact was visible on everyone, and the fighting and vigor slowed considerably. What was clear, though, is that The House of the Gray Bear and I were winning. We’d managed to somehow outlast the horde of vampires Aylash had set free upon us, and vanquished the surprise attack of Lenora Jeffries and her bastard band of traitors. I didn’t know at this point if Le Bouffon or Ballou were alive or dead, but I knew that we couldn’t lose now. We were too close. Too confident. One of Reginald's most physically imposing allies strode to the large double doors of the Winged God, and gracefully pulled them apart with his sculpted bulging muscles.

Then he was eaten alive. Aylash's experiments, the ones he said were too volatile to risk setting free, came surging out of the House of the Winged God, and they were insatiable. Unstoppable. Anyone who could retreat did so rapidly, and as I myself pulled back and ran in the opposite direction, I caught Aylash staring at me.

He was smiling.

Chapter Thirty-Six: Hope Out of Ashes

The Soulless, as Revall christened them, were tearing my counterparts limb from limb. Gang tackling and outnumbering French vampires four to one, they were decapitating, dismembering, and downright slaughtering our entourage in short order. Drempt up in Aylash Revall's warped brain, and drawn up in his laboratory, this truly evil 'final evolution of the vampire' was on full display. I couldn't help but think back to Warren Winston, and his delusional idea that the vampire would take over the earth and enslave humanity. If he had these sons' a bitches, he might have been right. Vampires frightened humans to death, and they were utterly scared shitless of these unbridled beast lunatics. I knew I would have to unleash the Luminastra to counterpunch against this heavyweight opponent, and do so quickly. I also knew Aylash would try to stop me, so I needed Reginald and others to distract him.

"Reginald, I need---"

"Way ahead of you, my Texan friend. Everybody, focus your attack on Revall. Do not let him get to Davis."

But Revall took to the sky, rejuvenated just enough that their efforts were useless. None of them had wings or superpowers flowing through their bodies. He, however, did. Gliding through the air with superb control, he fed the growing electricity within him and forced it on the crowd below, scorching huge swaths of land, property, and persons instantaneously. I focused my energy on doing the same to his soulless reinforcements. The energy began in my feet, and seized my calves, thighs, and hamstrings before swirling like a hurricane's eye in my gut. As it grew and grew, I threw my head backward and arms outward at my side, and let it wash over me in wave after consecutive wave. Revall's ravenous, mindless, killing machines were within fifteen feet of me when I stared them down and struck them down with the blue/white energy freeing itself from my hands. My bones stretched dangerously far, almost burning through my ligaments and coming unhinged, as I'd never expelled so much of this mysterious gift in one session. The bald, haunted house freak show that were the Soulless screamed with an ear torturing howl as they were annihilated and turned to burnt, frozen, ash. This fate didn't stop the ones that escaped it from advancing forward, and they also met their abrupt end. As

I prepared to unleash the Namtudari one more time, hopefully ridding the world of the Soulless before they ever had to endure them, I could feel the wind of Aylash Revall's wings as they drew near, and I turned just in time to face his blast of energy with my own, blocking his attempt to destroy me with my back turned.

He landed gracefully and in full sprint toward me when Reginald Duplante tackled him from the side, perfectly telegraphing Revall's descent. They both rose to their feet promptly, and began trading unrestrained blows, neither man gaining a clean punch. Sylvain Montreux entered the confrontation and Aylash dealt with the two of them while I and the other members of the Gray Bear fought off the remaining members of the Soulless, tossing their dead bodies into the river. All combatants then sort of stopped and watched the battle between the three principals ensue. We hadn't noticed that the few remaining humans inside the House of the Winged God had released everyone and everything from their enclosures. More importantly, we hadn't noticed Revall's half rhino/half hippo lumbering out of the main floor of the fortress and onto the yard outside. Just as it caught us all by surprise, forklifting an unsuspecting vampire some sixty feet in the air, I heard the mighty slap of a paw on the ground from near the bridge, and saw the fire-red eyes of The Abomination as he rose from the depths, not dead by a long shot. Everyone scattered in different directions, making sure to evade the rhino/hippo while Aylash continued to hold his own against Duplante and Montreux. Ballou made his way to solid ground on all fours, and stared at me, the only figure in between him and the other menacing colossus. Somehow sensing my thoughts, as well as assessing the situation in front of him, he growled and moved his head to the right. I swear he was directing me in his own language to get out of the way. It was the only semblance of complex thought I'd ever seen him project. I did as commanded right as Aylash's creature made a mad dash for Ballou. He moved to the side, and the rhinopotamus put on the brakes rather impressively to keep himself from sailing into the water below. Ballou attacked his right shoulder, and biting down hard on the hybrid creature's tough hide. He gouged deep lacerations on that hide before his enemy countered with a horn to Ballou's neck, causing him to jump back, bleeding and clearly wounded. The beast then jumped into a head butt that landed squarely between The Abomination's eyes, watering them, and causing an instant migraine. Ballou was enraged, and struck quickly, placing his entire mouth around the creature's face, biting through his extended jaw and snout. The rhinopotamus groaned an anguished whale's call, and blood poured from his open gash of a profile. Ballou reared back on his hindlegs and crashed down hard on the hybrid's back, digging in both paws until his front legs were deep in the monster's flesh. He pushed down and down until the rhino fell to his belly, and then he bulldozed him off the cliff and into the depths below. Ballou watched the creature sail lazily down the river out of sight, and then he laid down on his side and caught his breath, wounded but triumphant.

Against better judgement, I placed a comforting hand on the bear before turning my attention once more to

Aylash's battle with Reginald and Sylvain. How he managed to keep both men from ending him was astounding and masterful. I think if either of us had to face him one on one, we would have been done for, and secretly, we all knew that. There was just no comparing our skills with 4,500 years of life and experience, along with the supernatural side show tricks only he possessed. Still, Revall did appear to be getting winded, and I wondered when he might start to light up again with the Luminastra. This time, I was ready to intercept him with my own. In that moment of comfort, I'd failed to realize that literally everyone else had perished. All of Aylash's vampires, all of his demented creations, all of the Gray Bear, and the English. They were all gone. The only ones that remained were Revall, Sylvain, Reginald, Ballou, and me. Sympathetic to the horrible toll on vampire kind and specifically to my new associates, the odds of four vs one made me feel pretty damn confident.

And then Aylash killed Sylvain.

Sylvain and Reginald were weaving in and out of Aylash's reach, and alternating right and left strikes, when Revall studder stepped, causing Sylvain to throw a missing punch. Revall caught his left shoulder and spun him around to face Reginald. He then grabbed him by both shoulders and ripped his arms off, and followed that up by rabbit punching him, middle knuckle first, right to the back of the head, propelling him forcefully into Duplante's waiting arms. The look of shock on Montreux's face will never leave my memory, and he hurriedly repeated "I'm sorry" multiple times to Reginald as he laid him gently down on the ground. There was no time to console him as Revall immediately resumed his attack on Reginald, I rushed in and drug him by the legs to safety.

“Sylvain,” I assured him. ‘You’re going to be OK. I’ll help Reginald, and we’ll defeat Revall and get you back to Nis so they can work on you.” He just kept repeating “I’m sorry.” That’s when I noticed the pool of blood emerging from below his head. I carefully lifted it up off the ground and surveyed the source. The back of his head was as soft as pudding, and a dent had given way like a weakened dam to internal bleeding. Aylash was skilled beyond words at killing, and had done Sylvain in with as much insult as injury. Sylvain’s eyes were wide open, and it was as if he couldn’t stop saying “I’m sorry.” Then, he stopped talking or moving, altogether. I closed his lids, and crossed his arms over his chest. “I’m sorry. You seemed like you’d be a good captain of the Gray Bear one day,” were my last words to him.

The battle between Aylash and Reginald was now clearly in Revall’s favor, and I sought to outnumber him yet again, when Duplante stopped me in my tracks.

“No, Davis! This is my fight until I can no longer fight it. I need to defeat him alone.”

“Ridiculous,” Aylash laughed. ‘You’re assuring yourself a painful and unnecessary death.”

“Ever so confident. It will eventually be your undoing.”

Just then, Ballou rose from his rest, and began to charge at Revall. Reginald tried to stop him, but there's no reasoning with a wild beast looking to eat his maker. Revall sidestepped the bear's charge like a skilled matador, and threw a spinning back fist to Reginald's jaw, causing him to spin like a figure skater in the air, knocking him utterly silly. Reginald landed on his knees, and Aylash grabbed him by the head with both hands. He was attempting to crush his head, and Reginald yelped out in pain until Ballou sunk his teeth down on Aylash's right arm, yanking him from his clasp. Somehow, Aylash's arm wasn't completely severed, and Ballou tossed him backward approximately twenty feet. As Ballou spun around and began a full-on bull rampage, Revall's Luminastra Namtudari revealed itself again. I prayed for The Abomination to make it to Aylash's head before the process was complete, but my prayer fell on deaf ears. Even with a severely damaged appendage, Revall aimed both hands at Ballou and a white hot, almost crystalizing energy shot forth, hitting the bear mid-stride, splitting him open, and freezing his right side. As the bear stumbled forward horrifically, Aylash produced the same sword he'd used to execute Fuggerton, seemingly from out of nowhere, and swung it at Ballou's frozen torso. A million cracks formed and opened themselves up into the atmosphere, and The Abomination roared and groaned and wailed in absolute torment. Still alive, he tried to use his left hind leg to propel himself at Aylash, and his left front paw to swipe at him fruitlessly. Revall straddled him from the back and with the Luminastra engorging his muscles and equipping him with a temporary invincibility,

Aylash Revall gripped Ballou's face and ripped his head from his body.

Reginald Duplante sat with his head in his hands and wept for The Abomination, before rising unsteadily to his feet. He was prepared to kill or die, knowing that either was a waste of time. His life, his purpose, his leadership had led to nothing but bloodshed and massacre.

"Was it worth it?" Revall asked Duplante.

"Coming here? Killing you? *Not* killing you? At this precise moment, I'm not sure. I do know that sometimes the necessity of an action dictates its worth, no matter the outcome. The attempt, whether or not I, or perhaps Davis, succeed, was necessary."

"Fair enough. Let us finish this dance."

I could see Reginald's eyes as they looked at the remains of his furry symbol of Versailles and Paris' vampire kingdom, and I could tell that the spark of vengeance and justice had left them. He'd asked me to not intervene on his behalf against Revall, which made me wonder why I'd even come. Why they promoted me as the lynch pin to their victory. This late in the effort, though, I believe it was about Reginald's honor; his taking the Gray Bear on his shoulders one last time. I understood, even if I'd never been in a position where I could relate. Still, his heart had broken, and I felt he was not much longer for this earth.

"I wish you'd never been successful in your miserable experiments. I wish you'd been beheaded as a heretic and a lunatic early on in your ascension. The world would have truly been a better place. I've been capturing and murdering for over seven hundred years... because of you. Thousands of humans became something degraded... malevolent... because of you. You need to atone. You need the judgement of righteousness to befall you permanently."

"Then may you swing the axe, little man."

Reginald Duplante let the full breath of Aylash's insulting tone send shudders in the cilia of his ears, and then he leapt. He landed before Revall with punches, kicks, holds, scratches. He fought for all he was worth. Aylash blocked successfully, but Reginald's pace and delivery kept Revall on the defensive. A small window, though, where both of Reginald's hands were down, was all the space Aylash needed. He darted two fingers at Reginald's eyes, piercing them with his nails. Duplante, blinded and enthralled by searing pain, could not see Revall puncture his flesh just under the chin, grab his mandible with one hand and pound his face with successive, intensely powerful close fists. Reginald reeled, and began to drop to his knees, when Revall forced his head downward, double underhooked his arms, and lifted him in the air, head downward and legs straight up. In professional wrestling, this move would have appeared completely devastating, and been a grappler's signature finishing maneuver. In reality, it would not have injured the opponent. In a real life battle to the death, between vampires no less, it would be fatal. Revall took all his might and dropped all his weight to the ground, driving Reginald Duplante headfirst onto the unforgiving stiff terrain. Reginald's skull fractured exponentially, and his brain squished like gelatin just as the vertebrae in his neck imploded, introducing his cervical spine to his thoracic rather callously. Reginald Duplante died as soon as his head hit the earth. Aylash was nothing if not exact when killing someone once and for all. I knew he wouldn't make the same mistake with me that he had earlier in the evening. It was now up to me to kill Aylash Revall.

Anything short of that would most likely result in the deaths of millions more, Annie Moore and the small village once known as Selo Semce first.

Fuck that.

Chapter Thirty-Seven: The Final Conflict

An eerie, echoed silence. It fell over The House of the Winged God and the Crystal Mountain; over the river below and the lush, green forest of Suva Planina. My brain, however, was flooded with sound. Disturbing, disruptive, dissonant sound. The white noise on an old fashioned television from the 20th century: that's what the inside of my thoughts looked like. The darkness of the sky allowed a few new hues to meld into it, and that was my cue that dawn would arrive within the hour, if not sooner. My lungs swelled and the tension within me would not reduce their activity. I stood and observed Aylash, as he surveyed the demented, burning graveyard his property had now transformed into. I could tell that his mind had shifted into overdrive, infiltrated by thoughts and strategies I couldn't begin to comprehend. It felt like he'd forgotten I was even there, and a small bit of me felt a pain of sadness and insignificance. My body's memory of what it felt like in middle school.

“Are you ready to join your friends, now, Mr. McCarty?” Aylash disrupted the quiet contemplation.

I should be so lucky.

“You and I both know that I might not be disposed of as easily. No disrespect to the thousands of years of combined age the Gray Bear had on me.”

“Oh, I’m sure they feel none. I’m sure they don’t feel anything.” I could sense the intention in Revall’s voice. He was hoping to anger me. I wouldn’t take the bait.

“I almost killed you already. Your wings saved you from my Namtudari.”

“Yes, and I could have killed you a thousand different ways inside my castle. Yet, I let you live, naïve in my wish for a pupil, and manipulated by own narcissism.”

“At least give me some credit for planting that seed.”

“Acknowledged. Now, if you please, it’s time to die.”

Before I could get out a witty comeback for that, Aylash flew, not leapt, but flew into my chest with two fists harpooning me in the heart. My sternum collapsed like paper dunked in water. My feet departed solid ground, and I landed on the back of my head and neck, grasping hysterically for air. I sat up on my ass just in time to get kneed square in the face. The impact jolted me back to the ground like I was some reverse jack in the box. My nose, for at least the third time since I became a vampire, was broken. This time, though, the connection was more effective. The healing period, if I even survived this one-sided affair, would take much longer. I lay on my back staring at the stars, noticing how beautiful the sky looked, when Revall grabbed me by both feet and flew up in the air with me dangling beneath him. He lingered over the Bridge of Skulls and then let go. I managed to land on my back, on a pile of charred and slaughtered vampires. If he had dropped me from a higher altitude, I wouldn't have survived, vampire or not. However, he intentionally let me fall from a height that would only add to my suffering. I stumbled to my feet, groggy, and almost immobile. My back muscles had seized up. I could only laugh as I watched Aylash descend on me, feet first, scoring a direct hit to my chin with his left heel. I corkscrewed onto the bridge, colliding with the mangled flesh of my allies and enemies when I saw her. Staring at me as if she was still alive was the body of Tamlyn Bernard. We were face to face, within an arm's length. She had the same emotionless expression she carried through her days.

In hindsight, I'm glad I saw her. The guilt, shame, and rage it instilled in my insides provided the reaction I needed to snap me out of getting my ass kicked. More specifically, it built up the well of electricity and mist inside my gut that I would attempt to force into Aylash Revall's eyeballs. I spang up to my feet, which was surprising to the both of us, and I stood there pulsing with energy. Aylash tried to prevent my pending attack, throwing a punch to my mouth, but I grabbed his fist and held it tight. My electricity was starting to burn Revall's close fist when he kicked me straight in chest, further damaging my already destructed pectorals, and sending me pointing upward. The Luminastra Namtudari shot out of me, and straight up into the sky, singeing the clouds and force-feeding a soaking precipitation out of them. Aylash vaulted into the air, intending to come down on my face, but I rolled to my side, swept his leg with mine, and shot a thunderbolt of electricity along Revall's body that would have made Zeus proud. His thigh, hip, and left side were fried to a crisp, but he was still able to come down with a swinging hammer of a fist directly onto my forehead. My eyes watered and crossed for several seconds, and when I sat up, I noticed that his wounds weren't exactly there anymore. He was *healing* somehow! I dodged and ducked four punches in a row, but the perplexed look on my face must have amused him. He sought to pause the confrontation.

"You're wondering what has happened to the burn of the Luminastra."

"I am." There was no point in denying it.

"The added benefit of attaining the Spectralis Reptilios Invincibus is that it continues to regenerate my body for hours after I summon it. So anything you can manage to defile on me, save for complete annihilation, will heal."

My heart sank, my chest drooped, and Aylash's head roared back, bellowing a mighty laugh. Dave Chappelle couldn't have made him cackle harder. He was rather satisfied with himself. I thought I could startle him with a lightning right hook, but he blocked it easily. He blocked the next eight punches, then started peppering me with lefts and rights of his own. Jabs, crosses, uppercuts, etc. He was literally beating me to death. I refused to go down, though, so when he was tired of his handywork, he held me by the jaw, pushed my head back, and bicycle kicked me in the face. The impact caused me to backflip, my body carrying me several yards, and I came to an unflattering landing, face down and motionless. I could hear Aylash as he trampled over bones and skin on his way to finish me off for good. A miniature lifetime of fucking up and amounting to nothing filled my thoughts. Annie's face took over, then every single memory I'd ever had of her whizzed by my mind's eye, bullet train style. The thoughts of her either finding me dead on this battlefield or being raped and drained by Revall in the village plunged into me like a stainless steel icepick. *I failed you,* I thought to myself over and over as Revall's steps grew ever closer. *I failed you. I... I... won't... fail you. I can't fail you.*

"I won't fail her, Aylash," I mumbled inaudibly as he grabbed a handful of my hair and began to lift me up by it.

"What? What are you trying to say, you pathetic little man?"

"I *SAID*, I won't fail her, Aylash."

"Oh my child. My amazing boy. Your talent for delusion is truly amazing. Even now, even as you cling to life, you have this inspiring, almost annoying optimism. You haven't even given attention to your requirement for blood. Maybe the instinct to feed is rendered impotent when one is near death. I would only venture to guess, as I haven't been that close in some time. I hope you get to see your Heaven. You'll reunite with quite the large gr---"

Something sparked in my body, and it shocked Revall's hand. He immediately let go of my hair. I fell forward, trying to push myself up. Not only was I too weak to do so, but something had taken control of my body, not allowing any voluntary movement. I began sweating, and a virtually unbearable heat was building up within me. This wasn't the Luminastra Namtudari. This was something altogether different, and it was *painful.* I could barely lift my head enough to catch two details: the dawn emerging from behind the mountain, and Aylash Revall stepping backwards frantically. His face belied an angry, but astounded expression, and it made me wish I could read minds. My body shook violently, and my belly felt as if I was giving birth. White light poured from my mouth, eyes, and everywhere else, and I could smell the stench of burning flesh – my burning flesh – as whatever this was, cooked me from the inside out. My body levitated on its own until I was standing upright, and then my eyes opened. A rumbling murmur from deep in my lungs transitioned into an armor piercing steam shriek, and that shriek, along with the power and brightness of beautiful daylight, were about to exit me. They only had one place to go.

Aylash now felt, for the first time, that *he* was completely fucked.

Chapter Thirty-Eight: Catharsis

A seismic feeling, earth-shattering blast two hundred feet wide of white, all-powerful light and heat shot out of me, across the battlefield, into, and out through Aylash Revall. His insides opened up to the world, and the magic in his flesh tried to bind his two halves together as they had no doubt done many times over. Only this time, his endings were burnt and frayed, and non-responsive to his body's plea. A wounded master, perplexed and rattled, was now slowly coming to grips with his fate. For several seconds, his lips only managed gasps and grunts, until finally able to put together words so subtly.

"Do you see that?" he asked as he pointed to the horizon.

"See what?"

"The clouds. Instead of clouds I see only faces. The

faces of every person I devoured over the course of five millennia of existence. Of terror. They're sinewy, skeletal demons, angry and joyous in anticipation of their freedom. Of my ultimate demise."

"I don't see any of that. It's possible that the lack of blood, or your body going into shock, has caused you to hallucinate. I just see the tease of sunrise. The warning that I will soon have to seek shelter, or suffer. Suffering that you spawned."

Aylash could only laugh as he dropped to one knee, and began to tick tock his final moments on earth.

"You still don't understand. How blissfully oblivious you are. If I only had five thousand more years to teach you. To take you under my wing and mold the one who would take my place on the throne of the Winged God."

"Understand what? And you might want to make it quick if you wanted to squeak out one last bit of wisdom."

"The final transformation, you pathetic, miserable simpleton. The Palingenesia Solaris, the rebirth of the sun. You're now able to harness and draw strength from the sunrise and the sunset. You can walk in the day again. You can shatter mountains with your unleashed energy. You can wind soar without the wind. You can make the strongest armies, the strongest nations, bow at your feet. You are the strongest creature, living, dead, or undead, the world has ever known. I attempted many times in many ways to attain it. I came close, but as with all of my experiments, I became something else each time. Through some sort of blood heredity, or some cruel divine destiny, you – of all people – are the one. The---"

Revall began to cough and gasp for air, and he fell to the ground, laying on his right side. He looked absolutely ghastly, ripped open and cauterized by my new party trick. I just stopped and watched, half in awe at the privilege of ending the world's oldest single "human" organism, and watching it die. I hadn't yet begun to process exactly what he was proclaiming me to be.

"I hope that you're not expecting me to be grateful. I'm not. I'm living with a curse. And every level and every boss I beat in this twisted, crazy ass video game of a miniverse you created just makes me more unable to get back to a semblance of peace and normalcy. I was not created for this. This supreme underworld mindfuck... No. Fuck this. Fuck this, and fuck you! I'm done with you and this evil bullshit work of an insane demon vampire bitch."

My insides awoke with fire and my eyes glowed bright white. The mechanism with which to generate this Solaris was apparently anger, and I had gotten more incensed by the second. My feet rose off the ground as if propelled by the roaring thrusters on a NASA shuttle. My joints cracked and spit as my muscles grew larger and tighter. Those balls of pure energy once again emerged in my palms, and I aimed them right at Aylash Revall's face.

"Promise me you will continue my---" he croaked, and then...

Then I unshackled that energy from my body and commanded it to tear Aylash Revall apart. The majority of his body incinerated or evaporated instantly, and the small remains of his flesh flitted away, similar to feathers intertwined with butterflies, into the waking dawn. Tears of triumph and hopelessness streamed out of my eyes, and I was overcome by exhaustion. My body screamed out from within, and my mouth groaned in reply. I was drained. Utterly, completely drained. But the sun.

What of the sun, Aylash's words, and what it would normally do to my epidermis? I braced myself as bravely as I could and waited for the cruel, double-sided mirror of my limitations to reveal its complete self to me. As the rays clashed against my hands and arms, then my chest, nothing. At first. Then an uncomfortable radiance emitted along the edge of my skin, and I hypothesized that I'd made a mammoth error by remaining in the open. Normally, I would be able to run to shade. But I had no strength left. I'd be able to stumble warily at best, and crawl at worst. Either action would not be enough to escape the day. Was I to burn to death slowly, as the ashes of Aylash Revall filled my mouth with their taunting vengeance?

No. I didn't start to seize with the same unbearable pain I'd experienced before, sprawled out before my omnipotent nemesis. I was... stable, if still uncomfortable. *Was Aylash correct? Was I now... Sun Man?* The name seemed ludicrously stupid almost as immediately as I thought it, but the sentiment was authentic. I was clearly different now, and able to at least withstand the effects of the sun. Empowered with Vitamin D times one hundred billion. Just enough to keep me alive. But how would I get back down the mountain and to my beloved?

A savior emerged. I should have known.

Isabel and Igor rode up in a horse-drawn wagon. I couldn't believe it. It was as if I was on the set of some old western Mona would watch when I was a kid.

"The horses do not go out in the nighttime. They know the risk" Igor explained. "We would have been here sooner, otherwise. How come you are not dead?"

"That's a damn good question, Igor. I wish I had an answer that wouldn't make you think I was a complete lunatic. Do you think you would be able to help me into the wagon?"

"Of course."

He and Isabel both helped me to my feet, and gingerly placed me in the back of the covered wagon. The only thought that went through my head, and repeatedly, was *Gunsmoke. This reminds me of Gunsmoke*. We crossed the Bridge of Skulls, carefully trampling over the carcasses of two godforsaken armies, and as we were about to break through the imposing visage of the Crystal Mountain and cross the threshold of the forest, I had Igor stop. I delicately stepped out of the wagon, and faced the bridge, intending to muster one last bit of power to do my sun thing and destroy the House of the Winged God and the final piece of unified vampire bullshit tarnishing this earth, when Isabel placed her hand on my shoulder, and spoke in the most gentle voice imaginable.

"Whatever you're about to do, you don't have the energy for. It will kill you, and you will never see your Annabella again. And I need to remind you, this is our home. These mountains, this forest, even that horrid palace of the dead, it is our home. Please do not demolish the nature along with the evil. We can make sure the Winged God rots away and crumbles into memory. It is not your job."

I stared at her tender eyes, tracing the lines along her mouth, jaw bones, forehead, and corners of her eyes. I noticed the mats of gray and white hair entangled with her natural black, and I was honored to be in the presence of a kind, if boisterous, person who would get to grow old and experience normal life – and normal death. A once adventurous person who wanted to know the secrets of the vampire, but was wise enough to keep them at a distance. A kind person who was willing to risk her own life to assist, and then save, mine. I placed my hand atop hers, which had never left my shoulder, and just held it sweetly.

"Take me to my Annabella, then. Let's leave this chapter behind."

We parked the wagon at a barn, and Igor led the horse to his stable. Igor said it was strange that the horse, named Slivo, did not give them trouble when I got close to the wagon. He could smell the difference on me, the distinguishing scent of death that separated vampire from human. Normally it would cause him to back up franticly, defend himself, and gallop away if possible. This time, though, he just stood, solemn and uneasy, but cooperative.

Right before we got to Igor's doorstep, Annie burst out the door, and ran to me with a large blanket to shield me from the sun, a terrified expression on her face and chaotic tears in her eyes.

"What are you doing, you stupid, stupid man?! Get inside before you blister and suffocate to death!"

"Annie, Annie. It's OK. I'm OK. Something happened in my battle with Revall. Another---"

"Transformation? Shit. What is it with you and not being satisfied with your situation? What happened this time?"

"Well... let's just say... Me and the sun have sort of a tentative partnership going on now."

"OK. You look really, really bad. Like Aylash fucked you up good. But since you're here, I'm going to assume that... you... won?"

"Good assumption. Annie, I---"

"Annabella."

"What?"

"I want you to call me Annabella". *Hmmm. Didn't see that coming.*

"Oh. OK. Annabella it is... I have got *some* story to tell you."

"Great. I really want to hear it. But first, you need to get your wounds tended to, and then you need some sleep. Like a good 24 hours of sleep. And then, when you're up to it, you can tell me all about how you killed the big bad vampire who couldn't die... Oh, and..."

Annie's voice trailed off and she didn't finish her sentence.

"And, what?"

"No. Nothing. It can wait."

"What can wait? It's definitely not 'nothing', from your body language."

"It's just... A text. A text you got from Sinjin Pierce."

"Yes?"

"I don't know. His texts are so chopped up and weird, and you never know what's real and what's bullsh---"

"What did it say, Annie? I mean, Annabella."

She put her head down, looking at the floor, and bit her lip. Annie Moore's now famous, and familiar, 'oh shit' tell. If you see it at a poker table, she's most definitely bluffing.

"Here. You look at it." She sheepishly handed over the phone. Two different text messages, five minutes apart. 'Big problem. Ramifications. I knew sooner or later. Now later has become sooner. Calling in a favor' was the first one read.

‘And not just me. They want you too. They want you dead. Her, too. And they’re uniting.’

Annie studied my face as I read the messages. She was looking for any sign into my thoughts, but couldn’t wait for me to come forth.

“What do we do?”

“We go home.”

“Home to Abilene?”

“Actually, I’ve got somewhere else in mind”.

The End

Epilogue

If you're reading this, that means Annie finished transforming our story from an unbelievable work of fantasy into a *more* unbelievable work of fantasy. As it was happening in real time, I never had any of the poetic stanzas or psychological epiphanies she was able to express in this written document. Additionally, as my journey has become *our* journey, some things I wasn't actually there for. She was able to fill in the blanks and keep the words "in my mouth," so to speak, as much as possible. To say that she's a talented writer (at least in my opinion) would be an understatement. I really hope she lives long enough to publish these stories properly. And I hope to live short enough to not be around when she does. Reading this also means that basically a year has gone by since I defeated Aylash, helped Magdalena Minerva kill Miko, Sergei, Valentis, and his mother Margerie Duplante, thus ending the final two vampire Houses on the face of the earth.

And that's the problem.

I came back the U.S. to find a tornado of disorganization. A vampire uprising with no agenda, no order, no clear vision, except for one objective: to kill me. I enlisted vampires loyal to Sinjin, which, thankfully, there were a good amount of, and I crushed that threat with surprising ease, only to find myself... wanting.

So I took a piece of a conversation I'd had with Miko, Edsel, and Igor one night on the mountain in Nis, and moved Annabella and me Southeast – to San Antonio. Having so many isolated, ass-backward vampires in Texas didn't sit right with me, and even though I couldn't figure out why, I felt it was my responsibility to do something about it. So I built a house.

The House of the Lone Wolf.

Acknowledgements

I would like to thank the family and friends who supported me as I pursued this newfound passion and chose to keep Davis' story going. The generosity of the Dehlinger, Picon, and Dominguez family, as well as my parents, Gene and Alice, made it possible to keep my head above water.

My wife and kids allowed me to keep my sanity and my purpose over the last fifteen months. Without them, I have no idea where I'd be right now... but it wouldn't be pretty.

About the Author

William Xavier Chandler is a husband, father, author, and musician.

Of all his favorite places and past times, which include concerts, Dallas Stars games, art museums, Rome, New Orleans, various beaches, San Antonio, and Paris, William's absolute favorite place on Earth is on the couch at home with his beloved Carie.

He's lived his entire life in Texas, and *used to be* really proud of that. He's unlocked a newfound level of kindness, love, and maybe even (gasp!) *spirituality* in his heart, and hopes the rest of the world would do the same.

Made in the USA
Coppell, TX
23 February 2026

72582177R00207